Based on the true story of Amelia Farmer and Richard
Williams, forebears of the author.

Acknowledgements

This book would not have been possible without many years of historical and genealogical research conducted by my sister, Jacinta Marr. This research provided all the factual information, family trees, dates, convict records and other data that form the framework of this story.

Other organisations and people also assisted me in my research for this book. The Hobart Female Factory, Joan Marr, Sarah Parry, Captain of 'The Windward Bound', Woolmer's Estate, Mary Ramsay of 'Ratho', Bothwell, The Bothwell Historic Society, The National Trust of Tasmania, The Maryborough-Midlands Historic Society and The Archives, State Library of Tasmania.

Beyond Stone Walls

Teresa Marr

Copyright © 2016 Teresa Marr

Published by Vivid Publishing
P.O. Box 948, Fremantle
Western Australia 6959
www.vividpublishing.com.au

National Library of Australia Cataloguing-in-Publication data:
Creator: Marr, Teresa, author.
Title: Beyond Stone Walls / Teresa Marr.
ISBN: 9781925515015 (paperback)
Dewey Number: A823.4

For Jacinta

Prologue.

The huge, thick blocks of stone surrounded her with their implacable silence. The one she was touching felt reassuringly solid and her fingers traced the chisel marks that identified the craftsman who had carefully shaped and placed it to form the tiny cell that Amelia now occupied in the semi darkness. At that moment she felt an overwhelming gratitude to those stones, as they made her safe; safe from her husband, John Skinner.

The bruises on her face were still red, and would soon turn to dark purple, and the cut on her cheek was permanently to mar her lovely features. Her side was aching from the latest beating she had received at his hand, so she carefully sat on the narrow iron bed with the straw mattress, and inhaling deeply despite the jabbing pain in her ribs, leaned back against the damp wall.

Amelia was dressed in a simple grey gown with a petticoat underneath that was not fancy, but at least warm. Her boots were old, but still kept out the water, and spoke of a previous life that had been far better than the present one. She pulled her woollen wrap closer around her, and contemplated her situation.

Amelia's life, once so promising, as a member of a respectable family, had descended into one of poverty, desperation and pain. Tied to her husband as she was with five children, there had been little she could do to change it - until now. Her children were all that she lived for, and Amelia was determined to make them all a better life. Her strategy would ensure that they escaped their situation and started again, far from this filthy, rat infested town that offered them nothing but disease and an early death.

Old Mrs Fowler was to bring Evan who was two and still nursing, to her in Worcester jail. Poor Evan, Amelia reflected, he had spent half his short life in jail already. The other children would be all right temporarily, as her generous neighbour had assured her that she would look after them for a while if need be.

Charles, who was eleven, occasionally got odd jobs holding a gentleman's horse or unloading supplies for the shopkeeper, and he was to give Mrs Fowler whatever he could earn. Thomas sometimes went with his brother, but at eight, wasn't strong enough to carry boxes. She smiled to herself when she remembered the time that Thomas found a penny that had rolled under a stall in the marketplace, and how thrilled he was when he brought it home and presented it to his mother. Smiling, however, hurt her injured face, and she lay down gingerly.

She thought about her daughter. Martha would help Mrs Fowler in the house, as she was quite capable at ten years of age, and mind little Polly, who was four. Finding the most comfortable position possible, and feeling confident everything was going to plan, Amelia fell into an exhausted sleep.

Amelia's trial at the Worcester Assizes came in the days following; she was sentenced to seven years transportation 'beyond the seas', and Amelia had felt a strong surge of hope that all would be well. What followed, however, was three months of torturous waiting and as the weeks dragged by without anything happening, a familiar helpless despair began to overtake her.

Although Amelia had been put in a larger cell with several other women and their children since her trial and Evan's arrival, she almost wished she was back in the holding cells, as the bucket in the corner smelled foul with the bodily waste of so many. Even worse was the constant braying of coarse voices and shrill laughter when all Amelia wanted was to have blessed silence, where her daydreams of her family's new life could flow without interruption.

The news came without warning. The guard was accompanied by another man; an official in charge of transportation. He referred to a document when addressing Amelia and informed her that a ship was waiting on the Thames at Woolwich, the ship that would carry her across the seas. In a few days that journey to freedom would begin and her heart beat faster in her chest.

"When will my children be brought to me?" Amelia implored, but the men started walking away. "My other children!" she cried, clutching at Evan, suddenly in a panic. "I have five children!"

The men paused, and the official consulted the document. "Oh yes", he said almost absent-mindedly, "only your youngest child is to accompany you. He shall remain here with you until your departure." They turned and continued up the stone passage, their footsteps echoing in the chill silence.

Coldness clutched at her gut and spread through her whole body, enveloping Amelia in its icy numbness. She gripped the bars of the door with all her strength, her stricken face pale and her eyes staring. She beat with her fists on that dreadful stone, which had so recently provided a refuge, but now become an impenetrable barrier between her and the children.

For once the women cellmates were silenced by her heart rending scream and one of them caught Amelia as she collapsed onto the hard floor, hands and knuckles bleeding. "My other children!" she whispered, "what will become of them?"

The group of women balanced precariously on the wooden deck, the surface always moving, first leaning one way, then just as they gained their feet, it would tip up again.

Amelia staggered a little, the chains between her feet clanking and hampering her movement. Her clothes, although modest in cut, were filthy, and the torn hem of her skirts dragged behind, giving her the battered, bedraggled look of a woman abandoned. She felt the icy hand of fear clutch at her gizzard, as she contemplated the long and dangerous journey before her, as a convict woman transported beyond the seas.

"Name, year of birth and marital status!" barked the official behind the desk, as Amelia tottered forward, grasping the little boy firmly by the hand.

"Amelia...er...Hobbs, 1800..." she hesitated, then spoke more firmly, "widow."

The official proceeded to measure the woman's height, and scrutinize her at length, while making notes on her appearance in his ledger. "Height-four foot ten inches, hair-dark, visage-fair, oval face with high cheekbones, eyebrows-dark, scar on left cheek." He took some time recording all Amelia's details, and noted that she was accompanied by a boy who was two years of age.

"Evan," she volunteered, "his name is Evan."

The man looked up, then down again at his notes, but made no change. "Over to the smithie to get those irons off, then proceed to the hold to be issued with your clothes and bedding," he instructed, without looking at her face. "Next!"

After the frightening ordeal of having the iron rivets broken with a hammer and punch, and the heavy manacles removed from her painful and bleeding ankles, Amelia gathered her small bundle of possessions, and moved with difficulty to follow some others who were waiting to descend to the hold.

Evan managed the ladder by himself with difficulty, stretching his little legs and groping for each rung. His mother climbed down below him, to be sure to catch him if he fell. After collecting the bedding, and rolling it out on the shelf that was to be their home for the next four months at least, she lay down on it with Evan in her arms, exhausted. The little boy fell asleep at once, but events of the past kept replaying in Amelia's mind, keeping her awake.

Amelia could bear physical pain, but it was the pain of loss and grief that drained her so utterly, for now there was no turning back, and four of her children remained behind, many miles away. Her thoughts drifted to the tragic chain of events that had begun so long ago. It had all begun with one mistake and the ultimate consequence was the sorry situation in which she now found herself.

Years before, a pregnant Amelia had made the fateful decision to marry John Skinner. She had begun a life of pain and suffering from that day, as he was a violent, possessive man, and despite the fact that Amelia bore him four more children, the man never let her forget that her first child was not his own. The life she would face as a convict could be nothing compared to what had been left behind, Amelia was certain of it.

"Right you lot!" The large woman addressed those in the hold loudly, waking the children. "I am the matron on this voyage, and it is my job to make sure you know the routines of the ship which will be your home for the next... four months or more! Get into the clothes you have been issued, and move along with your other clothing and belongings to where the steward will stow them for you until we reach our destination. Then it is back down here with you until supper, while all of our... ahem, guests embark!" The homely woman smiled grimly, but not in an unkind way.

The Government Issue dress and pinafore were made of coarse, rough fabric, although thick enough to keep out the chill, and there was a woollen shawl to wrap herself in and a cap for her head. Amelia got up and dressed, and lifting the sleepy child, she struggled out with her possessions, such as they were.

"'Ere', gimme your bundle and I'll 'elp ya wiv it," said someone with an almost unintelligible cockney accent. "I can' see ya carryin' the boy and all ya stuff as well ya know - give it 'ere'!" The young woman had a rough appearance, but she had such an impish grin, partly due to the fact that one of her front teeth was missing, that Amelia liked her at once. She released the bundle which she had been holding tightly against her chest. "I'm Molly, Molly O'Meara," the girl went on, "and 'oos this li'le rascal then?"

"This is Evan," said Amelia, "and I'm Amelia Hobbs. Say hello to Molly, Evan."

"'Lo," said Evan in his little boy's voice, now awake properly. "Down, Mama," and he wriggled to be allowed to walk.

7

"Well, you are a big boy then, aren't ya now!" smiled Molly, as they followed Amelia and the other women through a narrow gangway into a large hold, where two men were handing out and stacking boxes.

"Take one o' these boxes, put your two bob's worf in i' and give i' 'ere for stackin", said one of the sailors rudely. "'Urry up! You wenches ain't got nuffin' that needs to be folded so careful I'll wager — so chuck it in and give i' 'ere!" He snatched the box and handed it to the other man, who asked Amelia's name, wrote it on the box and put it in the stack.

"Oh sorry about tha'!" Molly exclaimed as she dropped her wooden carton on the rude sailor's foot. "'Ow could I be so clumsy? — you must have go' in me way." She skipped out of the way of his boot nimbly, and called to the other man. "Molly O'Meara's me name Sir and don' you forge' it!" The two women, dragging Evan by the hand, scurried out of the door to the sound of expletives issuing from the sailor's mouth, as the other tried to calm him.

"For pity's sake Rick, leave 'em be. We've got too much work to get done today to bother about a sassy whore. She'll get what's comin'," said Jock, handing him another box.

"She'll ge' what's comin' all righ'!" yelled Rick, taking the box and shaking it in the direction of the retreating women.

"Oh dear," said Amelia, with a twinkle in her eye. "What a shame that gentleman hurt his foot so. It couldn't happen to someone who deserved it more!"

"I won' be pushed around by the likes of 'im," declared Molly pertly, "and don' you worry, I'm used to dealin' wiv angry fellas, 'e won' get the better o' me!"

There wasn't much to do while the long embarkation process continued, so the women sat talking to pass the time until they were allowed up on deck for supper. Molly claimed the sleeping shelf next to Amelia, and they were both glad to be near a friendly face. Evan slept, cuddled in the blankets while Molly told her story.

Molly grew up in a workhouse, couldn't remember her parents and had no knowledge of where she came from at all. She had been abandoned on the doorstep of the institution, and the authorities had no choice but to take her in. Her name was chosen by the matron.

There was never a time when she was not hungry, and had been so poorly nourished that her teeth had started to fall out. When the girl was fourteen, she ran away from the workhouse and moved into shared lodgings with some friends.

"But Molly, how did you pay for your lodgings and food?" asked Amelia, leaning back against the timbers.

"Ah, we figured a way," said Molly mysteriously, and continued. The three of them developed a method of thieving that proved successful enough to provide food, if not lucrative. Their scheme was to lure a man - one that was drunk was ripe for the taking, into a room. While one got his clothes off and kept him busy on the bed in the corner, the others would quietly grab his clothing, run down the alley. They hid there while they emptied his trouser pockets and tore the linings of his jacket to retrieve coins that had been sewn into the seams for safekeeping. The clothing too could be sold, particularly jackets or coats.

Molly and her gang shared lodgings with ten other women and girls, and more often than not, what they stole would again be re-stolen by one of the others by the morning if they did not get rid of it or hide it carefully before night fell.

"But were you not afraid for your safety, Molly?" Amelia felt sorry for her as she heard her story.

"There weren't much I could do abou' i'," said the girl. "We 'ad t' ge' food from somewhere, didn' we, overwise we woulda' starved. Well we did starve sometimes." Molly had known no other life but hardship and thieving, and she seemed quite cheerful about it. By the time she was sixteen, the girl had been convicted for several petty thefts, and she described the events that led to her arrest and sentence of transportation.

One of the unfortunate gentlemen had noticed the girls quietly slipping out the door with his garments and jumping up and wrapping himself in a blanket, he ran into the street calling 'stop thief!' The constable, who unfortunately for the girls was nearby, and after hearing the man's story, he quickly apprehended Molly and one of her cohorts, who were in possession of the booty and trying to sell the clothing and watch at a pawn shop.

"Me an' 'er was arrested, bu' the others go' away," Molly explained. The girl who had been left behind in the bedroom had dressed and escaped out the back of the building while the man was busy with the constable. The magistrate was tired of seeing Molly in his court and sentenced her to transportation for fourteen years. "Tha' was the third time I'd been up in fron' o' tha' magistra'e, ya see," she said in explanation. After relating her tale, Molly changed the subject.

"So wha' abou' you? How come a nice lady like you ended up in a place like this? I bet you come from a decent family an' all."

"Oh Molly," said Amelia sadly, "It is a long story, my decline. Yes, my family were respectable tenant farmers, then my mother died, and my father....." her voice cracking, she tried to continue. "I loved my father very much, and he was well respected in the community until I met..." her voice faltered again, and tears of helpless anger coursed down her face. "I'm sorry Molly, but... I can't talk about it now... I've lost too many..." She continued crying silently, clutching Evan to her tightly and Molly patting her on the shoulder.

After being called up for supper, the women stood on deck looking much cleaner and tidier than when they had embarked. The Matron explained that they would not be leaving the Thames until all the supplies were boarded, and as it could be up to a week before they sailed, it was a good time to learn about the basic routines and rules of the ship.

The Master, Alex Jamieson, with a very stern countenance, stood on the quarter deck looking down in silence, and Amelia felt a little afraid of him. The Surgeon, Sam Sinclair, was introduced, and he explained that there would be strict rations while onboard ship and that cleanliness was very important to prevent disease. A rigorous program of cleaning would be undertaken by the convicts every day. The women rolled their eyes and groaned.

The Surgeon continued. "I would like to see all of you, ladies, one by one over the next few days before we depart, so that I can assess the health of each of you and your children. It is my job to see you all arrive in Van Diemen's Land alive and healthy! Which is more than I can say for some of you at the moment," he smiled.

"I am determined that you shall leave this ship in better condition, and that will require your cooperation! We shall start the cleaning regime on the morrow, and it will continue, unabated, for the duration of our time together. Matron will be in charge of allocating duties, and I will begin your individual assessments imminently." He strode off, hands behind his back, nodding politely at the large group of women, and there was an immediate buzz of excitement.

"That gentleman seems like a very decent fellow, I must say!" whispered Amelia to Molly. "I trust with his care and attention, we shall all survive the journey in very good spirits indeed!"

"Capt'n looks a bit 'ard nosed though don't 'e?" commented Molly. "I wouldn't like to be on 'is wrong side, tha' I wouldn'! Look ou' – 'op in the line quick. I ain't gonna be the last to ge' me bi'!" And with her survival instinct honed in the workhouse, she grabbed Amelia and shoved her way into the midst of the women jostling to line up.

At the head of the throng was a large vat of soup, numerous loaves of bread, and several large barrels. They were allocated a bowl of mutton and vegetable soup, a chunk of bread, a spoon, and a tankard of wine with sugar and lemon juice, which had been mixed into a syrup. This concoction tasted very odd, and a little sour on the tongue, but the women were required to drink it in front of the Matron.

All nursing mothers were to receive an extra ration of bread, and although her son was two years old, Amelia was still nursing him, so duly received her extra piece and an extra scoop of soup for Evan. The women fell upon their food ravenously, as it was the best meal they had seen in months. If the truth were told, there was not much mutton in the soup, but the hungry women did not notice, as the repast was a veritable feast.

Chapter 2.

The next morning, a little more accustomed to the movement of the ship under their feet, the women were all required to bring their bedding on deck and shake and air it, while the sleeping areas were cleaned and scrubbed. Amelia and Molly were amongst the group of women who cleaned out their area, and they all grumbled a little, as they could not see how the sleeping space could be dirty after one night.

"The Master wants to establish all routines right from the off, ladies," explained Matron, supervising from the doorway. "Once we are under way, it will be extremely important to keep everything dry and well cleaned, as illness and disease come upon one very quickly on a ship, where everyone is living so close to one another. So stop your moaning and get on with it! Better learn how to do it properly now, while the waters are gentle."

The woman chivvied them all up on deck to leave the shelves and floors to air out, ensuring that the wood burning stove was stocked. These stoves, of which several were placed below decks, circulated the air and provided warmth, keeping everything dry.

Amelia was feeling a little queasy in the stomach, although the movement of the ship was no more than a gentle roll with the motion of the water in the harbour. She had no idea of what they were to encounter when the ship left the protection of the Thames. Leaning against the rail, she held Evan against her to steady him. He had been affected by diarrhoea since they arrived on board, and Amelia was looking forward to meeting with the surgeon that afternoon to talk about it with him. It was a long time since she had had the luxury of a consultation with a doctor.

She looked around at their ship which was splendid with gleaming timberwork, and it had three masts with sails tightly furled. The vessel's name was *'The Mary'* which had been her mother's name, so it must be a good omen, thought Amelia. She had heard some sailors say that the ship had made the journey already twice before and returned safely, so she felt confident that the journey would not be too arduous.

The Master stood on the quarter deck conversing with the Lieutenant, who, Amelia had learned, was in charge of the guard of soldiers that accompanied them. Several of the soldiers had their wives on board, as did the Master, and she could glimpse them in the distance at times but they mostly stayed on the lower deck, as no interaction was permitted between the convict women and the free ones. Interaction between the officers and convicts was also limited to daylight hours. They all slept and lived in separate sections of the ship, as well as the hold being locked at night to prevent intermingling.

A few of the sailors were a bit too friendly, however, and as they needed to move about the main deck to perform their duties, there was daily contact with them. Some of the women flirted with the men, making bawdy comments as they passed, and the sailors encouraged it, giving each other knowing grins and deliberately spending more time near the flirters without attracting the attention of the officers.

The Matron approached to fetch Amelia. "Are you Amelia?" At the woman's nod, she proceeded with her instructions. "Dr Sinclair is asking for you Amelia. Take Evan... is it? with you and go to the hospital for your assessment now." Amelia did as she was bid, determined to try and get some assistance for Evan, who was small for his age, and never seemed to do well.

"Good afternoon, come in Amelia," said the kindly surgeon, when Amelia knocked on his door. "Hello, little chap, what's your name?" Evan looked shy and hid behind his mother as she moved into the hospital quarters. It was a compact area with a number of sleeping shelves and hammocks, a cupboard for storage and a desk for the doctor in one corner. The ceilings were low, and although Amelia had no trouble walking upright, she wondered how Dr Sinclair avoided hitting his head constantly.

"How do you do Sir?" Amelia responded politely, and the man looked up at her with interest. He could tell by her speech that this woman was no sneak thief from the back streets.

"Sit down, Amelia. Now," went on the doctor, "do you have any health problems to report?"

"No," said Amelia, "although I want to talk to you about Evan..."

"We'll get on to the boy in a moment, I am interested in you first!" smiled the man. "Is Evan your only child Amelia?"

"Er, no... I have five children," Amelia hesitated on the brink of tears again. "I was only permitted to bring one."

The grim line of the doctor's mouth seemed to indicate his disapproval and he made a note in his book, but did not comment on this further. "Are you still nursing Evan?"

"Yes I am, he is often unwell, and I think I may help him if I continue to nurse him for longer."

"Yes, but we need to consider your health too," Dr Sinclair went on, looking at her keenly. "You are underweight; no doubt from a lack of nutritious food in the last few years, but not seriously. We shall see how you go with some better rations. You have been given the extra allowance for nursing mothers? Good. Now how did you get that wound on your face? It looks as if it is healing well."

"I...er was struck...by a ...man," Amelia stuttered, having being caught completely unprepared for questions regarding this. The doctor looked at her sternly for a moment, but did not press her for an explanation.

He examined Evan then, and asked about his history. Amelia explained that he was prone to bouts of dysentery, and required constant attention when he was ill. She hoped to have access to the hospital if Evan needed to be there any time during the journey, as he missed her if she was away from him for very long.

"Your mothering instincts do you credit Amelia, but now I have a question for you," said the man surprisingly. "I will need help, from time to time, in the hospital. As you are an experienced mother and obviously a caring person, I wonder if you would do me the honour of assisting me when required? It would allow you to spend more time here with your son if he is ill, and your help would be greatly appreciated."

"I thank you, Sir, for your consideration," said Amelia. "I would be happy to assist if you think I could be helpful."

"Well, everyone has to have some tasks to share the workload - and to keep them busy," said Dr Sinclair, putting his pen into the inkpot. "In this situation, I find it very important to keep the...er...passengers occupied, as it is very easy to sink into despair, if idle. Don't you agree Amelia?"

"I do indeed Sir. And...thank you." Amelia felt a wave of profound gratitude wash over her. The gentleman's consideration had been the first kindness that she had experienced for a long time.

"You may go. If Evan is still poorly tomorrow, bring him to me, and we can settle him in here for a time, to ensure he is taking enough water and keeping warm without having to be up on deck. I will see you each morning for some general cleaning duties to start with. Goodbye."

Amelia left the hospital feeling more positive. This man was genuinely concerned for their wellbeing, confirming the impression she had on the first day aboard.

The next day was Sunday, and as was explained to the women, there would be a service up on deck every Sunday morning and bible lessons afterward. Psalms and hymns would be said and sung on Thursday evenings. The Master was very desirous that the reform of the wretched women's souls should begin at once, even before they weighed anchor, and the way of God would lead them to repent their sins. They swayed with the deck and listened to the service, although some of the women giggled and jostled, attracting the angry stares of the matron.

"That'll be privy duties for those three for the rest of the week!" whispered a woman next to Amelia. She smiled wanly, while seeming to hold her stomach with one arm.

After the service, Amelia asked the woman's name. "Eleanor Clark is me name, I'm from London. You?" Amelia introduced herself, and feeling worried for Eleanor, asked her if she was quite well. The woman grimaced with pain, and trying to stand upright, she made light of it.

"Oh, its nothin'. I just get this pain in me guts sometimes, that's all."

"Eleanor, did you tell the surgeon about this?" Amelia enquired, reaching out to steady her. "You do look very thin, and there may be something seriously wrong."

"Nah, I didn't say nothin' to 'im. I've 'ad the pains for a long time, but if I tell 'em, they might send me back to the prison if we 'aven't left yet. I waited for a year in a stinkin' cell with five and twenty other women, without seein' the light of day. Please don't say anythin' to the doc, Amelia, at least not until after we set sail." Eleanor's eyes held such entreaty that Amelia agreed. She promised not to say anything to the doctor until after they left England, although she was determined to seek his help after that, as poor Eleanor looked very poorly to her.

At supper, Eleanor was standing in the line, when a big, tall woman with red hair and an equally red face pushed her roughly out of the way and forced her out of place. Amelia knew that the tall woman had already eaten. Eleanor shuffled to the back slowly, behind a couple of hopeful girls who had already eaten too but were trying optimistically for second helpings. She was obviously unable to stand up for herself. Amelia felt the blood rise to her face, and despite looking up a good six inches to speak to her, remonstrated with the bully.

19

"I say! Don't you push in on Eleanor like that! Can't you see she's ill?" she hissed, remonstrating with her hands. "She needs food more than you do, you look like you get enough for two people and there won't be anything left by the time she gets there!"

"Git lost," the big red-head grinned without humour. "If the puir thing is gunna keel over, I may as weel 'ave the use of 'er rations. 'S jus' survival, nuthin' more." And she stood stoically, arms stubbornly crossed.

She must be at least five foot five or more, thought Amelia, the woman looked huge to her, but nevertheless she made a stand. "I know this isn't the first time you've done this to her, I saw you this morning. Move out of the way, I say."

"Gonna make me, yer pipsqueak?" she said in her Scottish brogue, eyes narrowing menacingly and refusing to budge.

Amelia's mothering instinct was well and truly aroused, and she spoke firmly. "If you don't do as I say, I will report you to Matron!"

With reflexes faster than one would expect for such a big person, the bully's arm shot out and she grabbed Amelia by the throat with one hand. "An' you listen t' me, yer do gooder. Yer can lay off me, or I'll make sure you have trouble eatin' for a few days yersel', yer ken?"

"Bridget Duffy! Kindly remove yourself from the supper line and report to me at once. I will need to decide whether your behaviour will be reported to the Master." Matron stood there, incandescent with rage, a soldier by her side. Bridget dropped Amelia and reluctantly walked before the soldier to

20

Matron's quarters, her hard, cold eyes never leaving Amelia's until she was forced to duck her head to climb down the ladder.

Amelia hastened to Eleanor Clark and moved her back to the head of the line to ensure she received her full quota of food. Eleanor accepted her help gratefully.

Molly casually walked over. "I be' they'll pu' 'er in the box for a day for tha'," she said, pointing to the dreaded Black Box that was bolted to the deck. The wooden cell was made of stout timber, with air holes in the top. It was so shaped that it was impossible to sit or lie down with one's legs outstretched, and it had such a menacing aura about it that all the women had quickly become aware of its presence on board. "Besides, she'll miss supper tonigh' as well. Oh no, Amelia, you've made an enemy of 'er, tha's for sure."

Amelia thought of the vicious stare the Scottish woman had given her and shuddered. She hoped that she would not live to regret her intervention.

Chapter 3.

It was a little surprising, thought Amelia, that Molly O'Meara liked to spend her time doing cleaning duties or her leisure time on the deck with her, rather than the younger women. Amelia reflected that as she was over thirty years of age and Molly was not yet seventeen, the girl had never known the closeness of a relationship with anyone, and was in need of a mother figure.

Amelia, with the permission of the surgeon, had asked Molly to help her with the cleaning in the hospital, and as there were one hundred and fifty convict women on board, the doctor was already busily treating various conditions. Dysentery and other stomach complaints due to poor diet were common, and there were several cases of venereal disease in women that had been working on the streets as prostitutes. Evan was also staying in the hospital until his condition improved. At least he was safe there, thought Amelia, as there was always someone on duty if she couldn't be there.

She did not intend to reveal too much about her own past to Molly, but Amelia felt she needed to advise the girl against associating too much with the leering sailors, and while sharing their chores, inevitably, some of her story came out.

"Molly, whatever you do, do not risk getting with child to those no good vagabonds!" said Amelia, shaking the thin mattress. "There is no future for you with any of them. We are bound for Van Diemen's Land, and they will sail off again to – who knows where? Make no mistake, they are not interested in a relationship with you other than to their own benefit, and you will be discarded just as soon as they please."

"It sounds like tha' migh' 'ave 'appened to you once then, did i'?" asked Molly, her curiosity aroused, and she draped her bedding over a line to air.

"Well, it was a bit different for me, because I was going to marry the gentleman," explained Amelia, "but I did get caught. You see, my mother died while I was young, and my father loved me very much and did his best to raise me. We lived on a farm on Hanley Estate, and I helped my father with the chores. Then I met Patrick Wallace."

"Was 'e ya beau then?" asked Molly. I 'aven't 'eard you mention 'im before."

"Why yes he was," said Amelia sadly, leaning against the deck railing, "but meeting him was the start of my sad decline into the state I am now, you see."

"Why? Wha' 'appened?" the girl questioned, but then she hesitated. "...Did you ge' wiv child?"

"Yes", said the other woman, "and to explain what can happen, I will tell you my story - or some of it." The two women descended to the hold and began cleaning the area.

Amelia's childhood was happy except the dark times after the death of her mother, and she always felt safe and loved in the stone farmhouse. Frederick Hobbs loved his daughter and wanted to protect her and thought she should stay with him on the farm and not marry for a while. But the girl had fallen in love with Patrick who worked at a neighbouring farm, and they kept their relationship a secret from her father at first. The young man loved Amelia too; she entranced him, and he told her so many times.

"He was such a handsome gentleman Molly," she mused, "I had never seen such a comely young man." She went on. When she found herself pregnant, Patrick asked Amelia to marry him, as he was a respectable fellow and wanted to do the decent thing. The two were very happy. Amelia broke the news of their engagement to her father, and although disappointed, he liked young Mr Wallace, and felt the couple would be well suited.

"Bu' tha' is a wonderful story, Amelia," remarked the young woman. "Did ya marry 'im then?"

Amelia explained the events that unfolded. Two weeks before the wedding, tragedy struck. A dray loaded with logs had started to lose its load on a very rutted track, and while in the attempt to stabilise the logs, Patrick had been caught under them as they fell, crushing him to death.

"Oh me Lord!" exclaimed Molly, her mouth open and her eyes wide as she stared at Amelia. "What di' ya do then?" and she continued scrubbing a sleeping shelf as she listened.

There had been a man working on a neighbouring farm who had pursued Amelia for many months before she had met Patrick, but Amelia didn't like him very much, and neither did her father. His name was John Skinner. He found excuses to visit Frederick Hobbs's farm, and talk to the young woman in the village, and whenever there was a market he was always there, his eyes constantly on her even at a distance.

After Patrick died, John Skinner began his visits again. Amelia admitted to him that she was with child, and so it was with that knowledge that he asked her to marry him, and feeling that she had no choice, Amelia agreed.

"Bu' couldn' ya just 'ave stayed wiv ya father?" asked Molly. "'E would 'ave looked after ya and the baby wouldn' 'e?"

"I didn't know what to do," said Amelia, with tears in her eyes. "I was going to have a baby and I hadn't been married, so everyone would have branded me a loose woman. I would have become an outcast in our village. I made a decision, albeit a foolish one, to protect myself and my baby. Security was what I wanted, but I got nothing apart from poverty and grief." She continued to mop the floor as she continued.

John Skinner was a poor earner, and Amelia seemed to have the blessing, (or curse, depending on which way you looked at it), of becoming pregnant easily. They rapidly produced more children, but as the family grew, their situation became more desperate.

Amelia's father helped them by giving them farm produce from time to time, but his own living had been affected in the previous years and was no longer doing well enough to support all of them. John Skinner resented Frederick's kindly meant interference as he felt it was an insult, implying that he could not provide for his own family.

He beat Amelia quite often as he was ill tempered and often drunk, and it was one night when Mr Hobbs found his daughter covered black and blue with bruises, that he could no longer ignore her plight. The two men had a violent shouting match, in which Frederick Hobbs gave the younger man a thorough dressing down. To add insult, when Skinner tried to hit the man, he was so drunk that he missed completely, and Mr

Hobbs gave him a resounding punch on the nose which knocked his son-in-law to the ground.

"Oh me god!" exclaimed Molly, "I be' 'e didn' like tha' much."

"No," agreed Amelia. "He resented it so much that he decided to get revenge on my father." At the next livestock market, Skinner stole two sheep that were identifiable by earmarks, and put them in a shed on Mr Hobbs's property. He then spread rumours of the animals' whereabouts, and of Mr Hobbs's poor financial situation, which quickly reached the ears of the zealous young constable.

Having the wealthy owner of the sheep putting pressure on him to find the culprit, the inexperienced constable, being new to the area and not knowing Frederick Hobbs at all, inspected the property. When he found the sheep, he promptly took the older man into custody.

Mr Hobbs was transported to Worcester for trial immediately, and although Amelia travelled there with her four small children to plead his case, it was to no avail. Frederick Hobbs, good man, kind father, was convicted of livestock theft and sentenced to death. He was hung in the days following the trial.

By the time Amelia had finished her tale, she was in tears, sobbing for her beloved father and in anger for her hatred of John Skinner. She had never told anyone the full story before, and did not acknowledge the anger she had built up inside. Jabbing at the boards with her mop, she spoke with barely suppressed rage.

"He boasted to me of how he had done it! When he told me the tale of the set-up, he laughed! I will hate that man, as long as I live. I gave my father's name when I came on board, and said I was a widow. He is no longer my husband, and I hope the devil takes him to the depths of hell for what he has done!" she gritted her teeth through her tears. "If I had had the courage, I would have killed him myself!"

She took a deep breath, feeling a little calmer, but said sadly, "I can only say, that my poor father's death has at least prevented him from seeing the dreadful state that my life has become, and knowing the shame that my disgrace would have brought him!"

Amelia was too distressed to go on, but Molly knew there was more to her story. Did she mention four children? They continued cleaning and washing in silence until the chore was done, and checking on Evan, who was asleep, went back up on deck.

The weather had been cold and damp, although it was approaching summer, and it was a difficult task to keep the bedding dry while it took the air. The two women stood in companionable silence, watching in disgust the foul pool of excrement from the privies that had, over the previous week, slowly spread until it completely surrounded the ship.

"I wonder how much longer we are to wallow in our own filth in the river?" commented Amelia to Eleanor Clark, who had moved slowly to the rail and was standing next to them.

"I 'eard the Lieutenant tell Doctor Sinclair that we are sailin' on the morrow," answered Eleanor. "I wish they would 'urry up about it though, I 'ave two brothers already over there, and this pain's gettin' so bad that I'm wonderin' if I'm gunna make it to see them after all!"

Amelia now understood why the woman was so determined not to be put off the ship; she was going to her family, not away from them. The meaning of her words finally struck home, and Amelia put her hands over her mouth. "Tomorrow! Oh no!" she exclaimed, and she looked into the distance far away to the north west in the direction of her children. Their departure from London would make the separation from her children irrevocable, and it hurt tremendously to contemplate it. The other two women glanced at each other, not quite knowing what Amelia was thinking of.

Just then one of the sailors, whose name was Jock, sidled up to Molly. "Give us a quick cuddle then," he said grinning, and pinching her rear in a presumptuous manner. "I've got me eye on you, you're a fine lassie."

"Leave me be, Jock," Molly said, flinching away. "I'm sick of ya 'anging around."

Jock admired Molly's quick wit and independent spirit that he had witnessed in the hold that first day. "Oh come on," he persisted, fiddling with the rope he held in his hand, "I might be able ta get ya ou' of the hold some nights to come and keep me warm, if you've a mind to. It couldn't hurt, could it, jus' while we're on the ship?"

"Get away from her!" said Amelia tartly. "Haven't you got any work to do? You're a good for nothing scoundrel Jock!" The man grinned and winked at Molly, moving away at the shout of the first mate. "Until later, then."

"Until never, ya mean," commented Molly after he was out of earshot and responding to Amelia's stern look. "There's no way I'm goin' to get meself in a fix over someone like tha'. Don't worry Amelia, 'e's goin' to earn 'imself a clip around the ear, I'm not 'aving nuffin' to do with 'im," and she deliberately turned her back on the seaman. Amelia and Eleanor looked at each other and Eleanor raised her eyebrows.

"I hope that Molly is going to learn from my mistakes," the older woman told Eleanor by way of explanation.

The next day was drizzly and cold again, and the women's morning duties were completed to the shouts of the first mate issuing instructions to the crew readying the ship to make way. The ship was abuzz with activity, and by the time the chores were completed, the women came on deck as 'The Mary' started to slowly make her way down the river, bearing her cargo to 'The Land beyond the Seas.'

As they moved leisurely along the Thames in an easterly direction the smaller sails were hoisted, and Amelia Hobbs had her first view of the magnificent ship under sail. The sucking tide hurried their progress, and with good speed the banks of the river seemed to march by. By afternoon they passed Gravesend and put down the anchor to wait for another ebb tide which would enable them to continue towards the English Channel. The two women busied themselves with organising stores in the hospital and came up on deck again for supper as evening fell.

The ship weighed anchor and set sail once more with the tide. A brisk north easterly wind assisted their passage and as darkness spread and the vessel moved into more open waters, Amelia clutched the rail looking back at the land receding into the mist in the distance. She pulled her woollen wrap closer against the cold wind and wondered where her children were. She hoped they were still with Mrs Fowler, as the workhouse was the only alternative. She doubted that their father would provide for them.

She had never been overly religious, but at that moment with no other hope to help them, Amelia prayed for Charles, Martha, Thomas and little Polly as she wept. "Please God, watch over my little ones," she whispered in anguish, the tears flowing unchecked down her face. "Goodbye my sweet angels."

The boiling cauldron of hatred for John Skinner bubbled up into her throat so that she could barely swallow. Bitterly, Amelia finally acknowledged to herself that she would probably never see her children again, and would be tormented by their memory for the rest of her days.

Chapter 4.   Van Diemen's Land, June 1831.

As Amelia was sailing down the Thames, Richard Barton was contemplating his life, such as it was. He stood with his hands above his head, manacled to the post in the jail yard at New Norfolk, his muscled torso glistening with sweat, his scarred back exposed. He was awaiting yet again, the agony that he had already experienced once before. He had again been sentenced to twenty five lashes by Mr Edward Dumaresq, who was Police Magistrate of the district.

Barton was originally from the Channel Island of Jersey, and as a young man of sixteen, had moved to mainland England for work in Lancashire, and had lived and worked there for eleven years. He had never been in serious trouble before, but in a moment of foolishness he had agreed to distribute forged notes for an acquaintance in exchange for a handsome dividend, (easy money, so the man had said).

The forger responsible for making the notes had not been caught, but transportation for life meant Richard had to leave his wife and child behind in Lancashire, and he fervently hoped they would be all right. He tried not to think about the dreadful circumstances in which his wife had left him, several years before the forgery incident. She and the child had been taken in by her family and had lived with them ever since, so he knew that they would not be left destitute.

Barton had a good behaviour report from the prison and from the prison hulk, where he had been held on the Thames while waiting for departure from England. He also had a clean record since he arrived on the Earl St Vincent in 1825, and since being assigned, had worked in his primary areas of skill, brick laying and labouring. He was now thirty three years of age, and a fine physical specimen in the prime of his life.

It was since being sent to work at New Norfolk that the trouble started. This was Barton's third charge since being put to work at the invalid hospital in the town. The first charge had resulted in only a reprimand from Doctor Officer, and he had not referred the incident to the authorities. The doctor was reluctant to condemn the man when the circumstances were that Barton had been severely provoked.

Richard Barton had got into a fight with one of the patients of the hospital, a man who was extremely difficult for the doctor to manage and was prone to bouts of insanity. Doctor Officer was in the process of planning and building new facilities with a separate secure quarter for lunatics, so they could be separated from the other patients and the rest of the community. It was not ready as yet, and the man was free to cause trouble.

Sometime later in the same year though, one of Richard's fellow convict assignees had got hold of some rum from a Ticket of Leave man, who had been to a local grog hut in the hills. The men had shared the bottle, but got so drunk that they ended up in a fight, and Richard was brought before the law for the first time since his transportation.

This incident had been referred to Mr Dumaresq, and from the moment Richard saw the magistrate, he knew there would be no easy penalty. Mr Dumaresq was known to discipline prisoners to the letter of the law so there was no way that he could avoid punishment this time, and sure enough, the sentence was twenty five lashes.

Doctor William Officer was a decent man, and he would have prevented flogging altogether if he could. He had even tried to convince the police constable not to refer the matter, without success. Once it was in the hands of the magistrate there was nothing he could do.

The sentence had been an education in cruelty that no decent man could tolerate, but Dumaresq had watched the proceedings without flinching. Although that first whipping had been two years before, it had taken a long time for the prisoner to recover from it; the infections he had developed on his back from the open cuts gave him pain for many months before they healed.

On this latest occasion, Richard had allowed the building overseer to goad and bully him for some time, but eventually could take no more. He had a strong temper if roused, and had eventually abused the fellow and simply refused to work under him. Unfortunately this behaviour resulted in another appearance before Edward Dumaresq. Although the charge against Barton was minor and involved no physical violence, twenty five lashes were again prescribed.

Dumaresq had been given the position as magistrate after his lush job as Surveyor General was taken from him and given to a more deserving candidate. His brother in law, General Darling, the Governor of NSW, had used his substantial influence to convince the authorities to give him a replacement post. Magistrate at New Norfolk was the best position that

33

could be secured. Mr Dumaresq had come down in the world, and it was the convicts who suffered for it.

The magistrate was accompanied by his offsider, weapon in his hand. Richard had never considered himself a violent man, but a murderous feeling of desperation welled up in his gut as he saw the fellow approaching, and he knew that he would be capable of killing at that moment, if his hands were not tied.

The feelings of dread built up a terrible anticipation in Barton's memory, until he was writhing and struggling, giving hoarse yells of anger, even before the first cut landed. He would have prevented himself from crying out if he could, but the agony was so great that the air was rent with his hoarse cries. The rhythmic sounds were punctuated by the panting of the whip master, who was exerting himself to the limit with every stroke. He did not desist until the last cut was administered, and Richard Barton hung from the manacles, his back in bloody tatters again. The feeling of murderous rage was now replaced by a strong wish to die.

The doctor had little influence over the authorities, but he could try to control the damage. He treated Richard's injuries carefully, to try and prevent infection. He believed that the men worked much better and had more chance of regaining a useful life if simply kept out of trouble by work, close supervision and kind treatment wherever possible.

Having witnessed the current magistrate's proclivity for flogging, he was disturbed by the number of these punishments that had been inflicted on the wretched men in recent years. Doctor Officer abhorred the practise, so he did wish the man had managed to avoid another confrontation, however small. But Barton seemed to have a well of anger inside that was hard for him to control. What was worse, Dumaresq seemed to have taken a particular dislike to Richard Barton, and the situation was likely to escalate.

William Officer liked the big man, and knew he was a good worker and worthy of better treatment, so decided to help Barton in the only way he could. His solution, he believed, would be for the best.

"Mr Barton, I have written a letter to the official in charge of assignment in Hobart, and requested that you be transferred elsewhere," he said as he worked on Richard's back, rubbing in a salve. "The work you have done for me in the improvement of the buildings has been good, but I think it would be advisable if you had a change of … scenery." He went on, choosing his words carefully. "It would be likely that any further trouble, however insignificant, would be used as a reason for …further discipline. The next step, you know, is Port Arthur, and I would not like to see a man like you sent down there."

"Doctor Officer, do you mean I could get a transfer to another area, and so be under a different magistrate?" asked the man, flinching each time the salve stung his wounds. "Thank you Sir, you are a gentleman, and… your actions will likely prevent more deaths than one."

The doctor nodded and stood up, in complete understanding of Richard's cryptic words. "You will be safe in the hospital here for the next week, and will likely be moving on soon, if all goes to plan. The best of luck to you, Mr Barton. I hope you can find a good situation."

The order came in a little over a week. Richard was to be assigned to a Mr Patterson, in the district of Bothwell. It was several day's ride from New Norfolk, and by the end of the month of June he was settled, and sharing a hut with several other assigned workers, on the property of 'Hunterston' which was situated on the banks of the Shannon River near Bothwell.

Mr Patterson was a Scot, generally a kindly man, and he had his wife and daughter with him in the new land. He was unusually afraid of attacks by bushrangers and aboriginals as his isolated property had been invaded by the notorious gentleman bushranger Matthew Brady and his gang several years before. There had been much property stolen, and although the family had been treated with the utmost civility and respect by Mr Brady, it could have been very different had another man been in charge of the raiding party. The experience had been frightening for the whole family.

The inland area was freezing cold in winter, and resembled the Scottish Highlands with its bleak, windswept grassy plains. It was elevated, as from the town of Bothwell where they went for supplies; one had to make a gradual climb to a higher altitude for about ten miles before descending a short slope into the river flats area of Hunterston. The central highlands and its lakes were further on past Miena, and it was known that notorious bushrangers made hideouts there in the inhospitable terrain.

There were only a few groups of aboriginals left in the area by this time, members of the Big River People, but the settlers were constantly on their guard in case of attack. The previous October there had been a coordinated attempt to round up the aboriginals across the south, and many of the indigenous inhabitants had been removed. Richard knew this as Mr Dumaresq had been involved in the coordination of the men and in charge of conducting the drive in the New Norfolk district. Only Ticket of Leave men had been asked to be actively involved.

One day late in spring, Richard Barton and another assigned man had been instructed to take the cart to Bothwell to fetch supplies and be back before three o'clock. They were to clean out the outside privies when they returned, and Richard was furious. He had become angry and defensive since his harsh treatment at his previous workplace, and he refused to do as he was told.

"I'm not some shit shoveller, I'm a qualified bricklayer!" declared Richard to the other man. "There is no way I am doing that. Jack and Edward will have to do it."

His fellow assignee, Paddy Aherne, agreed. "Dere's a way we can get out of dis," he said in his thick Irish brogue. "It can accidentally, loike, take us till foive t' get back from Bot'well, and it'll be dark boi den!" So the plan agreed upon, the two men set off for Bothwell in the chilly air, their breath making steam each time they exhaled. Richard was glad of the dark beard that covered much of his exposed face, as there had been a cold snap before the warm weather would again approach.

The horse was pleased to wander at a walk to the town, past the grand properties of Cluny and Ratho, across the bridge and into town and the journey took three hours instead of the usual two. The men took their time loading the cart with supplies, and as they returned down the main street past The Castle Inn, Paddy looked longingly at the place.

"It would be grand to stop, just for one wee drink now would it not?" He went on, "we've still got a bit o' toime to fill in, or we'll be back too early and shovellin' shit before we know it."

Richard agreed. "Just one, mind. I'm not in a hurry to get another flogging!" Paddy looked at him with his eyebrows raised, but the other man did not elaborate. So tying the horse to a stout post, they slipped quietly in 'The Castle' and enjoyed a dram of whisky, feeling like real men again for a short while.

When they got back to 'Hunterston' it was dark, and Mr Patterson, realising their actions had been deliberate, was furious. The other assigned workers had indeed completed the dirty task alone, but the incident was not over. The next morning, Richard and Paddy had to accompany Mr Patterson to see the Magistrate in Bothwell, while he made a complaint about their behaviour. Richard was now regretting his actions as he had no way of knowing what kind of man the magistrate was, and his newly healed back prickled with anxiety.

The official in the area was Captain D'arcy Wentworth, and Richard's encounter with him was to change the course of his life. By the time Richard was called in to face the Captain, he was feeling very sorry indeed. But the man looked up from the paperwork and spoke to him quietly.

"Mr Barton, I can see by your record here that you had a bad time at New Norfolk. Good Lord, two floggings!" He sat in

38

silence for a moment looking at Richard. "I say, you don't want to continue down that path old chap. You have a useful trade, and your work will be in high demand here." He sighed, and continued. "Look, Mr Patterson tells me that you are usually a hard worker and an industrious man. You only need work well for him for a couple of years and you will in all likelihood earn a Ticket of Leave. He is a kind gentleman and will sponsor you if you do the right thing."

"Yes Sir," replied Richard, feeling a glimmer of hope.

"I'm not going to punish you this time," Captain Wentworth went on, "I will record a reprimand, but by God man, if I have you here in front of me again within the next three years, I shall have no choice. Do you understand?"

"Yes Sir, thank you Sir," answered Richard, feeling a wave of relief. He would do his best for Mr Patterson; he would work hard and get his Ticket of Leave. These men would do right by him, so Bothwell would be the place he would become a free man again! He left the Captain with new hope for his future, a future that would begin right that very moment.

Chapter 5.

The stiff wind and the rough waters of the Channel made for an uncomfortable night, and Amelia and Molly wedged themselves into their sleeping shelves as best they could. It was a new sensation, to run up the steep choppy waves and crash down the other side, and they all got out of bed in the early hours of the morning, as many of the women were feeling seasick.

They took turns vomiting into the night bucket until the Matron appeared above with the key to the hold. She looked decidedly green herself, and took no exception to the fact that all the women immediately staggered up on deck into the cold wind. Amelia was now very ill herself, and despite feeling extremely worried about poor Evan, down in the hospital cabin, she could do nothing about it. She stood next to a line of other women, and holding their hair back with their hands, they leaned over the side and heaved repeatedly.

After a while, Amelia could throw up no more, but still felt terribly nauseous. She and Molly went back down to their beds with difficulty and lay there, with the ship ceaselessly moving, tipping up and then crashing down again. The timbers creaked and groaned with the strain, and occasionally water splashed down the hatch, wetting the floor. Amelia hated the feeling of constant peril that she now endured in their wooden prison, and longed for the safe solidity of a brick or stone dwelling about her. In those long hours lying in her bed, she formed an internal picture of how it would feel to live in such a house where she could feel safe. Amelia made a solemn promise to herself that one day in her life, no matter what she must endure beforehand, she would have it.

Most of the women were absolutely unable to complete any chores or move about that day at all, so they alternately lay down groaning, or climbed the moving ladder to hang over the side once more. Amelia did manage to get to the hospital once, and Evan seemed to be spending most of his time asleep, although she commented to Molly that it was a miracle what children could slumber through.

Matron was lenient for one day only and then it was back to chores, no matter what the conditions. It was even more important to regularly mop and dry the hold area now that vomit fouled the hold, and water was coming down the hatch from the splashing, slapping waves and making the floor slippery.

Climbing the ladder to the deck whilst carrying bedding was a challenge, and every small task now seemed to be most difficult. Matron's wisdom in getting the women used to a routine while in calm waters was now evident, and at least the women knew what to do.

Those allocated to empty the night buckets were kept very busy with this disgusting job now that they were being sick into them as well as relieving themselves at night, and Matron made sure they all took a turn to do this chore. It was while Amelia was on a trip back from the privies after emptying and washing out a bucket that she saw the accident.

One woman was trying to climb down the ladder to the hold, when the seas threw the ship up violently. She was already off balance when the bow hit the trough in between waves with a jarring thump. Both her feet slipped from the rung of the ladder, and with a sickening crunch, she landed first on both knees on the rail of the ladder and then fell into the gangway below.

Amelia quickly passed her bucket to someone, and calling instructions for Molly to fetch Doctor Sinclair from the hospital, she moved towards the woman, being careful to hold tightly with her hands as she weaved her way along.

The poor creature was wailing in agony, holding her legs with her arms, while being tossed one way, then another. Amelia reached her side and kneeling next to her, tried to assess the injuries. There were deep cuts to her knees, and they were both swelling already.

"I'm Amelia," she said, "Molly has gone to get the doctor. Just think about breathing in and out, to help with the pain." The injured woman stopped crying out and with a huge effort, she took a large breath in and groaning with the pain, exhaled slowly. "What's your name?" asked Amelia.

"Fanny.....oohhhh......Fanny... Brown," she said through clenched teeth. "Where's the doc? I think I've broken me legs!"

"He's on the way now, he's probably trying to get to us without falling over too!" commented Amelia, to take Fanny's mind off her legs. "We will have to take you to the hospital I think. But look at the bright side. At least you won't notice if you are seasick anymore!"

Fanny smiled tremulously, then grimaced again as the initial shock had worn off a little, but the pain was still strong. She looked relieved to see the Surgeon appear at the end of the narrow corridor. He carefully stepped over the injured girl and Amelia moved out of the way to make room for him.

"You saw what happened, Amelia?" he queried brusquely. "Tell me." Amelia described quickly the story of Fanny's accident and the Doctor took a quick look at her knees. "Right, ask Matron to send me two sailors to help carry her. Can you please then come to the hospital? I need you to assist."

"Of course," said Amelia and as rapidly as she could, climbed the ladder in search of Matron. The woman, who had spent most of the last day leaning over the side with the rest, was a little better, and she organised the seamen, who, jauntily and with no sign of illness, strode to the ladder and swarmed down. Amelia went straight to the hospital under the deck amidships, and checked on Evan, who was still unwell and under supervision, and gave him a quick hug. She got the doctors desk, which doubled as an examination table, ready to receive the patient.

Surgeon Sinclair decided that the knees did require stitching and Amelia passed him the items he needed. It was a challenge simply to stay standing while the shipped tossed about, but the deft surgeon managed to complete the procedure. Amelia held the woman's hand while this was done, as although he had given laudanum, the process of stitching was painful.

She also washed the blood from Fanny's shins, and helped to bandage her legs with clean cloths when the doctor finished. The man concluded that although the girl's knees were severely bruised, he did not thing that the bones were broken, which was a blessing for poor Fanny Brown.

43

After helping to transfer the patient to one of the sleeping places, Amelia cleaned up with considerable difficulty. While concentrating on her tasks, her seasickness had abated somewhat, so she was grateful to be feeling a little better.

She and Molly resumed their normal cleaning duties in the hospital the next day. Molly seemed to take most things in her stride, and Amelia thought admiringly that the girl was a tough little thing. Fanny, however, had terrible aching in both her legs, and the swelling caused them to feel hot and tight. Amelia and Molly took turns to hold cold wet cloths on her poor, painful knees while they asked her about herself so that telling them her story might occupy her mind.

The Brown family rented a shop in the village of Winslow in Buckinghamshire. Fanny helped in the shop and their business was good, being a market town. At the market, she met a young man by the name of George Hunt. He was handsome and quick witted, and the girl fell in love with him. They decided to elope, and making their departure in the dead of night, took a coach to London where Mr Hunt had rented some lodgings.

Fanny, believing they were to be married directly, moved in with him, but weeks went by with no marriage and Mr Hunt kept making excuses why he had not arranged it. Fanny had started to become extremely worried by his strange behaviour, and did not know what to do.

One morning she awoke early and found that Mr Hunt had departed, along with the sum of two pounds, which was all of the girl's savings. She immediately wrote to her family to beg their assistance, but her parents, being strictly religious, refused to own her as their daughter, as she had brought shame upon the family.

Amelia was horrified at this, as she was disgusted by the villainous actions of the man, who, she thought, was no gentleman. "But Fanny, what did you do, without any coin, and nowhere to go?"

"I had no idea how bad the situation would get," said the girl. "I was starvin', with no way to pay for lodgin's or travel back to me family, but they did not want me anyway!"

She attempted to find employment but had no luck as her reputation was now ruined and positions were in short supply, so she came up with a plan that would hopefully help temporarily. Fanny sold some of the landlady's furniture at a local pawn shop, intending to find employment then buy the items back with her wages.

The anticipated position never came, and within two weeks that money had also gone and Fanny fled her lodgings and slept two nights in a shop doorway until she was apprehended by the constable. The charge of theft was easily proven, and she was sentenced to seven years transportation.

As she spoke, it was evident to Amelia that the poor girl clearly blamed herself for her poor judgement in going off with Mr Hunt but was bewildered by the rapid turn of events that had led her to this wretched ship. She wept as she told her story, and the other two women felt for her.

"I too, have made some terrible mistakes, that have led me here," said Amelia, who picked up Evan and sat down again, giving him her breast as she spoke. "I never dreamed that my life would go this way as I had a decent home on the farm with my father, and I was happy!" She choked a little on the word, aware of her rapid decline to despair. "But then I became trapped with my husband, and I could see no way out. I will tell you a little of it." The ship tossed and lurched while they talked.

Amelia was devastated after her father's death and she tried to run away from John Skinner, but he found her and brought her home, only to beat her so badly that she was unable to leave the house for a month. There was no money to pay rent, so the family were eventually evicted from the cottage in the village. Not only that, but he continually forced himself on Amelia demanding his matrimonial rights, and she soon discovered she was pregnant again with her fifth child.

"Tha' would be Evan then?" queried Molly. "Wha' happened then?"

The older woman continued. John Skinner rented a tiny conjoined cottage in the cheapest area of Worcester town and moved the family there, being the only place he could afford considering the pitiful sum he earned. Skinner worked only when he needed money for rum, and when he did get paid, spent most of his wages at the local pub, so there was little left for food. Sometimes Amelia's husband did not come home for days at a time.

"I hated living at that filthy hovel," Amelia shuddered, and she described it. It was made of wood and had one room below and two tiny sleeping rooms above, one for the four children and the other for their parents. There was a small room in a lean-to at the back which served as a washroom and laundry, and a privy at the bottom of the small garden.

The well, also in the garden, served eight houses, and there were always neighbours coming through the garden gates to fetch water. There was a coal hole next to the back door, but it was rarely filled, and the house was so cold that Amelia would wrap the children in blankets during the day to keep them warm.

The floor was dirt, and there was no drainage in the streets, so water came in when it rained and turned it to mud. There were no gas street lamps and in the blackest of nights, Amelia could sometimes hear the cries of people suffering at the hands of thieves or murderers as they tried to return to their poor hovels nearby.

"The worst of it though, was the horrible smell that pervaded everything, our clothes, blankets, the very walls of the house!" explained Amelia, grimacing. It was close by the livestock markets with their butcher's shops. The decaying flesh of cattle and sheep, the offal and scraps on bones were left lying around rotting on the ground, drawing flies and generating a stench that sometimes made Amelia want to retch.

To make matters worse, the privy carts emptied their contents in an area that was to one side of the markets, and the great pile of human excrement and slop was as foul a sight as it was offensive to the nose.

"Tha' sounds even worse than the work'ouse," commented Molly.

Fanny was also revolted by the description. "How could you ever raise children in such a place?"

The situation got worse as Amelia's pregnancy progressed, and some days, she did not see her husband at all.

This was a blessing in a way, however he did not bring home any coin and she and the children were hungry. If they were lucky and he left something, Amelia would buy a cut of mutton, as some broth with a little meat fat that was left over after it was boiled would feed the children for several days.

One day as she passed a butchers shop, she noticed a slab of bacon that was waiting on the large outdoor table to be sliced. There seemed to be no one about. Amelia grabbed the bacon, and wedging it under her arm, ran as fast as her growing stomach would allow.

Alas, a farmer driving some sheep towards the market saw her, and when the butcher came out of the house and looked around in confusion because his bacon was missing, the farmer called over to him and pointed to where Amelia was fleeing.

The constable had no trouble finding her in the cold house with her pitiful, starving children, and Amelia was arrested. As the police could not locate John Skinner, the children were given into the care of the workhouse.

"You 'ad four children didn' ya Amelia?" asked Molly. "Tha' must 'ave been terrible for you." Amelia nodded and described what happened next as she settled her son back into his bed.

Amelia waited in the stone corridor under the courthouse. She was in a line of people, men and women, all with chains upon their ankles, awaiting the magistrate to tell them their fate. One woman was sobbing, but the rest were silent. The only other noise was the scraping and clanking of the irons as the prisoners stamped their feet, trying to keep the circulation going in their legs. The sandstone blocks on the floor and walls bore the scars of this slow moving procession of misery; they were worn deep with the years of gouging by innumerable chains and countless stamping feet.

When Amelia's turn came, she was so stiff that she could barely walk with the manacles around her swollen ankles, and her feet numb with cold. She struggled up the stone steps into the dock to find there were a large number of people in the courthouse, and Amelia shrank from their stares.

The trial was very short. Conclusive evidence was heard from the constable, who had discovered Amelia with the goods, and the farmer who had seen her running, so a 'guilty' verdict was a formality. The magistrate was a thin old man with a severe face, wearing the white wig proclaiming his station. He did not look at Amelia as he placed the black cap on his head. "I hereby sentence you to be taken from this place and hung from the neck until you are dead. Take the prisoner down!"

"I remembered no more after the bang of the gavel as I must have fainted dead away in the dock," Amelia explained. "I awoke later in the holding cells to discover that the death sentence had been commuted to eighteen months in prison due to my advanced stage of pregnancy, so I was saved."

Evan was born in that prison several months later and when her sentence was complete, Amelia collected her beloved children from the workhouse. As the mother had nowhere else to go, she took them back to their hovel, back to John Skinner.

"What a terrible time you had," Fanny said. "So you were the victim of a blackguard too! How could a man be so uncarin' as to leave you and the children hungry and in conditions like that?"

Molly privately thought that the horrid house sounded like a better place to live than she had ever had, but then, she had never had to look after children either, only herself. The foul smell she would rather avoid though.

Another convict woman who helped supervise in the hospital came in to relieve them, and told Amelia and Molly to go up on deck for the midday meal. No more could be said then, but the three women gripped each other's hands for a moment of mutual understanding before parting.

They were still feeling ill, but tried to eat a little, as they had lost weight in the past days, not being able to keep food in their stomachs. In a few days, Amelia and Molly got used to the rough seas of the English Channel, but were relieved when they passed around the point of France at Brest. The seas were relatively calm for a time as they sailed south past the coasts of France and Spain, so the women became accustomed to their life at sea on board 'The Mary'.

Chapter 6.

There were eight children on board ship including Evan. The women, with Matron's help, had organised group supervision for the children for the mornings, while they completed their duties. The children would not then be under their feet while they were going about the chores on the open deck as it was not possible to watch them in such an unsafe environment while concentrating on other things. Some of the mothers had small babies who needed constant nursing, so they were taking turns to supervise the little group as their morning duty and Amelia was then free to help in the hospital.

Amelia was trying to hang up laundry on deck before taking Evan to the group, and she engaged the help of Eleanor Clark, who had no children, to watch the little boy while she completed the task.

"A ship is not a safe place for a two year old to play," commented Amelia to Eleanor, there are so many ways he could hurt himself, climb on things he shouldn't or even fall overboard!"

"I don't mind watching him Amelia," said the young woman. "I wish I 'ad children, but I was married for a couple of years to a fella, and never got with child at all. I think that's why 'e left me. That's why I thought, well, why not go over and meet up with my brothers in the colony? One of them has 'is Ticket of Leave already, so 'e gets paid for 'is work, and I could give 'im a 'and in the 'ouse, as 'e's not married. He can't write, 'imself, but 'e paid a scribe to write a letter for 'im."

"Eleanor, are you saying you deliberately got arrested so you could be transported to be with your brothers?" asked Amelia curiously. "That was a courageous decision. How did you know you would get to the right place?"

"Well 'e said in 'is letter that all the convicts were being sent to Van Diemen's Land, but that if I could swing it to come over, 'e would send a petition, by paying the scribe to 'elp 'im again, to try and make sure that's where I went." She went on, "a person with a Ticket o' Leave can sponsor someone, y' see."

Amelia was surprised at this revelation, as she thought that very few people would do something as mad as to be transported voluntarily, as she herself had also done.

"I have to admit to you, Eleanor, that you are not the only one to make the decision to deliberately be arrested. I wanted to go to the colony and thought it was likely that most women offenders would be sent out there, because they needed more females. Someone I met also had a letter from a brother who was in Van Diemen's Land." She paused and then decided to explain further. "Of course I did it for a different reason, to escape from my husband."

Eleanor did not look shocked at this. Instead she said. "I s'pose 'e used to beat you, did 'e?" and she nodded understandingly.

Amelia went on with her explanation. When in prison after the theft of the bacon, she had had much time to think. Realising how grateful she was to be away from her husband, she was startled to find that she also felt safe for the first time in years. If only she had her children with her! Amelia missed them terribly, and worried about their wellbeing constantly.

She kept reflecting on the contents of a letter that one of her fellow inmates had received. As Amelia could read, the illiterate woman had asked her to read it aloud to her. The letter was from the woman's brother who was in Van Diemen's Land. He had been assigned to work on a farm, and within a year or two, he was confident he would have his Ticket of Leave.

"He spoke in glowing terms of the amount of work available in farming or building over there in particular, and urged his sister to find a way to be sent there and if possible, bring their other sibling, a younger sister," Amelia explained. "He claimed that women were needed for domestic service, and maids were being paid twenty pounds per year."

The shadow of an idea started forming at the edge of Amelia's mind. While she was nursing Evan and spending many hours sitting with him in the cell, she thought about it more and more, until she could think of nothing else.

What if she were to be arrested for another theft? Most of the women she had spoken to were under the impression that a second offence would get you transportation. The illiterate woman, the recipient of the letter, assured Amelia that her cousin had been sent for seven years and had taken all three of her children with her.

"At the time," Amelia confided to Eleanor, "I was naive enough to assume that I would be allowed to bring my children too. I needed to believe it so that I could plan my escape from that man."

Amelia decided that it would be the ideal way to escape from John Skinner forever. Although he had threatened to kill her if she left him again, she could take the children and flee to where he would never find her again. Yes, she would do some prison time there and probably work for no wages for a while, but she would be free. Free from pain and fear, free from that cursed man, John Skinner.

Her obsession became a firm plan of action, and when Amelia finally was released, she collected the children and went back to him with a lighter step, knowing it would not be for long.

"So you did it, Amelia," asked Eleanor, "you got away?"

"Yes," confirmed the other woman, "but it did not all work out as intended."

Finally the day came to carry out the plan and Amelia was nervous but optimistic. John Skinner had gone off to the public house the previous night and not returned, so there was little chance that he would be home for days. She sent the children next door to her kind neighbour, who often watched the children for a few hours, and went to the market. Fingering some white shirts on a stall, she surreptitiously glanced around to make sure she had attracted someone's attention. Quickly, she stuffed two of the shirts into her apron and ran as fast as she could, while shouts of 'stop thief' rang out behind her.

Amelia darted into the garden, confident the police would find her, as the nosy resident from across the way was watching as usual. It was part of her scheme, as she knew the neighbour would speak to the constable. She opened the door and was unexpectedly met by a strong hand who grabbed her roughly. The slap was so hard, it knocked her to the floor, and she lifted her head and looked up to see her husband advancing on her. He was the last person that she anticipated seeing that day, so Amelia was completely taken by surprise.

"You useless, lazy woman - you whore, where 'ave you been? I jus' came 'ome to get me dinner, and wha' should I find, but nobody 'ere and no food, neither!" Amelia could smell rum oozing from the pores of his skin, but drunk as he was, the man's boot lashed out before she had time to move, and it caught Amelia in the small of the back. She shrieked, and tried desperately to scramble away. Cowering in the corner, she received another blow, but she managed to stand up by dragging herself up on the table with her hands.

The final punch she didn't even see coming. The vicious blow caught her right under the cheekbone and laid the skin open. As she fell unconscious to the floor, John Skinner staggered out the door without a backward glance.

The next thing she remembered was the constable leaning over her, as she lay in the kitchen with the two shirts stuffed in her apron pocket. Amelia recovered somewhat after a drink of water and she was able to get up, although a little unsteady on her feet.

She regained her wits quickly, and pressing a wad of cloth from her apron to her face to stem the bleeding, collected her wrap before leaving the house to accompany the constable to the jail. Amelia asked the constable if he would be so kind as to tell her neighbour what had happened for the children's sake. The police officer was a kind man, and feeling sorry for the woman, as he had found her in such a state, promised that he would do so.

"Amelia!" exclaimed Eleanor, after listening in silence, "is that 'ow you got that scar on yer face? That no good ruffian! You did right to get away from 'im, or you'd be dead, soon 'nuff."

Amelia told Eleanor of the terrible day the official came to tell her the ship was waiting and that four of her children would have to remain behind in England.

The news had come as such a shock that day that Amelia remembered it vividly. She had not been able to speak sensibly for that whole day afterward, and instead of sleeping, replayed in her mind everything that had happened over and over, her heart thudding at an unnatural pace, and her stomach churning. She had pleaded with the jailors to petition the authorities, but they were unconcerned by her distress and it seemed their ears were deaf to her.

When the day came to leave the place, the prisoner was duly put in shackles and chain, and bundled up the steps with her child and into the waiting coach without ceremony. She felt as though her heart had been ripped out. Completely powerless to stop the events now sweeping her to the other side of the world, the mother could only weep and cling to her little boy as the long journey to Woolwich began.

As she finished her tale, Amelia noticed through her tears that Eleanor was leaning over holding her arms across her belly, and seemed to be in distress not because of what she had heard, but because she was suffering from severe pain.

"Why Eleanor," she said, concerned, "has your pain returned?" The other woman could only nod, her face suddenly white, and her thin arms shaking with the effort of bearing the pain without crying out. "Molly, Molly!" called Amelia to the girl, who was nearby. "Quickly, could you please take this bedding down for me with yours and bring Evan to me at the hospital? Eleanor's been taken ill, and I must get her to Doctor Sinclair at this instant!"

Seeing the girl nod, Amelia wasted no time in putting her arm around Eleanor and almost carrying her to the steps amidships. Matron observed the women and knew there was a problem immediately. She hurried as much as she could with the tilting of the deck, to assist. Together they got the sick woman down to the hospital, and found the surgeon there.

The man spent some time examining poor Eleanor Clark, and Molly came in with Evan to wait with Amelia. The two women talked quietly to Fanny Brown while keeping their vigil. Fanny was still in the hospital after her accident, her swollen knees still painful, but they had improved somewhat. After he had finished, Doctor Sinclair came over to the women.

"Could you please help Eleanor into a sleeping place? She will be staying here. Then Molly, as Amelia needs to take Evan up, could you sit with her till I return? I thank you." He went to walk through the low doorway, and glanced at Amelia who was silently trying to get his attention. She raised her eyebrows to him, then looked at Eleanor. The kindly man shook his head sadly, and continued on his way and Amelia followed him with Evan. Before he went his own way once on deck, the surgeon turned and waited for her.

"You may as well know. She has a large foreign mass growing in her belly, in her womb I think. There is nothing I can do for her, save give her some laudanum for the pain. It is only a matter of time I'm afraid. I'm sorry Amelia; I know Eleanor has become a friend to you." He strode away, leaving Amelia feeling very upset and terribly sad for poor Eleanor, who was looking forward to seeing her brothers so very much.

She sat with Eleanor for a while after the cleaning was done, then after dinner she usually spent time with a group of the women who wanted to learn to read, sew or knit. The Ladies Association had donated a box of fabrics, needles and thread and wool to help the women find some industrious occupation whilst on their way, and learn some useful skills. There were also several books and Amelia was helping some women and older children learn to read and write.

Once the seas were not so rough, it was usually pleasant enough to spend the afternoons in this way in the warm hold. But that afternoon, Amelia could only think of Eleanor.

Chapter 7.

Later that night, after all the women had been locked below, Amelia became aware of surreptitious movement on the other side of the sleeping quarters. She lay quietly without moving but with her eyes open, trying to see what had awoken her. Two women were moving stealthily towards the ladder leading to the hatch. Someone opened the hatch from above, and the two quickly scurried up the ladder and disappeared from sight.

Obviously one of the sailors had obtained a key to the hold and was using it to allow their chosen 'partners' to come to their beds. Amelia remembered suddenly that one of the seamen who was very insistent with Molly had promised he would let her out at night.

"Molly!" she whispered. "Are you awake?"

"Yep, I am," she spoke quietly, "I was watchin' Catherine Morgan and Jane Kelly make the biggest mistake of their lives, going off with them two no 'opers!"

Amelia grinned to herself in the darkness knowing that Molly was congratulating herself for not making the same error of judgement. "Who are they going off with?" she asked.

"That bloomin' Jock O'Riley, and the smar' mouth Rick Tiller – you know the one 'oo was rude to you tha' first day in the 'old. They're as thick as thieves, those two."

"Is this the first time they've gone out at night?" Amelia asked, feeling like she'd missed something important that was going on.

"Nah, they've been out three times now," Molly explained. "'Aven't ya ever noticed before?"

"No," answered Amelia in surprise as she comprehended that each time she must have stayed fast asleep.

The next morning, Molly pointed out all the 'couples' that had been forming during the early days and weeks on board. Most of the seamen had favourites that they would flirt with, but Catherine and Jane were the only two that she knew about that were escaping their confinement at night to sleep with their chosen men, at least in their section of the ship.

"An' tha's no' the only kind of couple either!" Molly told Amelia mysteriously. When Amelia raised her eyebrows in query, Molly just laughed. "You'll find ou' soon enough," she said.

Amelia promptly forgot about Molly's cryptic words, but recalled them a few days later, when their true meaning became clear. In the meantime, she became much more aware of the nightly comings and goings and the relationships that were developing.

One woman, Ann Haydock, had been spending some time with the reading and sewing group, but did not seem very interested in actually learning anything. She simply sat and watched Amelia give her lessons. Amelia did wonder why she bothered to come, but the woman attended on consecutive days and much to her shock and surprise, Amelia discovered the reason that night.

She was drifting off to sleep, when a hand over her mouth had her awake with a jerk. Ann Haydock was sitting there, leaning over with her squarish unattractive face uncomfortably close and her foul breath hot on Amelia's skin.

"It's me, Ann," she said gruffly. "I thought a lovely woman like you might be missing some lovin' company. I can give tha' to ya. You don' mind makin' love to a woman do ya?" and without waiting for an answer, she began to nuzzle Amelia's neck with her whiskery chin, and her free hand roamed over her body and breasts.

Amelia wriggled and turned her head, trying to get the suffocating hand from her mouth, while at the same time pushing her away. The women persisted, and try as Amelia might, she could not get the larger woman off her. Suddenly a fury gripped her, and it was not driven by the revulsion of another woman trying to make love to her, but the very strong memory of John Skinner. She clamped down with her teeth hard on Ann's fingers, and fought as she had never fought before.

"Get off! Get off!" she screamed, and she thrashed about, slapping and kicking her assailant. "I am never going to submit to you, never!" Ann had no choice but to back away from such a forceful defence.

Molly, awoken by the melee, held Amelia until she calmed down, and through the gasping of her ragged breaths, the girl heard her say. "No... No... I cannot take this! It was just like John Skinner forcing himself on me again, I have that dream you know, over and over again!"

Holding her bitten finger to her chest, Ann watched Amelia's hysteria with a look of surprise and frustration on her face. After a minute she must have decided that her chances were hopeless so slipped quietly away to her own sleeping place.

Over the next few days, Amelia avoided Ann, fearing reprisals. However the woman made no further attempt to approach her, so she began to relax. After a while, she noticed that Ann spent more and more time with a woman called Eliza. Soon it became apparent that the two were a couple, as they began to share their sleeping place. Some of the women were very uncomfortable with this and Amelia heard them speaking about it from time to time. Amelia herself did not find the relationship between the two women repugnant, she was simply glad that Ann had another willing partner, so would hopefully not bother her again.

One of Amelia's previous conflicts had some consequences soon after though, as it became obvious that the big, red headed Scottish woman, Bridget, was looking for a way to get back at Amelia for her interference at the dinner line. Amelia found the woman watching her on occasions, and once, realised with a chill down her spine that Bridget was right behind her coming down the ladder to the hatch, and it would be so easy for her to give Amelia a kick...

One morning, Amelia got up and when she went to pick up her shawl before going up the steps, found it was missing, and she instantly knew who was responsible. Molly's was gone too, so they both went up on deck in the cold wind without a warm wrap. Bridget was already there, draping her bedding over a line, and Amelia strode over determined to have it out with her.

"Bridget, where are our wraps?" Amelia asked without hesitation. "I know you've been waiting for a way to get back at me - so where are they?"

"I ha'e no' got 'em," she said flatly, the colour rising in her ruddy cheeks. "Ask Rick or Jock, they migh' knoo somethin' abou' your wee wrap!" And she stalked off.

Rick or Jock! Those two no good sailors were somehow involved. Amelia turned and a flapping movement caught her eye. The two woollen wraps flapped prettily in the breeze, way up in the rigging next to the mid mast. Her eyes then fell to deck level and she caught sight of two grinning seamen standing directly below the items, arms folded on their chests.

"Ameeeelia, Moooolly, your warm clothes are up in the riggin'!" teased Rick maliciously. "We were wantin' a way to ge' back at yer two prissy wenches. Fink ya too good for the likes of us, do ya'?"

"Ya know Rick," laughed Jock, complicit in the crime, "I think I would 'a put 'em up there for that Scottish bitch without 'er even havin' to do you that...favour."

"Yeah, I bin waitin' for a chance to ge' even with tha' whore, Molly," agreed Rick maliciously.

Amelia thought for a fleeting moment that she certainly did not want to know what 'favour' Bridget Duffy might perform for one of these louts to get their cooperation in the scheme.

The problem was how to get the items down now they were up there? She certainly was not going to do a 'favour' for any of the leering sailors, and they were all looking over, enjoying the discomfort of the two women. There was only one solution. Amelia walked swiftly over to the rigging, and jumped up on it before she could change her mind, holding tightly with her hands and balanced above the ceaseless waves.

"Amelia! What are ya doin'?" called Molly in a panic. "Don' do somethin' as stupid as that' you'll fall and ge' yourself killed!" But her words had no effect as Amelia started to climb.

She tried not to look down, and soon her arms were aching with the effort of hanging on. The seamen all stopped what they were doing and stared open mouthed at the small woman who dared to defy them. She reached the garments and with difficulty, untied the rope that held them fast, and began her descent.

A large wave hit the ship, making it roll to the side. Molly covered her eyes, a vision of Amelia falling into the depths playing out in her mind, but she looked up to see Amelia gamely clinging to the rigging high up above the deck with a shout of laughter on her lips. Her hair whipped around her face and she glared defiantly at the sea, as if to challenge the waves to take her.

Molly reached out to grab her as she descended the last few steps to the rail, and when Amelia jumped triumphantly to the deck, the seamen gathered around smiling and clapping in admiration. Rick and Jock stood uncomfortably to one side, for once not the centre of their shipmates' attentions.

"Amelia Hobbs!" said an authoritative voice. "Come with me!" and Matron stood sternly near the hatchway to the hold.

Amelia gulped, and the smile fell from her face, as she handed Molly her wrap and stepped up to Matron, her chin raised, ready to take her punishment. As she looked up, she saw with dismay the cold, hard eyes of the Master appraising her from the quarter deck.

"We will talk about this...er... incident a little later," said Matron surprisingly. "Right now - you need to go to the hospital, Doctor Sinclair is asking for you urgently. Eleanor Clark is dying."

Chapter 8.

Eleanor Clark had now been in the hospital under the doctor's supervision for a week. In that time she had wasted away, with no appetite for food, and the large doses of Laudanum making her so drowsy that she simply lay there, her life slowly draining away. Her eyes were open, skin as pale as death, and she closed her fingers on Amelia's hand gently.

"Amelia, I will not now last the hour," she whispered. "I wanted to tell yer. I want y' to follow yer dream of freedom. Find another life, a better life, and don't look back." She sighed and closed her eyes for a moment, then continued. "There are good men in the world, yer can find one, an' start again."

"Eleanor my dear," said Amelia softly. "Know that I will write to your brothers and give them your love, and tell them you were on your way to find them. I will tell them that you are the one on your way to a better place, to freedom, so they are not to have a care about your happiness anymore."

A hint of a smile formed on the sick woman's lips as she spoke so quietly that her words were barely audible. "Thank yer, me friend." Her eyes closed for the last time, and in a few minutes Amelia noticed that Eleanor's breathing had stopped, and at last, she was free of all pain.

Amelia stood up and stepped back, allowing Doctor Sinclair room to come to the bedside. He shook his head, looked at his pocket watch and went to his desk to note the time of the woman's death in his log. He asked Amelia to cover Eleanor with a cloth, and to come back later to assist with the daily duties, when she was feeling up to it.

Amelia went to her sleeping place to be alone for some time. She mourned not only for her friend, but for others she had lost; her parents, her fiancé Patrick and her four children. Her tears dried eventually and shouldering the heavy burden of grief that was now her constant companion, Amelia went back to her duties.

The funeral was held on deck at eleven o'clock the next morning and all the women gathered for the service. Fanny Brown had improved enough to move out of the hospital, her legs now healing well. It was difficult for her to climb the ladders though, and needed help to get up on deck for the ceremony. She was determined to do it, however, as she had got to know Eleanor well during their shared time in the ship's hospital.

The Master stood alongside Doctor Sinclair, and read solemn words from the Bible. He then committed Eleanor's body to the deep, and the shrouded figure was cast into the sea. Molly in particular, was extremely badly affected by these events. She had never seen the ocean before coming on board the ship, and the thought of the body being lost to the deep was distressing and overwhelming for her.

"Oh Amelia!" the young woman cried. "I can' bear the though' of poor Eleanor bein' down there in the deep blackness of the sea, all alone. There migh' be monsters there, or vicious sea creatures wiv huge teeth. I 'ope I don' die on this journey, Amelia, I can' be thrown in there - don' ever le' them! Promise me?"

"Shhh... of course you won't die, you are young, and healthy. Don't give it another thought, Molly, try and put it out of your mind now." Amelia gave the distraught girl a hug, and led her away to the hospital, where the work there would distract them both. They paused on the way across the deck, for Amelia to ask permission of Doctor Sinclair to sit at his desk to write to poor Eleanor's brothers. The other women quickly dispersed to complete their morning duties, not wishing to dwell too long on the fate of their shipmate.

Later, after Molly left to hang up hospital laundry, Amelia had the blessed luxury of silence, as the hospital was temporarily empty of all patients, and she penned a letter to the men, explaining the sad events. She signed off, *'Your sister's friend in sympathy, Amelia Hobbs'*. She folded the letter and wrote the directions that Eleanor had given her.

As she reached over to melt the sealing wax, Amelia noticed the Surgeon's log still open where he had been writing his notes, as always, about his patients. The name 'Ann Haydock' caught her eye, and she paused, her dark eyes running over the copper plate script with interest. The doctor had evidently examined the woman for a minor ailment but also wrote a description of Ann's masculine mannerisms and her tendency to partner other women. He curiously described her as a 'pseudo male'.

Amelia dwelt on this for a few moments as she sealed the letter and left it on the Surgeon's table for him to put in the post upon their arrival. Was it possible to be a woman on the outside, like Ann, but like a man in all other aspects? Strange were the ways of the world, she thought.

Amelia knew that the incident of climbing the rigging would not go unpunished, and as she expected, she was called to see Matron that very evening.

"Amelia, I am giving you this opportunity to explain yourself with regard your extraordinary behaviour yesterday. You put your life in danger, and distracted the crew from their work. But I think you are generally a sensible woman and would not do so without good reason," said Matron in an even tone. "Well?"

"I afraid, Matron, that I must decline to answer," said Amelia quietly. "It will do no good to dwell on the problem." She was sure that she would have a serious issue with both Bridget Duffy and the sailors for the remainder of her journey, if she relayed the whole story and it was discovered that it was she who had caused trouble for them.

"You also, if you did notice, attracted the attention of the Master, and he has only been convinced to let me deal with you this time, because of a commendation from the Surgeon regarding your good work in the hospital."

"Oh," said Amelia, surprised. "That was very kind of Doctor Sinclair, I'm sure."

"Yes it was, rather," said Matron. "Any incident considered serious enough to be dealt with by the Master will result in severe punishment. So you have been lucky this time. You will be on privy duty for the next week as well as your other chores. Consider that the end of the matter." The older woman knew that Amelia was not disclosing everything about the incident; it was not in her character to cause trouble, but she could do nothing to ease the punishment any further.

"Yes, Matron, thank you Matron." Amelia spoke humbly, but inside was boiling with indignation, to be punished for the malicious behaviour of others. Never mind, she thought, smiling inwardly, as she had her own ideas on how to put the situation right.

A few days later, at mid-morning, Amelia was presented with a perfect opportunity to carry out her plan. Bridget Duffy had already brought her aired bedding down from the deck and gone off elsewhere. The entire sleeping area of the hold was empty while the women were going about their daily routine.

Amelia was in the process of emptying the last of the night buckets, and she stood, looking around cautiously, the bucket of strong smelling, yellow piss in her hand. She quickly strode to Bridget's bed and without hesitation, threw the entire contents of the bucket over the blankets. She then went quietly about completing the rest of her duties, and sang to herself as she worked.

The ruckus that exploded when the short tempered woman found her urine soaked bed was phenomenal. Fortunately for Amelia, Bridget Duffy had made herself extremely unpopular with many of the other women for her extraordinary selfishness and unwillingness to help. She had actively intimidated quite a few of the convict women, and subsequently had many enemies. There was no way that Bridget could know for sure which disgruntled person had been responsible for the foul mess. Amelia quietly told Molly that it was she who had taken revenge on Bridget Duffy, and the girl stared at Amelia with awe, before collapsing in hysterical giggles.

The women all enjoyed the sight of the Scot, washing and scrubbing blankets, loudly cursing as she worked, her red face almost puce with rage.

Not only did Bridget have to sleep without blankets for several nights until hers dried, but the smell, she complained loudly, never entirely left the woollen covers and stayed with her for the remainder of the voyage. Matron watched the unfolding events but chose to do nothing, knowing in her wisdom that somehow, justice had been served.

Soon after, the big woman from Scotland reported to Doctor Sinclair, as she was in severe pain.

"Och, I canna' eat, I can noo longer sleep, I ha'e noo relief from it. Wha' is causin' this pain?" She moaned, holding her face. Her jaw and neck were swollen, and her eyes were bloodshot.

The surgeon looked in Bridget's mouth and felt her neck. "I'm afraid that you have a bad tooth, Bridget," he explained, "and that tooth will have to come out."

She looked at him in horror, and got up ready to make a dash for the door, but Amelia was too quick for her. She took Bridget's arm, and speaking encouragingly, the woman was soon sitting down again. "Come Bridget," she said soothingly, "you can't go on in such pain. The surgeon is a very skilled man, and he will have the problem done with as soon as you like." Amelia began to feel sorry for Bridget as she had not a friend on board, and spent her time brooding alone.

"Bbbut how will he...." she stammered, still not quite convinced.

"I will give you a strong dose for the pain, and you will feel sleepy," said the kind man patiently. "Then I will pull out that painful tooth in a few moments. It will be very quick, I assure you. Amelia, if you will help me, let us ease this poor woman's suffering right now." And indicating the table, he stood to retrieve his instruments.

Amelia understood that they need to act immediately if they were to get the job done, and she prepared the table for the procedure. She made Bridget drink the draught of Laudanum, and with considerable difficulty, convinced the stubborn woman to lie down. After the draught had begun to take effect she relaxed somewhat, and the surgeon managed to get his metal forceps around the tooth and pull it out with one motion.

"That tooth has been bad for a very long time," he commented to Amelia. "It came out very easily indeed. This woman would have been in pain for months, in all likelihood, before she reached this crisis." Amelia thought to herself that this could possibly explain her tendency to be so bad tempered, but did not mention this to the surgeon. The doctor went on. "Now Amelia, you must pack the hole tightly for several hours, then get her to wash it out with salt water every few hours to aid healing and to keep the area clean."

Amelia did as she was bid, and over time the woman's pain began to subside. Bridget developed a kind of grudging respect for Amelia, and although reluctantly, did express her gratitude. "Ya knoo, we ne'er ha'e been friends Amelia," she said in her thick brogue, "bu' I ha'e to thank ye, for ye're help with the wee tooth. I' ached soo much tha' I hardly knew wha' t' do." Amelia was relieved, as it seemed the feud between the two was now over.

Chapter 9.

The weather, which was cold and damp, had gradually become warmer, and the good sailing conditions persisted, much to the relief of the women. Sea sickness had not been a problem once they all got their sea legs, but now another issue faced them. As they approached the tropics, the heat of the day became so high, that the women could hardly bear to be on deck in the direct sun.

With the help of some of the sailors, they had to rig some large tents or canvas shelters on the open deck to provide shade for the daytime hours. The humidity was also terrible and Matron decided she should issue each woman with a lightweight dress to aid in their relief. This was greatly appreciated, and the woman moved most of their afternoon activities to the shaded areas on the deck, where the sea breezes were cooling.

The areas in the bowels of the ship, once pleasantly warm and ventilated by the burning stoves, were now unbearably hot and the women working in the galley during the day were suffering terribly. For this reason Matron decided to cook a large vat of soup up on deck. It was hot, ready for serving, when Matron herself, a large woman and tending on the clumsy side, tripped on the leg of the stand that was holding the vat. The vat tipped up, slopping a large quantity of hot soup down the hatch that was just nearby. The screams of women that were caught under the hot flow were terrible, and there were two women that were badly burned.

Ann Henry and Lucy Hurst had received the worst of the deluge, and suffered severe burns to their backs and legs. Two others had more minor burns to their lower legs, from hot splashing fat. Amelia helped the surgeon tend the women in the hospital.

"It isn't the best time to suffer with burns, in this heat!" Amelia exclaimed, as she and Doctor Sinclair laboured over the women, applying cold salt water to the affected areas.

"They were lucky the soup didn't go over their heads", commented the doctor, "they would have had scars on their faces, and burns on the scalp under the hair would be difficult to treat."

Amelia shuddered, the thought was repulsive. "The hair would most likely fall off, would it Doctor?"

"Yes, and I have seen cases where the scarring on the head was so bad that the hair never grew back." he replied.

Amelia could not think of anything worse than to be forced to live the rest of one's life with no hair. Her own hair was thick and dark, one of her best features, and Amelia hated the idea of losing it. The burns to the women's backs were the worst, and once the wounds were dressed, Amelia helped the two women up on the cool of the deck under a shade each day, where they rested lying on their stomachs, cushioned by blankets.

Sluicing the skin with cold salt water seemed to be the most effective treatment, and luckily there was no shortage in supply of salt water, so Amelia was able to use liberal amounts. It took two weeks for them to be sufficiently healed to go back to their normal duties, but even then the two women could not move without pain, and they continued the salt water treatment for many weeks longer.

All the convict women continued to bear the hot weather with difficulty, but cheered up quickly when they received some exciting news. They would soon be anchoring at Cape Town to bring on supplies!

Doctor Sinclair had pointed out to Amelia that several women were showing the symptoms of scurvy, despite the regular intake of lemon juice. They had pain in their joints, swollen, sore gums, and red spots on the skin. It would be welcome for all to replenish their supply of vegetables and lemon juice. Fresh water was another very important cargo that would be loaded on 'The Mary' in large quantities.

It was well known that the south west winds sweeping into Table Bay in winter could be wild, and batter the ships anchored there with huge waves. The worst time for this weather pattern was from June until September, and many ships could not go into the port. On those occasions, they were required to continue sailing around the Cape of Good Hope, then north to Simon's Town, south of Table Mountain, which was sheltered by the isthmus.

As the month of August was nearing its end, and the weather had been mild, it was decided to anchor in Table Bay after all. As 'The Mary' sailed into the deep harbour, Amelia, Molly and many other women all lined the sides of the ship to view the spectacular sight.

The bay was surrounded by rugged mountains and hills, but was dominated by the magnificence of Table Mountain, a huge, rocky monolith with a perfectly flat top. The heat was clear and dry, although not quite yet spring, the sky was an uninterrupted expanse of azure blue.

There was much activity in the port, with many large merchant ships dotting the harbour, and numerous smaller vessels going back and forth from the ships to the jetty. Their ship was anchored off shore, and the Master went ashore with a small party of soldiers and officers.

The Matron held a meeting with the women. "We will be staying here in the harbour for about a week, weather permitting," she said, "and our main task while we are here is to wash." The women looked at each other, not quite understanding why this was to be, but the lady in charge explained. "We will be bringing on large quantities of fresh water, not only for drinking and for taking with us, but we will have an unlimited amount to launder all clothing, monthly rags, and blankets. This will be the last opportunity to remove all the salt until we reach our destination. All other afternoon activities will be suspended until it is completed, with the exception of the children's group, which will continue to allow the mothers to be occupied with their laundry duties."

She went on to delegate tasks and divided the women into groups. Extra lines were erected on the open deck, and as the days went on, these lines were constantly full of laundry, flapping in the helpful breeze. The weather remained ideal for this task, warm and dry with wind. Amelia and Molly set to work not only washing their own garments, but those belonging to the officers and soldiers too. It was wonderful to have soft, clean clothing again, particularly their undergarments, which were always stiff with salt, and did chafe the skin terribly.

The favourable conditions allowed the bulk of the washing and drying to be completed in a few days, and Matron was so pleased that she allowed time off in the afternoons for the rest of their stay.

There was a constant stream of visitors to 'The Mary'. Sailors and labourers loaded barrel after barrel of water, lemon juice and wine into the hold. Vegetables, livestock and fruits, as well as flour and sugar also were lifted from the transport boats onto the deck to be lowered down for storage.

The presence of all the strange males caused a good deal of excitement amongst the younger women in particular, and flirting, ribald comments and laughter were common. Some of the men stayed on the ship for the day or overnight, and there was many a secret tryst between them and the ladies, both below decks and in quiet corners. The officers seemed to turn a blind eye to this activity, indeed, some of them joined in, taking advantage of the bustle of comings and goings and the change in routine.

Amelia was occupied with her daily chores as usual, and spent the afternoons with Molly and watching Evan, whose health had improved in recent weeks, and his stomach seemed to settle.

The pleasant break was all too short, but as the ship weighed anchor and set sail once more, Amelia was quite pleased to have the ship back to normal, and a little more peaceful.

"They say we're to expect rougher seas and bigger waves once we round the Cape and travel across the open ocean," she commented to Molly, as they watched Table

Mountain recede into the distance. "I am not looking forward to the seasickness again, and I'm sure we shall all suffer by it."

"Across the open ocean!" shuddered Molly. "Ya mean, we won' even be able to see any land a' all?"

"Not a bit for many days," said the older woman calmly. "But then the next sighting of land we see will be Van Diemen's Land." Her stomach did a little flutter with the prospect. They were used to life on the ship now, and felt they were fairly well treated, but what would their new lives be like?

"I'll be 'appy to ge' off this cursed ship," said Molly, "and then I can stop thinkin' about fallin' in the sea and drownin'!"

Amelia hadn't appreciated that this danger was on Molly's mind constantly and particularly since Eleanor's funeral, the fear of falling overboard obviously never left her. When the day came that the last glimpse of the south coast of Africa disappeared over the horizon, and there was nothing but ocean as far as they could see in any direction, Amelia knew what Molly was thinking about, and endeavoured to keep her busy as much as possible.

There was always work to be done in the hospital, and although the two women who had symptoms of scurvy had greatly improved since the new rations of vegetables and fruit, there were the constant cases of bladder infections and dysentery amongst the population of one hundred and fifty convict women.

Chapter 10.

The industrious little group of women worked at their sewing and knitting each day while chatting and listening to the reading lessons that some were taking. Amelia was one helping with the reading and writing, and although she was making good progress with the older children, some of the women were making very heavy weather of the simplest sounds and letters.

She stretched her arms wearily, and leaving them to practise for a while, took Evan by the hand and went to sit next to a woman of about her own age. Her name was Elizabeth Walsh, and she was the mother of one of the older children on board the ship, a girl of about eleven years.

Elizabeth held some knitting limply in her hands, but seemed to have made no progress on the project. She simply sat in silence and stared into space sorrowfully.

"Are you having trouble with your knitting Elizabeth?" asked Amelia, lifting the tired little boy onto her lap. "Jane Kelly is the one to ask if you need help."

"Thank you kindly, Amelia," she said in a quiet voice, "but there is no point to it."

"What ails you? Do you need to come to the hospital?" asked Amelia. "You do look thin and ill, Elizabeth, perhaps there is something that the surgeon can do."

Elizabeth's voice was full of despair. "No one can do anything to help me. I have done some bad things, my family have disowned me, and I cannot stand before the Lord God as I am no longer worthy. I have been cast into the shadows, and I can no longer think about myself without repugnance."

Amelia responded hurriedly. "Indeed Elizabeth, you alarm me, by speaking so! We have all done things to regret, but there is no need to lose hope."

The other woman just shook her head. "I am not worthy of your concern. I cannot live with what I have done, but as desperate as I am to do so, I cannot take those deeds back either. Leave me be." As she turned away from Amelia, tears of hopelessness spilled from her eyes and ran down her cheeks.

Amelia did as she was bid, and left Elizabeth to herself, but now she was alerted to the woman's feelings, she observed her closely over the next few days. It appeared that she was pining so badly for her lost self-respect, that she was not even eating her rations. At midday dinner, she ate a little of the mutton broth, but her pudding went untouched. Three women sat down with her, and Amelia was pleased to think that she had other friends who were also concerned for her. Perhaps they would encourage her to eat. To her shock, the women made off with Elizabeth's bowl and damper, dividing the loaf among themselves as they went. Elizabeth herself sat apathetically next to her daughter, seeming not to notice.

"Molly! Did you see that?" Amelia exclaimed. She jumped up, and instructing Evan to wait there, she hurried around to the aft steps, but could see no one. Putting her head down through the hatchway, not daring to put a foot on the steps, she could hear women's voices, echoing along the gangway.

"Wha' a joke! Morag, di' ye see tha' stupid lass jus' le' goo of the bowl?" asked one, incredulously.

Another voice answered in a satisfied tone, "I told ye Elsie, I go' all 'er wee supper las' night, and Sarah go' 'er puddin' yesterday."

"Yeah," commented the third person in a strong cockney accent, "I fink she gone an' los' 'er wits, ya know. I been nickin' bi's of 'er stuff for weeks, an' she never even noticed nuffin'!" This was followed by a loud belch and a roar of coarse laughter from the group. Amelia withdrew her head, she had heard enough.

In a low voice, she told Molly what she had learned. Molly shook her head with disgust. "I's bad 'nuff tha' the poor woman's so poorly, wivout slappers li' them makin' it worse. Elizabeth reminds me of a girl I knew in the work'ouse. She was so down on 'erself for the sta'e of 'er life, tha' she go' sick and nearly died. Lucky she never though, bu' she was never the same again. I told 'er it wasn't 'er fault tha' she 'ad no family an' 'ad to scrounge to make a livin', bu' she wouldn't listen.

Amelia was afraid the same thing was happening to Elizabeth, and one couldn't stop eating and expect to live for long! She resolved that she would speak to Matron, say nothing about the other women who were taking advantage, but just try and help somehow. She approached her later that day.

"Er, pardon me, Matron," she said hesitantly, as she approached the supervisor, who was hurrying by.

"What is it Amelia?" Matron asked. She spoke not dismissively, but as if her mind was occupied elsewhere.

"It's about Elizabeth, Elizabeth Walsh." Amelia hesitated.

"Well, what is it, Amelia? I'm rather busy just now. Is Elizabeth sick? If so, take her to the surgeon."

"She's not exactly sick, Ma'am, but I am worried about her."

"Well if the problem is not urgent, it will have to wait, I am run off my feet with my current problems." The woman did not elaborate but continued walking hurriedly towards the quarterdeck. Amelia scurried behind her, hoping she would pause to listen.

"I have to see the Master now Amelia, please go and do something useful," and with that, she grasped the rail and began to climb, leaving Amelia staring up at her in frustration. She would just have to deal with the problem herself.

That evening, she had asked Bridget to point out the three women, as two of them, Morag and Elsie, were known to her, being fellow Scots. Before the call to go below, Amelia saw the group huddled together on the deserted aft area of the deck and resolved to confront them. She asked Molly to go with her, so they could speak to the women together. Molly was happy to defend Elizabeth, as she hated persecution of any kind. It was getting dark as they approached the little group.

"Good evening, I am Amelia Hobbs, and this is Molly," she began politely. The three rough looking convicts just stared at them, unsmiling. "I am a friend of Elizabeth Walsh...I saw you, er... taking her dinner. She is terribly down, you know, and she needs kindness and support just now. She has lost a lot of weight because she hasn't been eating, and I'm awfully worried that she is going into a serious decline. Could you kindly desist from what you are doing?"

There was a pause after this long speech, and then the horrid threesome burst out laughing showing their rotten teeth with gaps where some were missing. Somehow the laughter did not seem pleasant, but derisive, and it stopped quickly. The cockney woman took a step towards Amelia, her chin stuck out defiantly and her hands on her hips.

"Could we kindly desist?" her grin was more like a snarl, her eyes narrowed. "Could we kindly desist, girls?"

Morag answered, "I'm afraid we cannot desist, Sarah!" and snorted at her own joke as she spoke in a faux upper class accent. "I'm afraid my sister and I do no' understand the word 'desist' and even if we did, we would no', because *you* asked us to!"

There was more mocking laughter and the three women stepped closer, surrounding the two friends. Sarah snarled again. "I's no business of yours, wha' we do, and I'll thank you t' keep ya nose ou' of our business!"

Molly spoke quickly, feeling that the situation was rapidly becoming unsafe. "Now look 'ere," she said in a reasonable tone. "We 'aven't told the Matron or anyfing, we're jus' askin' you in a friendly way first, before we did tha'."

Sarah and Morag grabbed Molly and roughly dragged her to the rail. Elsie held Amelia's arm in such a fierce grip that the petite woman could do nothing. "Tell th' Matron! Tell th' Matron!" hissed Morag right in Molly's ear. "I'll make sure ye don' ge' a chance t' do tha' noo. It will be easy t' gi' a lass li'e ye a push, an' we would ne'er see ye again. Noo chance of tellin' Matron then!" The two tough women held Molly bent backward over the rail threateningly, the cold void of the ocean below.

To Molly, the crashing waves were menacing monsters ready to consume anything that was offered, and their insistent clamouring at the hull obscured any noise that may have been heard by anyone left on deck. The girl was so terrified that she could not speak and remained completely paralysed, her eyes wide in her bloodless face. She was convinced that the hour of her death had come and her worst fears were to be realised as she would be enveloped by the icy blackness, all alone, and sink to its depths to be devoured by the beasts that lived there.

Amelia found her voice and screamed. "Very well! Very well! We won't tell Matron. We won't! Let her go, let Molly go, I say!" She wrenched her arm almost out of the socket to get away from Elsie, and rushed to Molly as they allowed her to slide back onto the deck. Amelia felt dizzy with relief, as the women stalked arrogantly away.

"Ye better no'," said Morag, glancing back at them in warning. "Or ye're noo be'er than dead, the pair of ye!" And with that, the three disappeared into the darkness, presumably to go below.

"There now, Molly," said Amelia softly to the girl. "It's all right now, they've gone." Molly was in a complete faint, half sitting, half lying on the wet deck. "Here, let me help you up, we had better go below before we're stuck up here all night. Come Molly." She put her arm around Molly's waist and almost lifted her across the ship and helped her down the ladder.

Amelia made sure the girl, who was still unable to speak, was covered warmly. Evan was still sleeping where his mother had left him, and she lay down with him, her heart beat finally slowing. "Well Amelia, my girl, that was not one of your better ideas!" she murmured to herself. She reproached herself for putting Molly in such danger. But what else should she do?

Molly was much recovered by the morning, although very quiet after her brush with death. Amelia left her cleaning in the hospital, whilst she went on deck to hang the hospital laundry. On her way back, Amelia noticed that Matron had the large food store open, and she was supervising some women who were retrieving supplies to make the puddings for dinner. The big woman followed the cooks to the galley, where all the food was prepared, leaving the door open.

Quick as a wink, Amelia put her basket down, and slipped inside the door. She must act quickly before Matron returned. She looked around in the dim light at all the sacks and boxes. She opened the top of a large bag, and found it full of sugar.

Scooping handfuls of the stuff into her apron pocket, Amelia thought that she could perhaps help Elizabeth by giving her some extra energy until she recovered from the malaise that gripped her. She quietly closed the bag, and hearing footsteps on the level above, looked cautiously out the door to make sure no one was there before making her escape.

She took the sugar back to the hospital and found a small box to store it in. Later that afternoon, Amelia took some warm water from the pot that was warming on the wood stove for the hospital, and stirring a quantity of sugar into it, went to find Elizabeth Walsh.

Amelia did have some trouble convincing the woman to drink the fluid, and enlisted the help of Elizabeth's eleven year old daughter with some success. The three wicked women continued to take whatever of Elizabeth's ration they could get, but Amelia was too afraid to confront them or tell Matron. She could not risk poor Molly's life, or her own for that matter. She hoped the extra sugar would just keep the ailing woman going until the situation was resolved, and was unaware that suspicious eyes were watching her every move.

The second time Amelia took sugar from the store room, she thought with alarm that someone had seen her come out, as a movement caught her eye down the gangway. There was nothing she could do except continue toward the hospital, to hide the evidence. She opened the door and went inside, relieved to have made it back, only to experience a dreadful shock as the voice of Lieutenant Grey spoke directly behind her.

Chapter 11.

"Madam, show me what you have got in your pockets if you please!" commanded the soldier.

Amelia jumped and spun around to face the soldier. With him, looking severe, was Matron. Her heart skipped a beat and then it began to thud so painfully in her chest that she thought fleetingly it might explode. She stepped forward and opened the pocket of her apron with resignation. Surely, when they heard why she was doing this, all would be well. But Matron was looking stern.

"Sugar! And where did you get that from my girl?" the woman in charge demanded.

"From the store room. I was using it to help..."

"You have been discovered stealing stores from his Majesty's ship, and from your fellow shipmates," stated the Lieutenant. "This is a serious offence that will be dealt with by Master Jamieson. Make your way up to the quarterdeck if you please Madam. Follow Matron, I will be right behind."

Matron walked to the door and Amelia gave her a pleading look, but she simply shook her head. As they went out into the gangway and along to the hatch, several women were watching. Amelia turned her head as she stepped onto the ladder only to see the unmistakable, scornful stares of Morag and Sarah. Sarah said something quietly to Morag and the two laughed behind their hands, still looking at poor Amelia.

Molly went to fetch Evan from his children's group before dinner, as his mother had not returned from Master Jamieson. She had heard what had happened from some other women, who also told her that Morag and Sarah had been laughing as if their sides would split after Amelia had been taken away.

They sat with their bowls, Molly feeling helpless and hoping that Amelia would be back soon. The little boy was soon tired after he had eaten and as Amelia was not there to nurse him, Molly gave him a drink of water and put him to sleep in Amelia's bed. She went back on deck to find out what was happening.

The Master stood on the quarter deck looking down at all the convict women who gathered there. "Let this be a lesson for all of you. This woman has been found stealing from the ship's food stores. This is a crime against his Majesty, and all of us on this ship. For any of you that think you might like to try this, consider the punishment first. Three days in the Black Box. Lieutenant, if you please."

There were gasps and a loud murmur from the women as the soldier brought Amelia down to the side of the deck just below where the Master now stood. Lieutenant Grey opened the door of the box and pushed the helpless woman inside, banging the heavy wooden door decisively and fastening it with a large iron padlock with a key from his belt. One woman screamed with horror as the lock was fastened, and the memory of that scream echoed in Amelia's mind.

Amelia could now not hear any other sound save the relentless sea. The only tiny fingers of light came through the air vents near the top of the door way above her head, and they gradually faded as night fell.

She prayed to the Lord to help her live through the punishment, and recited the words of prayer she could remember, over and over. It was only possible to stand, or sit with her legs bent, and she alternated between the two, dozing and waking, dozing and waking, her unsuckled breasts becoming heavy and sore.

Amelia was given a small bread pudding and water twice each day, but had no other contact with any person. Time dragged by, and she no longer knew when it was night or day, or how long she had been inside the Black Box.

A fever came upon her and caused her thoughts to be jumbled. In her confusion the sick woman called out to God many times but could not understand why he did not answer; he had either abandoned her or did not exist at all, Amelia could not decide.

There was a bucket in the corner for her to relieve herself, but it had been twice tipped over, and the floor of the box was wet and slippery. If Amelia wished to sit down to rest her aching legs, she had no choice but to sit in the wet filth. She could no longer remember why, only that she must endure.

When Amelia was finally pulled out of the Black Box, she was wet, filthy dirty and her fever was high. Molly took her straight to the hospital, where the Surgeon ordered her to bed immediately. While Amelia was bundled in blankets Molly washed and aired her clothing. Amelia called out for her son; she needed to nurse him as her breasts were red and swollen from days with no relief. Doctor Sinclair was sure that was the cause of her fever.

While Evan did try to nurse, it did not relieve the problem as the ducts were caked with dried milk, blocking the flow, and Amelia's fever got worse until she became delirious. Molly stayed with her and surprisingly, the other woman to volunteer her help was Bridget Duffy. Evan also became sick from the upset in his diet, and the two women helped Doctor Sinclair not only in the daily cleaning duties that Amelia was accustomed to doing, but caring for the patients.

There was one other girl in the hospital, her name was Hannah, and she was being treated for chronic venereal disease. She had been 'on the town' for several years before being arrested for being drunk and hitting a gentleman over the head with a chair in order to steal his watch.

Amelia's fever eased, but she had lost a lot of weight, and Doctor Sinclair was very concerned for her welfare. "Amelia, you must wean Evan, you are wasting away, being sick yourself and trying to nurse him as well."

"No, no!" Amelia cried, feeling desperate to hold on to that bond with Evan, and concerned for his health. "I must feed him as long as I can. I lost all my other children, I don't want to lose him too!"

Doctor Sinclair thought he understood why the mother was so attached to her son, but he persisted, hoping to convince Amelia to look to her own health, as he thought the boy would survive. The issue resolved itself within days, however, as the fever, the days without suckling and Amelia's weight loss inevitably resulted in the loss of her milk altogether. Evan was weaned, whether she wished it or not.

Amelia asked after Elizabeth Walsh, as in the days of her illness, she had not thought about the other woman, and suddenly remembered with a start, that no one had been making sure she was eating.

"I 'aven't 'ad time to look after Elizabeth," said Molly, guiltily. "I 'ave 'ad me 'ands full lookin' after you and Evan, and doin' me chores. Besides, I ain't gettin' on the wrong side of them slappers for no one!"

As soon as Amelia was able to leave her bed, she went looking for Elizabeth, and was alarmed and distraught to find her skeletal and with no energy, as if the melancholia had taken her completely. She refused to go to the hospital, so Amelia went to fetch the surgeon, walking slowly and holding carefully to the railing, as she herself, was still feeling weak from her illness.

By the time she found the man, and told him of her fears for Elizabeth, another woman came rushing along the gangway to tell him that a woman had collapsed up on deck. He looked at Amelia, and quickly climbed the ladder, to go to the person's aid. It was Elizabeth. She lay on the hard boards of the deck, pale and still.

The surgeon checked her heartbeat, then felt for any breath and sat back, shaking his head. "We're too late, she has breathed her last. May God have mercy on her soul."

Amelia was inconsolable. She had known Elizabeth was declining and had not been able to help her. Molly meanwhile, explained Elizabeth's story to the Surgeon, as he was at a loss as to understand why she had died. "Ah yes, I have seen that before," he nodded. "Some men and women, being convicted and sent away from everything they have known, are unable to reconcile before God what their life has become and become convinced that there is nothing to live for, hence the decline."

Molly went on, emboldened by this understanding. "Ya do know tha's why Amelia took the sugar don' ya? She was feeding i' to Elizabeth... cause she wouldn' ea'." She ventured nothing about the involvement of the three vicious women. There was no point risking their lives by telling now.

The Surgeon, thus enlightened, thought no ill of Amelia for her actions, and resolved that he would continue to value her assistance in the hospital. He did not know why she had chosen to take the matter into her own hands rather than seek help, but it certainly had proved a mistake. Although it was regrettable that the punishment had such a dire effect on a nursing mother, there was nothing to be done about it now, so he put the matter aside.

Chapter 12.

A funeral service, as before, was held on the deck for Elizabeth. The same procedure was followed, and the women watched sorrowfully as the body was tipped over the side. Molly could not watch, and sobbed uncontrollably into Amelia's bosom. "I forgo' abou' 'er," she sobbed. "'Cause I was lookin' after Evan and you was sick, I forgo' 'er. If I'd told Matron, maybe she would've lived."

"Molly, Elizabeth wanted to die," Amelia said, more firmly than she felt. "Once someone is determined to die, there is not much one can do about it, no matter how hard they try. All we can do now is to be kind to her daughter. Perhaps you could spend some time with her." Molly nodded, unable to speak of it any further. She looked up to see Matron watching them.

Matron was also feeling the burden of guilt. Amelia had tried to talk to her about Elizabeth before all the business with the sugar. She suddenly knew now why Amelia had taken it, and felt a lurch in her stomach when she remembered that she had been too busy to listen. Now Elizabeth was dead, and Amelia had suffered so much, then lost her milk. She would pray that God might forgive her.

Evan remained in the hospital, as his dysentery persisted long after Amelia was up and about. She spent a good deal of time with him after her duties were done each day and this was how she came to hear the news. Amelia hurried to tell Molly.

"You will never guess what has happened Molly!" she whispered urgently. "Come over here." In the quiet of the area near the mizzenmast, she imparted her secret. "Both Catherine Morgan and Jane Kelly are with child. I told you that would happen!"

Molly was staring at her, open mouthed. Amelia was determined to make sure Molly understood the situation. "They are with child from those no good sailors, Molly, they will now have the burden of children that they did not want, and will take them into an uncertain world. We don't know what our future holds, but I would not wish to be giving birth there. They will get no succour from the men!"

Molly's face cleared. "Well tha' explains i', don' i'?"

"Of what are you talking Molly?" queried Amelia, confused.

"The Doc and Matron must 'ave figured ou' someone was lettin' Catherine and Jane ou' a' nigh', since they've got 'emselves pregnant since we lef' England. Those two have been locked up in a separate area a' nigh' for the last week. So no nigh'time 'anky panky. 'Aven't you noticed Amelia?"

"No," Amelia responded, and again realised that she had been oblivious.

As predicted, the weather worsened, and huge seas and battering gales blew the ship constantly, sometimes lessening briefly then strengthening once more.

The only blessing was that as they travelled in a south easterly direction, the weather had gradually become cooler, so it was more comfortable for both passengers and crew, who were used to the colder temperatures of England.

The women were all seasick again, and spent their time leaning over the side, or lying in their beds whenever they could. Many days passed in this monotonous fashion and everyone, including Matron, lost weight as a result of the inability to keep down their rations. It seemed that one day merged into the next, and night into day, until at last a call was heard from way up high in the rigging.

"Land Ho! Land Ho!" called the sailor on watch, and everyone rushed up on deck to look. It was an hour or more before it could clearly be seen, a blue grey land rising from the sea. The big waves continued to toss the ship until they rounded the southern-most point of Van Diemen's Land, and mercifully, the more sheltered waters gave all those on board blessed relief.

The travellers on 'The Mary' were treated to the most fascinating sights as they sailed the waters around the south coast of the island. Amelia heard the sailors calling out and pointing to something in the water, and she dragged Molly and Evan to the side of the ship.

"Oh my Lor', it's a monster from the deep!" quailed Molly, terrified, and she cringed back. But the sailors seemed excited rather than frightened, and as the ship got nearer, there it was. An enormous whale that was as long as the ship, wallowed at the surface. Water and air blew forcefully from a hole on its head, causing a fountain accompanied by a whooshing noise.

The creature seemed to roll on its side to watch the people on the ship, but was not afraid, as it spent some time doing this. Then leisurely submerging its great head, it dived under the water with a slow rolling motion, its huge tail flipping up in the air before descending into the depths. Molly looked so horrified that Amelia laughed at her.

"Molly those creatures are not monsters, they are whales, and are generally gentle animals, although they are very big!" she reassured her. Molly and most of the other convict women had never heard of whales, although Amelia had read about them in books and found it awe-inspiring to see one for herself.

One of the women suddenly pointed into the water at the bow of the ship, as dozens of dolphins played in the waves, joyfully leaping and diving, while swimming very fast.

Molly lost her fear as she became engrossed in their antics, and began to point things out to Evan. "Look Evan, tha' dolphin 'as a baby wiv it," and she smiled gleefully at him. "Look, its stayin' righ' next to 'er, just li'e you do wiv your mama!" The little boy smiled and pointed with his finger too.

It took several more days of sailing, past large islands and between peninsulas to make their way into the mouth of the large river, and with a breeze behind them and travelling at a pretty clip, by the end of that final day the ship gently sailed past the rolling hills into Hobart Town.

It was a beautiful area as the harbour was deep and there were picturesque hills all around. The town had as its backdrop a large mountain, which rose up gradually steeper behind the township, culminating in a sheer cliff face near the summit.

They anchored in the harbour slightly off shore, and the women were told they would be disembarking only after all the formalities were completed and everything was made ship shape. This was likely to be several days. It was now October, and the middle of spring, with warm temperatures in the mornings, but cold afternoon breezes and chilly at night. Fluffy clouds sped across the sky. The women all thought that it was odd to be October and yet be springtime and they were kept busy as usual with cleaning and laundry, washing down the hold and sleeping places and cleaning the privies.

Officials came and went from the town, lists were made and notes written. Inspectors came to look at the state of the ship. The convicts themselves were interviewed one at a time, and the names of the two dead women were noted and crossed off the disembarkation list. Finally, Matron addressed them for the last time.

"Well, ladies, it is our last evening together on 'The Mary'. After our supper there will be a service on deck that you are all to attend as is usual for a Thursday. Each person will then go to the hold to collect the belongings that were brought on board." The large woman went on. "You may sleep a little while you are waiting if you wish, but you will be awoken in the early hours of the morning to leave the ship by boats. Make sure you wear your warmest clothing and carry the rest." She paused, "and may God's blessing go with you all in your new lives."

Some of the women were weeping, and Amelia realised that the fear of their new lives was overwhelming for some, now that their cloistered life on the ship was at an end. After the service, Molly went to the hospital to speak to Surgeon Sinclair for one last time, to thank him for his kindness. She could hear voices in the sick quarters, and could make out Matron's voice.

"Well, congratulations, Doctor Sinclair," Matron said cordially. "This has been a most successful voyage, compared to some of the fiascos of the past!"

"Thank you, Madam," murmured the man, and then he spoke more strongly. "I am glad that we only had two deaths, as I did hear that on some of the earlier journeys it was not unusual to have thirty of the poor wretches die at sea."

"It was due to your care, Doctor," insisted the grateful woman, "and also to the fact that the voyage was relatively short."

"Yes, I agree that a longer sea trip of six months or more would have produced more casualties, but these days the seas are charted quite well, and past experience helps the masters choose the easiest path to Australia. But still, four months is a triumph, and with the necessity for only one stop in port. Master Jamieson shall have our congratulations!"

The conversation seemed to be over, so Amelia tapped on the door. Matron passed out of the room with a nod to Doctor Sinclair and a smile at Amelia. After thanking the Surgeon for his assistance with Evan, she went to the hold and prepared Evan and their belongings. The women dozed a little on their sleeping shelves before being awoken and given the order to go on deck.

It was dark, the deck only lit by lanterns, and a cold breeze made the women shiver. They gave their names before handing down the little boy first, who cried as his mother let go his arms and a sailor took him. The first group of women climbed down a ladder into an open boat, which took them to shore, where they would be marshalled before leaving the docks.

There was little sound save the wind as they approached the wharf. Some street lamps lit up the waterfront buildings with a dull yellow light. It looked eerie and dirty just like a dockside area in England, thought Amelia, as she lifted Evan up the ladder into the arms of a waiting seaman and climbed to the top herself. She glanced back down at Molly who was preparing to climb up, then put out one foot and stepped onto dry ground for the first time in over four months. They had reached Van Diemen's Land.

Chapter 13.   Hobart Town, October 1831

The group of women waited shivering on the wharf. The whole waterfront area was silent and deserted, although come daylight, it would be bustling and noisy like any port, supposed Amelia. It was four o'clock in the early hours of the morning, and the disembarkation process was underway.

"Why would we come ashore at this time of the morning?" asked Amelia of her companion, Molly.

"Per'aps it's t' save us bein' stared a', you know?" replied Molly. But she didn't really care, she just wished the ground would stop moving! Matron had warned them about the strange sensation of standing on solid ground after such a long time at sea, but it was very disconcerting to experience it.

Amelia doubted that the officials would much care about the humiliation of the women walking through the streets in daylight, there must be another reason. She was unaware that parading one hundred and fifty new women in the streets would cause a near riot in the woman-hungry colony, and that in the past, men had rushed at the poor girls being unloaded from ships and simply carried them away!

When all the women were assembled in the dim lamplight of the waterfront, they were formed into lines and instructed to begin walking. Guards walked in front accompanied by a local guide and others to the sides and the rear of the party. Amelia, carrying two year old Evan, and being a small woman herself, hoped they would not have to walk too far. Most of the women were underweight. Despite the reasonable rations on the ship, poor health on boarding, limited exercise and bouts of seasickness had prevented any substantial improvement in their physical condition.

The air was cold, but the breeze had gone now they had left the open waterfront behind, and in some areas it was so dark, the women could not see where they were walking at all. Amelia was struggling with her possessions and Evan, so Molly took her bundle. "'Ere, give me tha', she said in her strong cockney accent, "you've go' your work cu' ou' just carryin' the li'le fella!"

"Oh Molly, you are so kind," said Amelia breathlessly, as she struggled up a slope. "I don't know how I would have lasted the journey on the ship if it wasn't for you!"

"I'm gra'eful to you, Amelia, for 'elpin' me and lookin' after me. I's been a bi' like wha' 'avin a mother must be like, I wager, although, ye're no' as old as me mother would be o' course," she said hastily. Both the women chuckled softly. Although they were about to begin a new and challenging life as transported convicts and both felt very anxious, Amelia shook her head in wonder at the positive energy that Molly exuded. She could still find a way to make her laugh despite their circumstances, and Amelia regarded this ability as a real gift.

Suddenly an unearthly sound rent the air! It sounded like a loud cackling, then a whooping, evil sounding laugh. They all stopped, terrified, and some of the women screamed in fear.

"It's just a bird!" called their guide who was from the local police guard, and the other guards repeated the information. "Keep moving!"

"A bird!" said Molly fearfully, "I' sounded more li'e an evil banshee than a bird!"

Amelia agreed that it was a very disturbing sound, and walked with less confidence, wondering what other strange or dangerous animals there may be in a place like this. The guards next to them carried lanterns, and as the procession continued through the dirt streets and out of the town, the night became darker and darker.

She felt as if she were in a strange dream, with the ghostly noises and the darkness only interrupted by the light of the nearest lamp which seemed to float along on its own. The long lines of women stumbled along, focusing on the light, not able to see the ground in front of them.

A flurry of movement made them jump back in fear! An animal sped through the line of people, causing the frightened women to scatter in all directions. Jumping quickly on muscular legs, and making a heavy thumping sound each time it touched the ground, its gait was most unusual. Its large strong body was the size of a man's with a long tail curving behind, and it appeared suddenly as if from nowhere and then disappeared out of sight again just as swiftly. The gasps and shrieks of the women showed how frightened they all were. They had never seen anything like it!

"That is called a kangaroo," said the guard next to Amelia conversationally, although the shaking in his voice indicated he must have had as great a shock as they.

"W..Will they attack us?" asked Amelia, concerned not only for herself, but also for her son.

"No, ma'am, they feed only on grass, and they make good eating too, I'm told. We must have frightened it," the man informed them matter of factly.

"Us, frigh'en tha' animal?" laughed Molly shakily. "'Scuse me Sir, bu' I think i's the other way 'round!"

They continued on their way up the dark track, and now that the town was behind them, the scurrying of many smaller animals could be heard around, which made them all jump and tremble. Other new sounds were very strange too. A loud gurgling, growling noise came from up a tree, and this woke Evan, who had been peacefully sleeping in Amelia's arms until then. Although they hurried by the tree, Evan started to cry and struggle, and Amelia shifted him to her other hip, her arms aching.

"I'm going to have to stop," she gasped to the guard, putting the screaming child down. "I can't carry him any further. Please!"

"You can't stop 'ere, Ma'am, he said politely, we've been walking for about two and a half miles, so only another half a mile to go now."

Half a mile! Amelia could hardly put one foot in front of the other. Evan would not walk himself or go to Molly, so she picked him up again and by shifting him constantly from one side to the other she managed to struggle on, Molly still lugging both bundles of clothing.

The temperature had noticeably dropped since the group left the river, and the air now had a touch of iciness about it. The two women could hear the sound of rushing water getting closer, and in the dim light of pre-dawn they saw a huge, sinister stone wall loom up in front of them. They all trooped along the wall to where stout wooden gates stood. The gates swung open with an eerie creaking, and light spilled out. They had reached the Female Factory.

The doors closed behind them with a dull clang, and Amelia looked around, putting Evan down and leaning against the wall in exhaustion. They were standing in a large covered porch area inside the wall, and the uncertain women crowded together for warmth.

Ten at a time, they were called into a large receiving room at the side. They were told by a strict sounding woman to strip off all their clothes and wash thoroughly. There was a bucket of water and a bar of carbolic soap in front of each convict. It was discomforting to strip naked in front of everyone else as well as the guard in the corner, and cold too, but they had no choice but to follow orders and Amelia dipped her soap into the water.

"Oh!" she called out in shock. The water was icy cold, probably straight from the rushing stream nearby, she thought. She washed herself and dried her body with her old clothes. Shivering, she put on the clothing provided. It was a uniform consisting of underclothes, a dress, pinafore, shawl, boots and gloves. Although the material of the dress was of a rough, scratchy material, Amelia supposed it would become more comfortable after wearing in. She turned her head in consternation, as screams could be heard coming from the small room adjacent. What could be going on in there? Then Amelia heard her name being called.

"Amelia Hobbs! You will be known as number eighty six. Take your cap and proceed through the door." She dragged Evan by the hand into the other room and stopped in dismay. The two girls that were already there were kneeling on the floor, their long hair being cut off in reams. One of the girls was sobbing. Amelia recognized Hannah, who she had treated in the ship's hospital at one time. The girl stood up, arms over her head, trying to hide the short, ragged boyish cut of her hair, tears streaming down her cheeks. She stumbled out in distress.

Amelia was forced to kneel and suffer the same indignity as the others. As she waited for the shears to do their work, she thought of her father, and the life she had once had, of her children and John Skinner. Once more, she had no choice but to submit, and as the long thick dark hair fell to the hard stone floor, it was as if her old life was also shed. Amelia, as had the other women, cried tears of exhaustion and humiliation, but resolutely stifled her emotions. This was the beginning of her new life.

As the group of women stepped out of the vestibule area into the yard, the matron of the institution looked down at them from the window of her lodgings on the second floor above the receiving room. She noticed the child walking with the small, dark haired woman. There's one for the orphan school soon, she thought.

She cast her eye over the factory from her vantage point. The facility was enclosed by a high stone wall, and lined on all four sides by narrow two storey buildings. Yet another double level building extended down the centre, dividing the outside space into four sections, or yards. The women were taken to the assignment section, where the accommodation was crowded dormitories. Amelia and Molly managed to stick together and made sure they were in the same room.

Once each person had claimed a sleeping place, they were told to wait outside. It was cold, but the cap they now wore on their heads helped protect them from the wind, and their shawls were wrapped securely around their bodies and right up to the neck. While they waited the two friends observed their new home in the dawn light.

Other women were going about their early morning chores, emptying buckets in small cell-like structures which from the smell, they took to be the privies. As they looked around it became apparent why the place felt so wintry.

"Cor, look at them walls!" exclaimed Molly, turning around on the spot. They're so 'igh, y' can' even see the sky." The young woman was right. The monstrous, towering stone walls cast a gloom of cold, solid finality over the place. Amelia supposed they might get sunlight briefly, just in the middle of the day when the sun was at its highest. The ground was wet and the lower part of the building's walls were damp and mossy. However it was not the buildings that caught Amelia's eye, but another forbidding sight.

"Look Molly, we are right in the shadow of that mountain." Amelia tried to see the top, but it was hidden from sight by huge trees that strained towards the light and filled the gully, as if marching in succession up the foothills. They could hear the torrent of water nearby gushing down the rivulet, and Amelia guessed that its source was the mountain, and although freezing cold would at least be clean.

A bell was rung, and other women, obviously inmates, started making their way through a door into the neighbouring yard. Guards gestured for the new arrivals to follow, so they proceeded through the door into an area which obviously housed the kitchens and laundries. Amelia and Molly lined up and duly received their ration of gruel and a lump of bread. The matron came to address them after they had eaten.

"I am Mrs Winters, Matron of this centre, the Hobart Female Factory. You will begin in the assignment yard, where you will wait to be allocated to a master who will take you to your place of work. If you are not assigned immediately, there is much work here, which I will direct you to do. I hope you decide to work well, as life will be much better for you if you do so. If there is any disobedience or refusal to work, you will be sent to crime class, and then after a period of punishment and hard labour, you will have to go through a probation period in the corresponding yard to prove to me you are worthy of assignment.

"You will rise at five, remove your waste, wash yourself and tidy your bedding, and be in your yard for muster at six o'clock daily. Rations will be provided at seven o'clock, and at eight, your working day will start. Prayers are in the Chapel at four every afternoon. All new residents wait here, and I will provide you with mending from the laundry to work on. Tomorrow, some gentlemen are coming to select workers at ten o'clock, so you will be asked to assemble in the assignment yard, where I will explain the process. All women with children, come and see me now. Dismissed!"

Chapter 14.

Molly went to fetch her mending, and Amelia walked with trepidation towards the group of mothers and children. Matron stood beside a man who sat at a table with a large ledger open before him. "What is your name?" she asked one woman, "and your number?"

"Me name is Margaret, but I can' remember me number." the confused woman answered.

Matron sighed with impatience, and after consulting with the man and his book, she said, "your number is ninety-two, and don't you forget it! You will be known by that number while you are here, not your name!" She went on to ask further questions, and then it was Amelia's turn.

"Name and number!" barked Mrs Winters.

"Amelia Hobbs, Ma'am, number eighty six."

Matron looked slightly mollified. "Well at least one of you remembers her number. The name and age of your child please?"

"Evan, Ma'am. He is two and a half years coming up next month."

When all the members of the group had given their details to be recorded in the ledger, Matron pointed to the four eldest children. A girl of eleven whose mother, Elizabeth, had died on the sea voyage was included in this group; and Mrs Winters ushered them together. "Right, you lot will be going straight to the orphan school." She nodded to a guard in the corner, and he came over and tried to take the children to the vestibule near the gates.

The mothers of the selected children started to wail and cry, and Mrs Winters spoke to them sternly. "Brace up! You are convicts, transported here because you broke the law. You are the property of the British government now, and once the children are of an age to be moved they go to the orphan school. We don't have room for them here, and perhaps they can get some education and become useful citizens. Once you have served your sentence, you may go and retrieve your child from the school."

This speech did no good, as the women continued to cry and cling to their children. Finally mothers and children were separated and the gates opened, revealing a carriage outside, presumably to transport the children.

Once they had gone and the grieving mothers sent back to the assignment yard, Matron gestured to the rest, who had younger children or babies, to follow her. The woman took them to a building next to the kitchens, which was in two levels. There were two rooms, one upstairs and one down, each was packed with nursery cots, one next to the other in rows. There were many children there, all infants up to around two or three years of age. They were sitting or lying in filthy beds, or standing holding on to the sides, dolefully staring at the newcomers. Matron gestured for the new children and babies to be allocated a space, and the mothers were forced to leave them there under the charge of several convict women, who were obviously supervising them.

"You can come and see your children when you have finished your daily work and at mealtimes," explained Matron. "Those that are nursing can continue to do so, but as a rule, the babies are weaned at six months." She ushered the women down the stairs to fetch their allocated mending for the day, and sent them away.

"Six months!" declared Amelia to Molly. "That is too young to be weaned! Many of those babies will die, I am sure of that! Thank the Lord that Evan is older and has had the benefit of nursing longer," she said fervently.

"The orphan school," murmured Molly, "sounds a bi' li'e a work'ouse." She looked up at Amelia. "Will Evan 'ave to go there do y' think?"

"I have no doubt he will Molly," confirmed Amelia, tears coming to her eyes as she tried not to think about it. "But he's here now, that's what matters. Molly, I've been thinking," she said urgently. "If you get the chance to be assigned to a master, you must go. It is an opportunity to make a more comfortable home than here, and if you work well, you will earn your freedom. I heard that you can get a Ticket of Leave after only a few years if you are recommended by good behaviour."

"I s'pose i' depends on 'oo your master is too. Ya could be lu'y to 'ave a kind one." Molly paused, reflectively. "All righ' Amelia, I will try, but... wha' if we are separa'ed?" she wailed. Amelia had no answer, but privately thought it unlikely they would be assigned together.

The bustle in the yard at ten o'clock indicated it was time for the gentlemen to pick their new servants. Mrs Winters chivvied the women into two long lines, their numbers having swelled significantly with the new arrivals. She explained the procedure for their benefit.

"You will curtsey nicely to each gentleman as he passes, and if he likes the look of you, he will drop a handkerchief in front of you. If you accept the post, you must pick it up and present it to him. The first gentleman has a farm, so only those women with farm experience must step forward.

Amelia took her place in the line, as she had milked cows and fed livestock, but she hoped with all her might that the man did not pick her. She wanted to stay with Molly and Evan. The well-dressed gentleman strolled down the line, looking intently at each candidate. Amelia kept her eyes downcast, and tried to be as insignificant as possible.

Perhaps she did not look strong enough for the required work, as he dropped his silk kerchief in front of a young, cheerful looking woman. She promptly picked it up, folded it neatly and presented it to the man with a quick curtsey. "Wish me luck!" She said to the girl next to her and followed her new master to wait at the receiving room to be recorded in the assignment lists.

The next two men wanted domestic servants so all the women stood forward. There was a scuffle at the end of the line, as two or three women would not line up. When the guard forced them to do so, they refused to curtsey, turning around and presenting their backs towards the gentlemen.

The guards forcefully grabbed the women by their arms, and threw them to the ground. Amelia recognised them, Morag, Elsie and Sarah, the tough trouble-makers from *'The Mary'*, who had threatened to throw Molly over the side. "Off to crime class!" Matron barked, and the three were herded unceremoniously away.

The potential masters, who had been disconcerted by the behaviour of these women, resumed their inspection of the others in the line-up. One young woman, no more than a girl, was selected, and the other, to Amelia's dismay, cast his kerchief in front of Molly. The girl looked at her, nodded in affirmation, and then bent down and retrieved it with a shaking hand. She handed it to the elderly gentleman, and he indicated that she should follow him. As Molly passed her companion she paused. "Goodbye Amelia. You 'ave been a be'er friend to me than anyone ever 'as. I 'ope we mee' again. Goodbye!" and marching away with a determined step, she did as she was bid.

Amelia watched her friend trying to be brave, but she knew that Molly was terrified. The young woman knew little of life in a gentleman's house, but she had some cleaning and laundry skills from her work on the ship, so it could only be hoped that she learned quickly. Amelia closed her eyes for a moment, and prayed that the young woman's master would be a kind one, and when she opened them, Molly had vanished.

Chapter 15.

Amelia relaxed against the wall in the corner of the assignment yard, eyes closed and face raised to the warmth. It was the only one place in that yard where the sun reached warming fingers down to ground level for an hour or two in the middle of the day. She turned around and let the sun caress her back, enjoying a brief moment of bliss.

She studied the huge blocks of stone that again enclosed her world. The sight of them was familiar, their stoic presence somehow comforting, and she traced her fingers over the grooves and chisel patterns that covered the surface whilst allowing the welcome heat to soak into her body.

Molly had been assigned two weeks earlier, and Amelia's life was a duller, lonelier existence without her. She hoped that the girl was doing well and controlling her cheeky tongue. She smiled to herself, remembering her friend's quick wit and sense of the ridiculous.

After the midday meal, Amelia had been to see her son who seemed in reasonable health. He liked to play with the other children although he didn't usually have much energy. Poor Evan, he missed Molly too. She was lost in her daydream; so much so, that when the woman behind her spoke, it made her jump.

"'Ello Amelia. I came to ge' some sun too!" It was Lucy Hurst, one of the women that Amelia had treated for burns from an accident with hot soup, during their sea voyage.

"How do you do, Lucy?" asked Amelia, turning around again and leaning against the warm stones. "Are you not working in the kitchen anymore?"

"No, thank the Lord," replied the young woman heaving a sigh of relief. "I 'ave done my shift there for two weeks, so I won't 'ave to go back for a while. I didn't like the work much, but I did hear a lot of interestin' things while I was there."

"Oh?" said Amelia, tilted her head curiously, "what in particular?"

"Well I 'eard what happened to the 'orrible threesome after they behaved so badly on that first day when the Masters came." She put her finger to the side of her nose, and Amelia leaned closer with interest. "They were sent to crime class, first to the dark cells for three days on bread and wa'er, then to the washtubs for a fortnight. They are still there, in the yard next to the kitchen. You can hear them swearin' and cursin' all day!"

"The dark cells?" questioned Amelia with a shudder. "What are they?"

"Tiny stone cells with just a fold up bed and a bucke'. They ge' no light at all, so you're in the pitch black, except when they open the 'atch to give y' rations."

"I hope I never have to go in there," said Amelia, remembering her experience inside the dreaded 'Black Box' on the ship, "but are the washtubs so bad?"

"The factory, that's this place," explained Lucy, "takes in laundry from the 'ospital, schools and the like to 'elp pay for the place. All the washin's done in big tubs with freezin' cold water direct from that rivulet y' can hear runnin'. You have to use carbolic soap, and they have their hands in that stuff for nine or

115

ten hours a day. I 'eard that after a few days, the skin all peels off ya hands and they get so painful it 'urts to put 'em in the wa'er." She related all this with glee, as Lucy had borne the intimidation from the three women on the ship as many had.

Amelia did chuckle to herself, imagining the tough women swearing at the top of their voices all day, yet forced to work. Somehow she didn't think that it would improve their behaviour much though. "Once they finish at the tubs, will they be back in here?" Amelia was hoping not, and the thought of a raging mad Morag, with sore hands and vengeance in her mind, made her shudder. She would not be very pleasant to have around to say the least!

"No, after the two weeks are finished, they go to the other yard, it's called probation class, and they 'ave to mainly work on weavin' blankets and sewin' there. Y' do get a bi' of meat though. They have to prove that they deserve to come back 'ere for assignment before they are moved back.

"We won't be seeing them for quite some time then!" laughed Amelia. "Good, what a relief! What happened to Ann Henry, your friend from the ship? I saw her a few days ago."

"Ann was a very good friend on our journey," confirmed Lucy, nodding. "When we both got burned so badly with that soup, we spent a lot of time together while we was recoverin', and I got to know 'er very well. She is a good girl, Ann, and she was assigned just yesterday, when we 'ad that whole group of men come to choose. I think I 'eard that the man was a publican. But I miss 'er already." The tears threatened to spill over, and Amelia put a hand on Lucy's arm.

"I miss dear Molly too, more than I ever would have imagined. I pray for her every day," said Amelia, with her voice catching in her throat with emotion, and the two women shed a tear together. "But it is good news that she is still with her master, she must be getting along very well there and I hope it continues, for her sake."

"Did you know there are three more masters comin' tomorrow?" asked Lucy pensively. "They've all finally 'eard there are new women 'ere, so they're out to find new servants."

The next morning the women lined up for inspection, as usual. The lines were shorter now, as already about thirty of them had been assigned. There were two men who looked like country gentlemen and a well-dressed, middle aged couple walking through the gate together. Once again, the inspection process began, and Amelia stood looking at the ground, waiting. A pair of shiny shoes and some dainty slippers stopped in front of her.

"Can you read and write?" asked the gentleman in a cultured voice, looking down at Amelia suspiciously, "as we need someone with an education."

Amelia, startled, looked up and saw the well-dressed couple staring at her intently. She answered the man clearly. "Yes, Sir, I can." Then she looked down at the shoes again. A silk handkerchief floated down from above and landed next to her boot. As if in a dream, Amelia picked it up, folded it, and handed it to the man with a curtsey.

"Wait over there," said the man, and they continued along the line, obviously seeking a second servant. Amelia walked over and stood with resignation next to Matron, where he had indicated.

Suddenly, she straightened up in horror. "Mrs Winters!" Amelia whispered urgently, a clenching fear mounting in her stomach. "What about my child, my son?"

"He was sent to the orphan school this morning with nine other children. So don't worry about him, he's already gone." Mrs Winters spoke matter-of-factly.

"But," Amelia said loudly, shocked. "I didn't even say goodbye! He won't know where he's going. He'll be afraid!" But Matron just shushed her.

Amelia slumped helplessly, and was reminded yet again by the brutal convict system that she was not in control of her children, herself, or indeed anything in her life. By the time the couple came to collect her, Amelia was full of such misery that she stumbled after them to the coach, scarcely able to see through her tears, and too distressed to think rationally. She had known that Evan would go to the orphan school at some stage, but was hoping that it would not happen so soon.

Mr and Mrs Giblin resided in a stately home on the waterfront just in the south end of Hobart Town, near the battery that had been built fifteen years before to defend the town. The couple alighted from the carriage in the drive at the front of the house, and Amelia and her fellow assigned worker were sent around the back to the housekeeper. The housekeeper showed them the kitchen, laundry and the room where they were to sleep, and told Amelia that part of her duties would be to watch the two small children, and to help them with their reading and writing.

I don't want to watch someone else's children thought Amelia in despair. I only want my own. Evan, Evan! The thought of him crying for his mother in a strange place brought Amelia to tears again. She made a decision that she would go to him. In her irrational state, Amelia gave no consideration to the consequences should she follow through with this idea, she could only resolve that she must leave this place and find the orphan school. Find her son!

Later, after listening to all the instructions from the woman in charge, Amelia ventured a question. "Begging your pardon Ma'am, but where is New Town?" She knew the orphan school was called St John's and was situated in a place with that name.

"What on earth does the likes of you need to know that for?" asked the housekeeper, vexed. "But since you ask, it is north of Hobart Town, about three miles."

The two convicts were locked in the first floor room to sleep that evening, but it was a simple matter for Amelia to squeeze out the small window, and carefully climb down the trellis to the dark garden. She froze once reaching ground level, watching for signs of movement, but seeing no one, made her way out into the street and wavered, wondering which way to go.

She hurried downhill until coming across the rocky shore and then towards where she thought the main town would be. Following the river was not easy, and the streets seemed to twist and turn until Amelia lost all sense of direction. Surely she must have covered three miles already!

Seeing larger buildings up ahead, Amelia thought that she must have reached the main part of Hobart Town. Following the water to the familiar wharf area, she then turned and climbed the hill in an inland direction, attracted by the noisy sounds of a public house not far hence. There were many unsavoury characters loitering around the street in the front of the tavern. Amelia walked hesitantly up to the group.

"Pardon me, but could any of you gentlemen direct me towards New Town?" she asked politely.

There was a silence as all the men turned to look at her, then they burst into raucous laughter. One particularly uncouth man, with filthy clothes and a strong smell of sweat, sidled closer. "Ooohh, what 'ave we got 'ere?" he asked in a knowing voice, and circled Amelia like a cat stalking a mouse. "I live in New Town, as it 'appens, and I could take you there."

Amelia backed away, "I would much appreciate it Sir, if you could just point the way up the right street, I don't want to put you to any trouble."

The men looked at each other, grinning. "Oh leave de poor wench alone," said one in an Irish brogue, exasperated. "She doesn't want de company of de loikes of you!" And he held his tankard of Guinness in one hand and waved his other, in what Amelia presumed was a northerly direction up a long, straight street that was lit occasionally by street lamps. "Go up dat way, lass, about t'ree miles to New Town. Boot be careful how ye go, dere are scoundrels about!" and he raised his eyebrows in the direction of his fellow drinker.

She thanked the helpful man, and hastily followed his direction. Another three miles still! Amelia supposed she had

120

taken the long way from Mr Giblin's house. There was little activity on the street; here and there she could see a pub with people spilling out onto the street, but she avoided these and slipped past on the other side of the road. Amelia felt vulnerable, and kept looking behind her apprehensively to ensure she was not being followed, but could see no one.

Suddenly, a man stepped out from behind a tree and grabbed her arm! "Well, have you found New Town yet?" asked a cruel voice, and Amelia recognised the sneering drunkard from the tavern.

"Please let me go Sir, I need to get to New Town!" she said urgently. "Please Sir, I have to go to my son."

"Sir, this, Sir, that." the man grimaced. "I ain't no Sir! And you are a foolish woman for goin' out on your own at this time o' nigh'. You'll soon regre' it!" And he held her in a vice-like grip and dragged her further up the street. Amelia screamed at the top of her lungs.

"Help, someone! Help me!" She was desperate to get to Evan, and this man would not stand in her way.

Terrified, she fought the man, struggling with all her might, as Amelia knew that her life may well depend on freeing herself from the man's clutches. With difficulty he picked her up, heaving the writhing woman over his shoulder and made to carry her away.

A door opened beside them, and a gentleman rushed out from a large house that was situated right on the street front. He saw Amelia being bodily lifted, and called out in an imperious voice.

"Unhand that woman at once, you brigand!" And he called back into the house. "Charles! Help me out here at once!" and another man came running from the building. Amelia's attacker dropped her in a heap and sprinted away into the darkness. One of the men pursued him while the other came to pick Amelia up from the ground. "I say, are you hurt?"

The second man returned, being unable to catch up with the offender in the dark. "Dammed lout," he said, breathing heavily, his hands on his knees. "This place is full of scum like that."

The men questioned Amelia about why she was out by herself in the street at such a late hour. Without mentioning that she was a convict servant, she answered that she was on her way to New Town to collect her son who was waiting for her. Amelia insisted upon leaving and continuing on her way, against the advice of her saviours. "I thank you gentlemen, for coming to my aid, but now I must go and return to my son." The men were not convinced and stood on the street looking after her.

"Charles, when you ride down past the constable's post, do you think it might be a good idea to stop and tell him of this incident? I don't believe that woman's story. I think she's a runaway." The other man agreed to do so, and went to fetch his top hat and his horse.

Amelia made it another mile along the route to New Town, being far more cautious about being seen, scurrying from shadow to shadow. The sound of hooves came from behind her, approaching quickly, and Amelia looked around in the near darkness to try and find a place to hide. She hurriedly stepped through a gate and stood silently behind some bushes, hoping the horses would pass by. They stopped close by, however, and two men's voices could be heard as they called to each other.

"She can't have gone much further than this. Let's go back that way!" called a voice, and the frightened woman heard the sound of a horse moving away. Amelia quietly crept out of her hiding place and turned north once more, almost colliding with the second horse which was standing quietly in the road, its rider waiting for her.

"Oh!" she squealed in fright. Trying to run was futile, as the rider urged the horse to follow quickly, and a strong arm reached down and held her fast in an iron grip.

The man dismounted, and Amelia immediately saw with dismay that he was a police constable. "I thought I saw something move!" he said with satisfaction, holding her arm and pulling her into the lamp light. He called to his comrade. "Sergeant Wright! I have her!" There was an answering shout and the increasing sound of hooves indicated that the second horse was returning directly.

Amelia was put up on the saddle in front of the constable and taken to the police post back toward the centre of the town. Here she was questioned, and unable to give a satisfactory answer as to her identity and her presence in the street alone, she was put in a cell till the following morning. Amelia cried all night, thinking about Evan, and bitterly disappointed that her mission to see him had been thwarted.

The next morning, resigned to telling the truth, she explained to the officer that her son had been taken from her to the orphan school and she was trying to get to New Town to find him. Sergeant Wright felt sorry for the distressed mother, but could do nothing but report her to the convict authorities.

Amelia was taken to Mr Giblin's house, but the couple refused to have her back. She was to be returned to the female factory and punished. The police cart took her directly there, and as they approached the forbidding mountain, an imposing stone building at its foot came into view and an obliging constable told her that it was the Cascades Brewery.

Amelia disembarked at the stone wall of the factory to the familiar accompaniment of rushing water. Back in the receiving room, she learned that her punishment for absconding would be three days solitary in the dark cells on bread and water, then fourteen days at hard labour.

Mrs Winters brusquely gestured with her hand and a guard came and dragged her unsympathetically away, as the matron looked on rigidly with her arms folded. Amelia was taken through the thick wooden door that designated crime class, and it was securely locked behind her. There were no women in the yard, but long rows of cells indicated where they might be.

The corridor was dank and damp and all light receded except for the guard's lamp. At the very end of the corridor a door stood open. Amelia was pushed into the cell and she had a brief glimpse in the lamplight of an iron bed with a straw tick and a bucket in the corner, before the door thudded closed behind her and the silent blackness became absolute.

Chapter 16.

Her eyes were open but Amelia could see nothing. She lay on the dirty straw mattress and stared into nothingness, hour after hour, thinking of her children. It dawned on Amelia that she had been a fool to entertain the notion that she may be able to take her son with her to wherever she was assigned, and even more of a fool to think that she could get Evan out of the orphan school.

They were now trapped in the relentless juggernaut of the convict system, and Evan would have been marked for transfer to New Town soon after they arrived as he had been amongst the oldest children in the nursery yard. From the moment they departed from England, it was inevitable that he would be taken from his mother to that institution.

Amelia was powerless to help her youngest son for the present, and she could do nothing but hope and pray for Charles, Martha, Thomas and Polly, left behind in England. Were they in the workhouse? Surely Mrs Fowler would not agree to have them permanently, and it was a forlorn hope that their father may have taken responsibility for them.

Evan had now been taken from her too, but as Amelia endured her solitude, she made a decision that although it may not be possible at this moment, one day she would go and find her son, and bring him home with her.

After three days in the dark cell, Amelia was weak from lack of food and the searing light hurt her eyes when she came out from the dark. She was put into another cell, where there was a little light, and given a basket of old tarred ropes. Her task was to pick the ropes apart, separating the strands and putting all the fibre into the basket for collection. These old fibres would be mixed with tar and become caulking for repairing ships timbers.

Listlessly, Amelia plucked at the ropes until late in the day she was let out to go to chapel. The women in crime class were kept in a separate walled off section of the chapel to the other women. After the service had finished, they were taken back to their individual cells for evening rations, in isolation.

Fourteen days passed excruciatingly slowly. The work was tedious, and there was no company or conversation to help pass the time. Amelia's fingers became sore and dry, until the skin split on the ends, and it became very painful to pull apart the strands of rope. She tried to use her fingernails, but they soon tore off, leaving nothing to protect her at all. Lucy had reported of the harsh conditions at the washtubs, but Amelia would have rather had been there than alone in her cell. The day finally came when she was to be moved, and Amelia entered probation class.

The mutton soup and bread that was provided at midday was the best meal that Amelia had enjoyed for some time, after the basic rations of crime class. There was not much meat in the soup, as the officers took their helpings first and made sure they got the largest chunks. All the same, the fat was satisfying, and there were a few vegetables in it too.

Each day, the women were occupied working at sewing and weaving until after the midday meal when they were to have a short break for exercise in the yard. Again after chapel in the evening there was an opportunity for socialising and fresh air, and Amelia had her first chance to look at the other women in the yard. As expected, Elsie and Sarah were there, and causing trouble for the guards, but Morag was not to be seen. Amelia assumed she was in crime class for bad behaviour, and this assumption was soon proved correct.

It became apparent that there was a well organised racket going on, with food parcels being thrown over the walls to the women. At regular intervals throughout the first week, when the yard was clear of guards, a signal rock was thrown over the wall telling the suppliers on the outside that all was well. Immediately, a package would fly back in return and the women would scurry over and throw themselves upon it, snarling and fighting over it like dogs.

"It be mine, so ge' ye're filthy hands off it!" hissed Elsie.

"Go an' ge' you're own ruddy parcel, ya trollop," snapped Sarah, slapping at the hands of another grasping woman.

Having got possession of the bundle with difficulty, the two women would spirit it away to their sleeping quarters and immediately gulp down whatever food items lay within, lest they were caught. The packets often contained tobacco, and some luxuries such as soap, which the women would trade for other items within the factory.

Amelia kept to herself, afraid of the women and not wanting to be sent back to crime class. But she watched them, and on her fourth day in the probation yard, it happened. The signal rock was sent, the parcel flew over, the second it landed four or five women pounced on it and at the same instant, the gate opened and Matron and a guard entered.

"What the devil is going on here?" exclaimed the guard, reacting swiftly by swinging his truncheon, and the women fell away, leaving Sarah, the tough cockney, at the bottom of the pile holding fast to the illicit hoard. The man reached down and wrenched it from her grasp.

"You'll be joining your friend, Morag, at the wash tubs for a month, as you are clearly the ringleader here," said Mrs Winters briskly to Sarah after she had recovered from her surprise and got to her feet. "We will have to make sure we break up this little operation will we not?" and she looked at the guard who nodded.

The five women looked sullen and made rude gestures. One jeered at the woman in charge, "Fink ya can stop us, do ya', well ya can', we do wha' we like!" and the whole group around the parcel roared with laughter.

"You are all incorrigible women!" exclaimed the Matron. "You have no hope of being assigned or having better conditions, as you insist on behaving thus." She went on. "You others will also be sent back to crime class for two weeks, as it appears you are all members of this gang. Oh yes, we shall get a mountain of laundry done! And if any of you so much as say a word out of line, it will be the iron collar for you!"

Mrs Winters strode to the gate and called another guard. Sarah, Elsie and the three other women involved were all taken back to the wash tubs, leaving Amelia feeling relieved to be free of them, as trouble seemed to follow wherever they went. But she would not have to see them again, as if everything went to plan, she would be back in the assignment yard before they returned.

It was approaching the end of November, and the temperatures were warmer in general. No longer did the women need to crowd into the small patches of sunlight to try and get warm. Amelia was allowed back into assignment class, and although losing weight, felt she had handled the conditions of her punishment as well as possible.

Hannah was still awaiting assignment, and she caught Amelia up with the news on who had come and gone. Some of the women who had been assigned previously were back already, like Amelia, for various offences, and others had left the factory for work. "Lucy Hurst has gone to a farm... and Amelia, there have been two cases of scarlet fever here in the factory! I don't know who, but I heard the doctor talking to Matron about it. They are worried about it getting into the nursery!" For the first time, Amelia felt glad that Evan was no longer a resident of the filthy, overcrowded nursery building, and she closed her eyes, giving a silent 'thank you' to God.

"Have you heard anything of Molly?" asked Amelia, "she isn't here, but has she been back?"

"Not that I know of," answered the girl, "she must have been lucky, and got a good master!" Hannah herself was eager for assigned work soon, and told Amelia there were more masters due to arrive for selection in the following days.

Amelia's next assignment was to one of these, a Mr Boyd and his wife, who lived in great style in a large house in the town. Mr Boyd was a court magistrate, and he took great pains to present himself as a gentleman. Amelia could tell by the manner of his speech that he was not gentry, but a self-made man, perhaps moving into his present position from the military.

She did not blame the man for that, but he put on such airs and Mrs Boyd acted like she was a duchess or suchlike, so that Amelia found that she did not respect the couple at all. They were also quick to find fault with one's work, and spoke unkindly and impatiently to all their servants. One evening, Amelia found herself alone in the house with Mr Boyd, as his wife had taken the carriage to a 'ladies only' cards evening.

"Amelia, bring me a glass of port," he said abruptly. When she had done so, he put the glass aside.

"Is there anything else, Sir?" enquired Amelia while looking hopefully toward the door, expecting to retire for the evening.

The man reached out, caught hold of Amelia's arm and gave her a swift pull. She was off balance and staggered towards him. He encircled her in his arm and drew her roughly onto his lap.

"Mr Boyd! What do you mean by this?" snapped Amelia sharply, struggling to get away.

"There is something else I require," he said self-importantly, "and it is up to the likes of you, wench, to provide it." The look on his face left Amelia in no doubt of what service he expected.

Amelia thought quickly, "that is not part of my duties Sir, and I will thank you to let me go!" She sat quiet for a moment as if waiting for him to release her. Suddenly she tore her arm from his and leapt away. She ran to the door and wrenched it open, but he was hard upon her heels.

"If you do not let me go, Sir, I will report your behaviour to the authorities!" Amelia said loudly, trapped partway through the door as he held the handle, preventing her from opening it further.

"Who would believe you?" sneered Mr Boyd, "I am an important person in this town, and it would be my word against yours, a convicted criminal!" he spat. "This will go on your record as a charge of insubordination!" But as she slipped out of the door, he made no move to stop her, and Amelia escaped to her room. She probably would be sent back to the factory, but it would be just as well, she reflected. Amelia could see that her present situation could become very difficult indeed.

She was not sent back, but a charge was recorded on her record with a reprimand. The work in the house was not so unpleasant, but since the incident Amelia was on her guard at all times, careful not to be left alone with the master of the house. There came a day that the man found her changing sheets in a bedroom, and she was alone save for another servant in the garden, as the mistress was in town. This time Mr Boyd manhandled Amelia onto the bed, his hand clamped over her mouth to stop her from screaming, and he pawed at her body, trying to tear away her clothing.

There was a loud knock on the front door and the master got to his feet abruptly, straightened his clothing, and left her to go downstairs. Amelia fell back onto the duvet, exhausted but relieved; she was saved! She quickly finished the bed and silently departing the house by the kitchen door, hid in the garden shed until the mistress' carriage returned. She was called to see the lady, and by then, Amelia had a plan.

131

"You lazy, good for nothing woman!" the mistress spoke indignantly, in her faux upper class accent. "You were left with a series of tasks to complete by the time I returned and they are not done! You have scarce completed any of your work. What do you have to say for yourself?"

"I thought, as I felt tired, that your ladyship might do her own laundry and cleaning today!" snapped Amelia, "as that's probably what she did in the days before she left England!"

The woman stepped forward and slapped Amelia across one cheek. "How dare you speak to me so!" she berated Amelia, "you are nothing but a common criminal!"

Amelia stepped back, holding her face. "No real gentlewoman would have acted as you did just now. You are the common one!" and she stared at her defiantly.

Of course Amelia's plan worked. The lady of the house would not stand to have her in the house any more, and had her charged with gross insubordination. So, as hoped for, the convict worker was sent back to the factory, free from the presumptuous Mr Boyd. She knew full well that what the master had said was true; nobody would believe her in preference to a court magistrate. It would be more likely that reporting Mr Boyd's actions would only get her sentence extended, so the simple answer had been to abuse her mistress instead! A month at the washtubs, thought Amelia gloomily. It was worth it though, to escape the constant threat of abuse, and she was duly received at the factory and sent back to crime class.

Chapter 17.

Amelia did not mind the work of laundry, as a rule, but the strong soap and freezing water did affect the skin on ones hands very badly. When they were not immersed in water, Amelia tried to keep her hands warm and dry. She even managed to get a lump of mutton fat from one of the girls who worked in the kitchen and rubbed a little into her skin at night and in the mornings before she began work, which did help. It was whilst at the tubs that Amelia witnessed the use of the Iron Collar. It was Sarah, one of 'the incorrigibles', who earned two weeks experiencing the delights of that device of torture.

The wash tubs, lined up side by side, were all in use. Amelia was down one end of the line, and Morag, Sarah and Elsie were all at tubs further along. The furtive looks and coarse laughter were signs that a plan was afoot, and as the guard walked past Sarah's tub, she suddenly upended it, the surge of cold water soaking the man and knocking him off his feet. Sarah saw her opportunity and leapt onto him, pummelling him with her fists and banging his head onto the ground. Shouts from the guards overlooking the yard had other guards come running, and they dragged the crazed woman off their comrade.

"Ge' off me, ya no good sons of whores! 'E deserves all 'e ge's, the dir'y bastard. 'E keeps givin' me the eye, bu' if 'e comes in me cell and wants i' again, I'll make sure I've go' a knife, and I'll cu' i' off!" The guards paid no heed to Sarah's words, but hauled her away to the dark cells.

Amelia was shocked to conclude from what she heard that the guard had taken advantage of Sarah when she was in her cell alone, forcing himself on her. Although she disliked and feared the woman, Amelia was surprised to find that she suddenly felt sorry for her.

Sarah reappeared after three days in the dark cells wearing the iron contraption that was to remain fastened around her neck night and day for two weeks. There were sores rubbed raw on her flesh, and bruises up her neck from bumping the collar against doorways. The thing weighed around nine pounds, and had long spikes sticking out to prevent one lying down or resting one's head. The woman worked at the tubs with the device in place although she became weaker and weaker, obviously unwell, and exhausted from being unable to sleep. The sight of the raw, infected flesh around the girl's neck and shoulders was horrible to behold, and all the women at the tubs worked in silence, as Sarah's suffering affected them all. Finally, in the second week of her punishment, Sarah collapsed.

The doctor was sent for and he examined her on the wet ground of the wash yard, where she lay in a contorted position, her head hanging from the collar that prevented her from falling flat to the ground. "She has a serious infection where this – instrument of torture..." he paused in disgust, "has been resting on the collar bones and completely worn away the skin. The thing is resting on bone alone, and the putrid infection has spread all over the area!" He looked up at Matron. "I have wanted these barbaric contraptions banned for years."

"But doctor, these women are ...incorrigible!" she spluttered. "If they are already in hard labour and behave thus, what else are we to do with them?"

"Well, at least it could be taken off at night!" said the man indignantly, "so the poor creature can sleep. That would not do enough to rid her of this infection though. She needs to have treatment immediately or I fear for her life!"

The two proceeded to argue in whispers about the proposed course of action, and eventually a guard came with a key and the collar was removed. Sarah was taken from the yard but never returned, and they heard some days later that she had died of her infection. Morag and Elsie became even more sullen and uncooperative, obviously grieving for their friend and angry about her treatment. Amelia kept her distance, as she was only too well aware that it would not be a good idea to antagonise the women, and in time, she was removed from crime class again.

Now February, it was unbearably hot, with a scorching wind blowing across the yards, turning the ground, which had once been mud, into a fine dust that coated everything and got into one's eyes. Back in the assignment yard there was much bustle, as many new arrivals from a ship that had docked in Hobart Town the week before were settling in or moving to positions with assigned masters.

Amelia, sweltering although in the welcome shade of the wall, struck up a conversation with a woman called Charlotte, who as it happened, was from Worcester.

"Are you from Worcester too, Amelia?" she asked, as they languished in the heat, waiting for dinner to be served.

"Yes, I grew up and lived at Hanley William, a little village on the Hanley Estate just west of the town," answered Amelia. "What tales do you bring of Worcester?"

"The only report I bring is terrible!" Charlotte paused, red eyed, as if remembering with sorrow. "I left there in October, and a terrible scourge of the Cholera was sweeping through the town. At least eighty people had already died in Worcester alone! Two of my sisters died, and I know not what happened to my brother, as I left England before I got word of him. I suppose I was lucky to be on the ship, out in the river, and the sickness did not reach us there."

Amelia stood with her mouth open, stricken. "Cholera! But that is a terrible thing! My children- they would have been in the workhouse..."

"Them work'ouses, they were affected worst of all, I heard there was scarcely a child left alive that was there!" Charlotte looked sad. "I'm so sorry to bring you this tragic news, Amelia."

Amelia sank to the ground, hands over her mouth. Could it be that Charles, Martha, Thomas and Polly had all died from the dreaded disease? It was torture to think of it, but although she imagined the worst and yearned, day after day, night after endless night, to know the truth, Amelia was never to be sure of their fate.

The mood of the people in Worcester was ugly. The bill for voting reform had been defeated only a month before and there was widespread anger and resentment toward the upper class. The wealth threshold for voting was to have been lowered, enabling many middle class merchants and professionals to have voting rights. 'Rotten Boroughs' were common, where voting in the area was restricted to one or two wealthy landowners, giving them disproportionate representation in parliament. But the wealthy protected their own, and the bill was overturned, despite the 'Night of General Illumination', where many thousands across London lit candles and lamps to show support for the reform.

John Skinner was lolling in a chair in 'The Bull and Horn', just down the street from his hovel. He had a large tankard of rum held in his hairy fist, and was drinking with his new friend Thaddeus Rush. Rush was recently up from London, and brought news of unrest in other areas.

"I'm tellin' ya Skinner, there's goin' ta be a rio'! I can tell, from wha' happened in London. As soon as the people 'ere ge' word of the reaction of them Londoners, the same thing will 'appen 'ere! You mark my words! And tha's good news for the likes of us," he ended in a satisfied tone, swilling a large mouthful of liquor.

"What do you mean?" asked John Skinner, his hand clamped tightly around the receptacle as if it might try to escape. "How can any of that affect us? We were never goin' to get the vote anyways, we're still too poor."

"Ah, there's always a profit to be 'ad my friend!" the man said mysteriously, "'specially when there's change in the wind. All the fella's in the mob will be runnin' around, tryin' to ge' attention for this votin' stuff, and we'll be takin' advantage of the confusion to grab some choice items to sell for a pre'y penny!"

Thaddeus Rush knew all about selling things for a pretty penny. In London, his chief form of employment, aside from drinking rum, was operating as a body snatcher. He usually operated at one of the many London graveyards, and would wait for a new funeral before going to work. As soon as night fell, he would dig down at one end of the grave until he could get a good grip on the corpse, and pull it right up out of the ground.

There was a shortage of bodies for dissection at the numerous training colleges for surgeons around London, and he could be paid anywhere from eight to twenty guineas for each one, depending on the current demand and the freshness of the specimen. Rush was in the employ of several doctors who asked no questions, and paid him on the spot.

John Skinner was amazed at the coin that could be made from such activities. "Twenty guineas! A police constable only earns about twenty shillin's in a whole week, that's only one guinea!" He was getting worked up, and thumped on the table in emphasis. "Rowan over there, who used to be a silk weaver before the glove trade died a few years ago, made five shillin's in a week, and you are tellin' me that these doctors will pay *twenty guineas* for one body!"

"Well, I'll admi' tha' was the most I ever got paid, 'cause that particular stiff had never even been buried! I knew the young fella 'ad died a' the work'ouse, 'cause I watch the comin's and goin's there closely, in case I see the doctor 'urryin' in, ya see. I just walked in, pretendin' to be a family member come to claim the body, an' took 'im righ' down to King's and go' me twenty, straigh' off!" Rush grinned at the memory, and took another gulp of the warming liquid.

"Why don' ya keep doin' it then?" asked the man called Skinner.

"No' long ago, there was a couple o' ressurectionists, which's wha' I prefer to call me trade, y' know, and one of 'em was called Burke. Well, Burke an' 'is offsider go' a bi' clever, see, and they go' a 'omeless woman an' a street vagrant tha' no one would miss, ya know? Took 'em down a lane, and 'it 'em over the 'ead wiv a lump a wood. The bodies were still so fresh when they go' 'em at the college, they were still warm. Someone got suspicious, and the two of 'em was arrested and 'ung for murder. Since then, people don't like ressurectionists much, they think we're all 'Burkers'.

They seem to 'ave go' a bi' funny about their dead relatives bein' dug up too, so the police 'ave 'ad a big crack down on folks li'e me. There was also gettin' so many men in the business, tha' we would be fightin' over 'oo go' the la'est stiff, ya know? So I decided to try me lu' somewhere else like."

"Don't think anyone is in that line a business up 'ere, that I know of," said Skinner.

"It used to be too 'ard to ge' the stiffs down to London, where the medical schools are, they'd stink too much after. Bu' I

139

though' now the railway's 'ere in Worcester and i' goes righ' through to London, i' wouldn't take too long ta ge' 'em down there. Trouble is, ya'd 'ave to take 'em on the train in daylight, in a box or a bag or somefin'." He sat and mused about this problem, whilst finishing his rum. "I still fink it's worth doin', 'cause their ain't as many 'angins as there used to be, and tha's 'ow the doctors used ta ge' most of their bodies. Prices will be ge'in 'igher!"

"No, they're not 'angin' 'em, they're sending a lot more people to the colonies now," said John Skinner, "like my dear wife! Bluddy useless woman, gettin' herself transported and leavin' me with four whinin' mouths to feed. I jus' sent 'em to the Union Work'ouse, I ain't go' enough to feed meself!" He spent no longer than a moment contemplating his actions, then looked up enthusiastically. "Well, if there's goin' to be a riot, we better make sure we don't miss it then, a bit o' lootin' sounds like the ticket!"

The two men kept their ear open for word of any mob activity and indeed, did their best to spread dissatisfaction with the outcome of the voting rights bill in various public houses throughout the town. They were amongst the first to hear of the planned protests and welcomed the chance to be involved in the Worcester riot that broke out a few days later.

Many people were arrested and more had sore heads, as the unsavoury characters of the town were appointed special constables against the mob, and they enjoyed wielding their cudgels. The Seventh Hussars eventually cleared the streets, and there was little damage other than some broken windows, and of course, some looting.

As the riot act was quickly read and the mob dispersed effectively, the proceeds of the Worcester riots were slim for John Skinner and Thaddeus Rush. Other rioting followed at Nottingham, and the castle was set afire. Momentum was building, and word reached them of some big riots planned in Bristol for the end of the month, and as it was only sixty miles on the train, the two men were determined to be there in the hope of some richer rewards.

The twenty ninth of October came, and all the trouble-makers of the region had gathered in Bristol. Some men and women were there to genuinely protest the defeat of the voting reform bill, others to achieve their own ends, like some thieving, and still others to express general dissatisfaction with their poor lives. The gathering grew larger, and with some carrying lanterns and clubs or other weapons, the mob began its surge through the city.

"Rush, if we stick together, we might be able to get some better stuff, and keep watch for the soldiers at the same time!" called Skinner, as they deliberately inflamed the mob's desire for destruction by throwing rocks and smashing windows. The more chaotic the situation became, the more chance of slipping into houses unnoticed, so the two men awaited their opportunity.

Ladies and gentlemen rushed out of their large homes in the main streets and ran for their lives, in the hope of getting shelter at the barracks or at the home of a well armed friend. One such well-dressed man ushered a lady carrying a child out of a house up ahead, and made off down the road, followed by servants wearing aprons. Smoke billowed from the neighbouring house, and the noise of screaming and shouting was deafening.

"'Ere, there's our chance for some real boo'y!" yelled Rush, and he grabbed Skinner by the arm as they darted to the building. "I'll wait 'ere and keep an eye out, an' you go see wha' you can ge'," he panted. "I don't fink I can run up the stairs!"

Nodding in agreement, and having a cursory glance up and down the street, Skinner took advantage of the confusion and bounded up the staircase. Within no time he had his bag laden with silver, ladies jewels and a fine jacket. He bid a hasty retreat down to ground level, to be sure of an escape before being overcome by the smoke, when the gentleman owner rushed back in accompanied by two strong friends. They almost collided at the foot of the stairs in the hall.

"Ah ha!" shouted the man. "We have you!" and the three men collectively wrestled the offender to the ground. "Call for a soldier!" the gentleman yelled, and one of the men ran outside, ostensibly to find a man of the law. He returned quickly.

"We shall have to take him to the square! Some soldiers are there, I can see them in the distance although the rest have followed the mob," he declared.

They dragged the intruder outside, and Skinner noted bitterly, desperately swivelling his head to see, that there was no sign of Thaddeus Rush anywhere. The men manhandled Skinner between them up the smoky street that was littered with broken glass and the bodies of men that lay where they had fallen to musket fire or sword.

When they reached the town square, the thief was forced to lie on the ground face down, and one of the hefty gentlemen kneeled on his back to prevent his escape. In due course, with the crowd brought under control, a soldier came to assist them.

The gentleman explained his actions, waving his arms indignantly. "I am the owner of a house down there," he indicated, "and when the mob came, I knew some no good thieves would be waiting to loot all the houses, so I took my wife to safety and went back with reinforcements! We found this piece of garbage," he gave Skinner a kick, "trying to make off with my possessions!" and he triumphantly held up the bag of loot they had found in John Skinner's hands.

"Come along to the Jail house Sir, and I will make a record of what you have told me. Thank you too Sirs," the officer said, nodding formally to the other two gentlemen, and yanking Skinner to his feet, "for assisting in the capture of one of the criminals involved." He pulled his pistol out from his belt, and pointed it at the offender. "Now march, you scoundrel!"

John Skinner was duly taken into custody, and when the bodies of the thirty dead were dealt with, and the remaining participants seized, he stood trial in Bristol. Five men, the organizers of the riot that had been apprehended, were executed by hanging, and dozens of other men convicted with various sentences.

The Magistrate was clearly in a hurry to get through his unusually large workload for the day. He quickly came to his verdict and pronounced in a solemn tone, "John Skinner, I hereby sentence you to transportation for the term of your natural life."

Thaddeus Rush leisurely made his way back to Worcester, with a few choice items that should make him some profit in his pockets. He had seen the men rush back toward the house, decided instantly that he would not risk his neck trying to save Skinner and quickly melted into the shadows, evading capture. After all, he was a creature of the night, and it was in darkness that he felt most comfortable. Sure that John Skinner would not be returning to his house in Worcester, Rush claimed the place and took up residence there. He sold the items gleaned from the riot at a pawn shop and spent his time at the public house, plotting and planning his new bodysnatching venture.

A few days later, he started to feel ill, much more so than was normal for a morning after drinking a bottle of rum, and he had terrible stomach pains. Rush scuttled out of the house to the privy in John Skinner's garden a number of times that morning. On one of his visits to the garden, there were a number of people gathered around the well, and they were pulling something large and wet out of the deep hole.

Rush put his hand over his mouth and ran back into the privy with all speed. He had started vomiting too. When he emerged, he stopped and looked at the object of interest. The partly decomposed body of a small man lay on the ground, and the people were leaning over it, one of whom looked like a doctor.

"He must have been in there for a fortnight at least, mebbe a month!" said the man dubiously. He turned to the woman next to him, "you say you found him when you went to fill up your bucket with water for your house?"

Rush felt weak at the knees. He had been drinking water from the well too. There had been reports of illness going around, but then again, there always were stories about something so he hadn't taken much notice. He found that his knees were not just weak, but actually aching painfully, and he decided he needed to lie down. Thaddeus Rush staggered up the stairs and collapsed on the bed, the cramps in his legs getting more severe. The infection was doing its work, and advanced dehydration was already setting in...

Chapter 19.

In early March, Amelia was assigned to a Mr and Mrs Smith, who had a farming property near Melton Mowbray, north of Hobart Town. It was hot and windy, and would be an unpleasant place to live if it not for the river. The Jordan River was deep and clear, its sources were several smaller rivers coming down from pristine lakes in the high country.

The Smiths ran sheep, and although the property was not a particularly large one, the neighbouring farm was big and employed a great number of convicts and Ticket of Leave men. The two properties often coordinated their activities; the sheep were shorn at the same time in order to share the work gangs, and machinery was shared between the two in what was a most convenient arrangement.

Mr and Mrs Smith lived in a large, comfortable brick farmhouse with verandahs all around to shade the windows from the hot summer sun. There was a large two level, wooden shearing shed, a shed for farm implements and equipment, and the large stone carriage house with stables. They had ten convict workers in all comprising two household servants, and eight men working on the farm. The men lived in their quarters over the shearing shed, and the two women shared a room above the kitchen.

Amelia shared duties with a fellow servant by the name of Siobhan, and she was a young girl from County Wicklow, in Ireland. She was cheerful enough, although sometimes lacked good sense, and seemed to have little in the way of household skills.

The housekeeper was Mrs Gaunt, and she and her husband were employed by the Smiths to run the house and garden. Her husband was in charge of the large, productive vegetable patch, the pigs and chickens and the formal garden, and he sometimes had a convict worker assisting. The woman was very efficient, and she gave Amelia a tour of the kitchens, cellars and laundries while she explained her duties.

"Down here is where all the food is stored," she said, as they descended some steep stone steps down under the house, and they emerged into a cool, spacious underground cellar. "The rooms go right the length of the house - through there, see? And these stone shelves are where the milk, butter and cheese are kept." Amelia felt the cold stone shelves with her hand and found that they were thick and heavy, providing a large number of individual compartments that maintained a cool temperature even in summer.

"What keeps it so cool down here?" asked Amelia. "It is hot outside, and yet this is an ideal storage temperature for food."

The housekeeper pointed to some large gratings on the floor. "Those pits are filled with water and there are several of them down here. The air circulates through those vents, see there?" She pointed up to the top of the walls. "They are at ground level under the verandahs. So the air comes in there, and as it flows around the rooms, water evaporates from the pits, and keeps the air cool! Being underground also protect us from the heat down here." Amelia had never seen a larder so efficient and was very impressed with the way this was done. The shelves appeared to be well stocked with food and there were several sides of mutton hanging in a huge walk-in meat safe that had its own heavy wooden door to keep the room secure and free from flies.

The kitchens were at the rear of the house, and you could step into them from the courtyard at the top of the cellar steps. The laundries adjoined this courtyard too, and a wooden door led to the vegetable garden and the chicken pens. Amelia's daily work was to start with milking the house cow and feeding the chickens each morning, and then work in the laundries and kitchens for the rest of the day. These were all familiar tasks, and Mrs Gaunt seemed a reasonable woman, so Amelia fell asleep that first night in a comfortable bed feeling very optimistic indeed.

A week later, Amelia was out early in the morning. The milking was already done and she was feeding the chickens. She loved to watch the little ones, dashing out from under their mother's wing to snatch a little morsel, then scurry back under again. The hens clucked over their food, the sun shone warmly on Amelia's shoulders and she sighed.

She could not believe her good luck, being sent to this place. The sound of the pigs and sheep were familiar, and the rhythms of farm life came back to her so naturally that Amelia could almost believe she was home again, where she grew up with her father on their smallholding at Hanley William. She put the basket down for a moment and stretched, enjoying the rare moment feeling safe, happy and hopeful for the future, then went inside to begin her day's chores.

John Skinner stood next to the farm shed. He had come over from the neighbouring property with the overseer and another man to fetch the large dray, which was to be stacked with grain from both properties to be sold in Hobart. While the other men checked the wheels and hitched up the horses, he looked around. He had only been in Van Diemen's Land for a week, and had been sent straight to the property as they had a shortage of workers.

His only complaint so far was the lack of rum, but had been assured by the other convict workers that a supply was on its way from a local sly grog shop, and a Ticket of Leave man was to deliver it in the coming days. Skinner had traded a jacket for some coin, and he intended it to be of good use, trading for goods or buying rum. It couldn't come soon enough for him, as his hands shook and his stomach craved for the warm, comforting liquid.

He stood in the sun, lounging against the wall, lazily watching a woman feeding chickens in the yard next to the house. What he wouldn't give for a night with a woman! Almost as much as for a bottle of rum, he grinned lasciviously.

He straightened up and stared intently at the woman, crushing his cap between his fingers. There was something familiar about her. She was small, with dark hair under her cap, but it was too far to see well. The way she held her head to the side, and brushed her hands on her apron just so... It couldn't be! He blinked and stared even more keenly. He could almost swear that the wench was his wife, Amelia!

Just then the overseer, who had the horses ready, called Skinner to come and help. He reluctantly tore his eyes away and went to hoist a bag of grain onto the dray with the help of his fellow worker. He quickly glanced back at the house, but the woman was gone.

The rum duly arrived from the Ticket of Leave man, and the convict workers, unbeknown to their overseers, decided to meet down at the river that evening after their work was done, to drink it. They secretly spread the word to some of the household servants at the homestead, so that the women could join them.

One of the men had struck up an acquaintance with Siobhan, after working closely with the men at the neighbouring farm a number of times. He decided to fetch her from across the river, and sent a message to tell her he was coming and to ask the new woman if she wanted to come too.

He crept quietly up to the room above the kitchen and turned the key that was in the lock. Siobhan was waiting for him and fell into his arms. Amelia did not want to go, the smell of rum was not one she relished after living with her husband for many years, so the couple slipped away, leaving the key in the outside of the door so Siobhan could get in later. Amelia hoped that the girl would keep her wits about her, but somehow she doubted it.

While the property owners assumed the workers were all in their beds, a great party was in progress down at the bridge next to the river, where a large quantity of rum was consumed. John Skinner spoke to the Irish girl from across the river and ascertained that the other domestic worker next door

150

was indeed Amelia. She was using her maiden name for some reason that Skinner could not fathom, but he was unaccountably angry about it, and the fact that she had not come down to the river.

His need for rum was strong and had been unsated for so long, that the man consumed a good deal of it, all the time looking darkly towards the other house and brooding about the presence of his wife, so nearby.

Skinner decided to pay her a visit, and wove his way unsteadily over the bridge and up the road to the house where Amelia slept. When asked about their accommodation, Siobhan had innocently told him that they slept in a room over the kitchen, and helpfully described where the stairway was located.

Even as befuddled with drink that he was, Skinner easily found the building and stared up at the small window knowing that she lay within. No dogs barked, so the convict found the stairs in the dark and climbed up, confident that he would not be heard by anyone in the main house, which was some distance away. The key was in the door, and it opened easily, so he stealthily stepped over the threshold and closed the heavy door securely behind him. The steady breathing in the bed on the right told him immediately where she was, and seized by a surge of fury, he strode over and clapped a strong hand to the sleeping woman's mouth, dragging Amelia out of her bed.

She was jerked awake with such a shock, that Amelia, bewildered, could not comprehend what was happening. Her startled shriek, through thick, dirty fingers, was muffled by the hand clamping tighter, and she found that she could barely breathe.

Quickly regaining her wits and remembering where she was, Amelia could feel the power of the person who had come into her room and attacked her while she slept, as he held her with a vicelike grip. The distinctive, sickly smell of rum and unwashed body assailed her nostrils. It was a familiar stench, and it brought back unwanted memories, memories of pain and humiliation. It could not be him! She was in Van Diemen's Land!

She struggled, in a panic to twist around and see the man who was roughly dragging her upright by the hair, and in the moonlight from the window she saw him. A person Amelia thought never to see again in all of her life, the man she thought she had escaped. Indeed it was her husband John Skinner, and her eyes widened in horror.

"Ah, I see ya recognize me at last ya stupid wench!" he slurred. "Knowin' you was over 'ere in a nice warm bed was just was too much for me ta resist, not havin' had a woman for so long." His lewd grin revealed the man's rotted teeth and she shuddered with revulsion. It had rapidly become obvious what Skinner's intentions were and he forced her head back, lowering his bearded face to hers, and the harsh bristles on his chin scratched Amelia's neck, finally goading her to act in her own defence.

The petite woman fought furiously. She bit down on the filthy fingers with her teeth, so that his hand was jerked away and she could breathe more easily. "Get away from me, you repulsive brute!" she exclaimed, and yanking her hair from Skinner's grip, ran for the door.

He was there too quickly, crossing the floor with two rapid strides despite his level of drunkenness, and he laughed, holding the barrier closed with ease against her frantic attempts to pull it open. It was an evil, mocking laugh that frightened Amelia to the depths of her being. "Oh my God, have mercy!" she cried. "You are a devil from hell!" She was tiring fast from her efforts to escape, so she screamed at the top of her lungs. "Leave me alone! Someone, please help me!"

"Ye're my wife, and ya can dammed well shut up, and give me what I want!" he hissed, grabbing her arm and throwing her across the room with the brute strength of a madman. She slammed against the wall and collapsed like a rag doll, but quickly scrambled up and backed away from Skinner, who was advancing on her menacingly.

"I'd sooner go to hell!" Amelia retorted with feeling. "You'll have to kill me first!"

"'Ave it your own way, then," the man said softly, and struck with one hand, giving Amelia a resounding cuff around the head, which sent her reeling and staggering onto the hard boards. He followed the blow with a mighty kick to the stomach which rendered Amelia completely defenceless, and she writhed on the floor in agony.

John Skinner kneeled over her, arrogantly daring her to try something. She flailed at him weakly with her hands, hoping against hope that Mr Smith had heard her scream and would come, but she was losing the battle.

Another clout to the face knocked Amelia senseless, and she drifted in and out of consciousness while Skinner raped her. In Amelia's more lucid moments, she could hear the sound of feral grunting like a wild animal, and she wished for death to come and take her away, so that this life of torment and suffering would end.

At last, John Skinner lurched to his feet leaving his victim sprawled on the hard floor and stumbled for the door buttoning his clothing. It was at that very moment that it burst open, revealing Mr Smith and Mr Gaunt, the latter holding a shotgun which was aimed threateningly at the brigands' belly.

Mr Smith was holding a lantern, and he took in the situation quickly. "By God, you villain! Get back against the wall, or take a blast from both barrels! Hold him there Mr Gaunt, while I fetch some rope to tie him up!" and he hurried out, only to be back momentarily, followed by a terrified Mrs Gaunt.

Skinner was wild eyed and crazed looking, and still looking for a way to escape, despite Mr Gaunt and his gun. But there was nowhere to run, and Mr Smith, a large man, seized the villain and threw him on his stomach on the hard boards, and holding him with his knee between the shoulder blades he tried to tie Skinner's hands behind his back. When he resisted, Smith took hold of the man's hair in his fist, and gave his head a resounding 'whack' onto the floor.

"There, that should calm him a little!" he said with satisfaction, and completed securing the prisoner without any further trouble.

"Cover her up, my dear, while I help Mr Smith with this fellow!" called Mr Gaunt to his wife, and the housekeeper nervously edged into the room, keeping one eye anxiously on the captive.

Mrs Gaunt grabbed a blanket from the bed, and covered Amelia, who remained lying inert on the floor and seemed to be completely unresponsive, although her eyes were open. The housekeeper's eyes were filled with compassion, and a tear dripped from her chin as she leaned over and spoke gently. "There we are, my girl, that's better is it not? We've got him now, Mr Smith and Mr Gaunt are taking him away, so don't you worry anymore." She kept up a stream of soothing words, and Amelia listened to them, holding onto the tenuous link with consciousness.

"I told you I heard something Gaunt, it's a good thing you thought to arm yourself first! Well, my good man, we'll take this fellow down and lock him in the large meat cellar for tonight. You can send a messenger to the Sergeant at Green Ponds first thing in the morning." The other man nodded, and between them they heaved Skinner to his feet and pushed him out the door and down to the cellar at gunpoint, his curses and shouts drifting back up the stairs to the women.

"She's me damned wife, I can do what I want to that bluddy wench, she's got no right to refuse. You can't lock me up!" But his words had no effect on his captors, and he was bundled into the stone room and the door securely locked.

After the men had gone, Mrs Gaunt helped Amelia up, and although her legs would not support her, the housekeeper managed to lift her onto her bed, and cover her with warm blankets. She left the room then, promising to return quickly, and she brought water, cloths and Mrs Smith who was in her nightclothes with a warm shawl draped around her.

The two ladies tended Amelia's cuts and bruises, washed her face and body, and gave her water to drink. Amelia, benefiting from the ministrations of the kind women, rallied somewhat.

In the morning, Amelia tried to get up but found that she was so stiff and tender with pain and the ache in her stomach and one shoulder was so bad, that she simply could not rise, and fell back on the pillow.

Siobhan, who had been found and brought back hours before, awoke. She had been briefly informed of the events while being hustled back to their room in disgrace. Taking one look at Amelia's damaged face, with one eye swollen completely shut, and her obviously painful attempts to move, she scurried downstairs to fetch Mrs Gaunt to tend to her. She was afraid of the unpleasantness that this morning would bring for her, but she knew that her punishment would be nothing to what Amelia had suffered.

Siobhan blamed herself for the attack on her friend. If only she had not told that man where they slept! He had seemed so interested in Amelia, and if she hadn't consumed so much rum, the girl may have recognized that he intended no good and said nothing.

Amelia was kept in bed for a week before she was able to resume her work, and although her face was still black and blue she felt more normal again, but could not speak of her ordeal. She overheard the Gaunts talking in the garden and in that manner discovered the fate that had befallen that hateful man.

"He tried to give the excuse that she was his wife! But her name's Hobbs and his is Skinner, so they knew that couldn't be right, and the Sergeant would hear no more about it. He said that was not relevant anyway, because he attacked a servant of Mr and Mrs Smith, and the woman is the property of the government besides. Not only that, but the rascal had also consumed a large quantity of illicit rum, which is a very serious offence!

"They've sent him to the coal mines near Port Arthur, and that's a place not many come out of alive!" Mr Gaunt told his wife, who was listening avidly, her hand on her husband's arm, and she shuddered at the mention of that dreadful place.

"Will the Gardiner family lose many of their workers over the events of that night?" asked Mrs Gaunt. "After all, there were many who were drinking rum, as Siobhan confessed to me."

"They only caught one other out of his quarters, the fellow with Siobhan, so they must have all gone back before the alarm was raised. He only got a reprimand, because he hadn't drunk any rum, but he was out of his quarters at night without leave," the man clarified.

"I hope we don't lose Siobhan!" said Mrs Gaunt suddenly, "it's so difficult for Mrs Smith to get to Hobart to pick out new girls."

"No, she only got a reprimand from the magistrate too, the same as Amelia," he said.

Mrs Gaunt was shocked. "What do you mean 'the same as Amelia'?" she demanded.

"She had a man in her bedroom without permission." said Gaunt.

"But that is ridiculous!" snapped his wife, stepping back from her husband with a disgusted expression. "Amelia didn't invite that criminal to her room!"

"Well we don't know that," said Mr Gaunt, shaking his head. "Nevertheless, the authorities don't differentiate between those that are invited and those that aren't. She was found with a man in her room, and that's that! It's an offence to be put on her record."

Mrs Gaunt stalked into the house, shaking her head with disbelief at the injustice of the system. Poor Amelia! The kindly woman hoped that she fully recovered as she was a good worker; most of the women they had in the past had few skills and even less inclination to work!

Amelia did recover physically, although slowly, but continued to wake screaming with terrible dreams night after night, which upset poor Siobhan. In her nightmares, Amelia ran and ran, trying to escape someone who pursued her, then the scene changed, and she was trapped in a room with a crazed John Skinner, and she hammered on the door, trying to get out, while he got closer and closer until his hands were around her throat!

As Amelia went about her work, she often paused, convinced that she could detect the rancid odour of sweat and rum combined, but could not find any source for it.

She started to improve gradually over the following months and began to rediscover her enjoyment of life on the farm again, until she realised that the worst had happened. The signs were unmistakable, Amelia was pregnant.

Richard Barton had been working for Mr Myles Patterson for several months, and had come to respect him as a kind and fair man. Mr Patterson placed much store in Richard's bricklaying skills, and had him constructing workers' cottages at Hunterston. It was early January, and hot, exhausting work, as Bothwell was a dry and exposed inland area and there had been particularly high temperatures since the New Year.

Although he expected them to work hard, Mr Patterson ensured his convict workers had plenty of water, food and rest, and summoned the doctor if any needed medical treatment.

Richard often reflected on the good advice he had received from Captain Wentworth the previous year, advising him to ensure that he remained in the service of Mr Patterson. In the six years since he had been in Van Diemen's Land, this was by far the best situation that Richard had enjoyed.

"Ah, there you are, Barton," said Mr Patterson, as he came around the corner of the new cottage, and found the man mixing a new batch of mortar. "I want you to take the dray with the surplus hay down to town on the morrow. The Reids at Ratho need some extra fodder, and you are to deliver it before noon. Mr Reid has already recompensed me for the supply, so there is no need to collect his payment."

"Yes Sir, before noon it is Sir. I should have this wall finished today anyways," replied Barton genially.

His Master walked around the building site, assessing the man's work, a thoughtful look on his face. "There is another task that you could perform for me while you are there, if you are so inclined," and he waited, allowing Barton's curiosity to build.

"What task is that Sir?" asked the convict eventually.

"I have a letter I would like you to deliver to Captain Wentworth. I have had so many requests from fellow landowners in the district for your services that I thought it was not right to deny them." Patterson sighed, and smiled mysteriously.

"What do you mean Sir?" asked Barton, "does Captain Wentworth need some bricklaying done?"

"Why no, man. I'm not legally able to lend you out, so to speak, until you have your Ticket of Leave. So I thought it best that I sponsor you to get it." Barton's eyes widened, but before he could speak Mr Patterson continued. "On one condition, mind; that you continue your good work for me, on a paid basis of course. When I have no work for you, you will be free to offer your services around the area. I think it about time you received financial reward for your skills!"

Richard was frozen, dumfounded, but at last found his tongue. "Sir, do you mean..."

"Yes, Barton. This is a letter recommending you for a Ticket of Leave, that I wish you to deliver tomorrow. You will receive a response from the convict office in due course. It is the first step in securing your freedom." He handed Richard the letter, his eyes twinkling. "I suppose if you take Paddy with you tomorrow you would like leave to stop at 'The Castle' for a drink or two?" Barton nodded enthusiastically and Patterson laughed. "Of course you may, I think this deserves a little celebration - as long as you are back by five, and in a fit state!"

"Yes Sir, we will!" Richard paused reflectively, "I would like to express my... gratitude, for your assistance, Sir. Without you, I may have been sent to Port Arthur. You have been the makings of me and you do not need to ask for my loyalty Sir, you already have it. You shall have first priority for my services whenever you have need of them."

"Well, well, we will need to wait for the result of the application first. But I have no doubt it will be granted." Mr Patterson put out his hand and Barton wiped his own hand carefully before grasping it firmly. "Good luck to you Barton." And with that he sauntered off, well satisfied.

It was the fifth day of January, and Richard and Paddy drove to 'Ratho' in high spirits. The property with the elegant homestead was situated by the River Clyde, just out of town. Once the hay was unloaded and stacked, the two men continued on into town meaning to stop for a pint of Guinness. Unusually for midday, there was a large crowd outside the inn, and once the horse was watered and tied, they hurried over to see what was happening.

A large man stood on a box, addressing the crowd, and for the first time, they noticed that a group of aboriginal people stood to one side armed with spears, their black skin painted with patterns in white.

"Oi don't loike dis at all!" said Paddy, stopping in trepidation. Dese 'Big River People' are particularly warloike, an' dey don't appreciate us bein' here at all!" He turned as if to retrace his steps back to the dray.

"Wait Paddy," said Richard, curious. "No one else looks afraid. Let us hear what this man is saying," and he walked boldly up to the group of townsfolk. Captain Wentworth was there attending the gathering at 'The Castle', as were most of the tradesmen and people of the town, so there would be no need call by Wentworth House to deliver his letter.

"My name," said the man on the box loudly, "is George Augustus Robinson, and I have been appointed by the government of Van Diemen's Land to negotiate a truce with these aboriginal people. I have done so with the help of Truganinni and Woorady here," and he gestured to two natives who stood nearby. "They have agreed to accompany us to Hobart Town and are to be relocated, along with the rest of the Oyster Bay People, to Flinders Island, off the north coast of the land."

The townsfolk all turned to each other with a buzz of conversation at this, but the man held his hand up. "I beg you folks, allow me to finish. Our people have been fighting with theirs since we occupied this land, and we hope that this bloodshed will now end, and these people can live in peace, as can we. To demonstrate their willingness to cooperate, the remaining members of The Big River Tribe would like to perform a corroborree, or sacred dance, for your entertainment." He jumped down from the box and gestured for everyone to move back, giving the tribes people a large space in the centre.

A fire was lit in the stone surround that had obviously been built for the occasion and the flames leapt skyward. The people began their ritual, a strange, stamping dance, accompanied by sticks that were tapped together in a distinctive rhythm. They swirled around the fire, occasionally giving a guttural yell "ugghh" and the stamping of their feet added to the rhythm. It seemed that part of the dance was intended to imitate animals or birds, but it was like nothing anyone had seen before, and when it ended with a great shout and stamping in unison, there was silence.

All those present were filled with a sense of nostalgia, as although the two groups of people had fought with each other, they both understood that this unusual rite was being performed in this place for the last time. Some townspeople started clapping, and most joined in, but the smattering of applause sounded inadequate somehow, for what they had just witnessed.

As Robinson prepared to depart for Hobart, the crowd dispersed, and the two convict men went over to Captain Wentworth. "Excuse me Captain," started Richard, and the gentleman turned. "Mr Patterson asked that I deliver this to you Sir. He has written a letter sponsoring my Ticket of Leave, if you would be so kind as to send it to the authorities."

"Ah, Barton. Thank you, yes I will deal with this in due course. I told you he'd do right by you did I not?" The magistrate looked satisfied.

"Yes Sir, you did. And thank you for that advice Sir."

"Well now," he looked at the men, an unreadable expression on his face. "Who'd have thought you would see something like *that* when you came to town today! And never will see again in this region..." He paused enigmatically, "thank God, poor devils!" and turning on his heel he added briskly, "give my regards to Mr Patterson."

Whether Captain Wentworth spoke with regret for the lives lost in the conflict, an ancient culture destroyed, or in relief for an end to the problem, was not clear.

Richard and Paddy, now firm friends after working together since spring, enjoyed a pint or two and then returned to Hunterston. They told of the events of the day, and Mr Patterson and his family were interested to hear about the departure of the aboriginals, but mostly relieved that the danger of attacks had now passed. Mr Patterson had always felt vulnerable in his isolated situation next to the Shannon after his incident with the bushrangers, and Richard felt pleased that he could bring him such comforting news.

Several weeks passed, and a messenger with post for Mr Patterson rode down the road to Hunterston. Only ten minutes later, Mr Patterson appeared on the work site waving a letter. "It's come, it's come Barton!"

Richard rushed over and breathlessly enquired what the letter contained. "What is it Sir?"

"Your ticket! It's your Ticket of Leave, it's been granted!" and the two men shook hands, Richard struggling to hold back his emotions.

"Thank you Sir, thank you Sir," he repeated, shaking his head, a flush of colour in his cheeks.

"It says that your registered place of residence is Hunterston, and you have to attend a monthly muster at Shannon's hut, down by the river. They will check your name off and ensure you are in the right place. You must make sure you are at these musters, and go to church each week. Do not attract the attention of the constable or the magistrate, lest

165

your free certificate be delayed, or indeed you can be taken back into labour for a time. But it's the first step. Congratulations Barton."

Richard raised his eyes and stared at the blue sky in contemplation. He noticed a bird flying in the distance, and suddenly he had an inkling of what it would be like to be free of the chains of servitude. He was on the path to freedom for the first time in seven years, and he would be forever indebted to Mr Patterson, his master no longer.

Over the next three or four years, Richard Barton made himself indispensable to the people of Bothwell. He built barns and farm cottages at Ratho, houses at Dennistoun and of course, continued his work at Hunterston. He put away all his wages in savings, and thought of the day when he might buy his own house. His Certificate of Freedom awaited him, and he meant to obtain it as soon as possible.

Chapter 21.

"I have to tell her," stated Amelia, hands on her hips in a matter of fact way.

"But Amelia, you'll be sent back!" objected Siobhan, clutching at the wet towel she was hanging. "I don't want you to go!" she wailed. But it was no good. Amelia could hide her condition no longer, and Mrs Gaunt would find out soon enough anyway. She nervously approached the woman in the kitchen garden.

"Mrs Gaunt, I need to talk to you." Amelia said quietly, and the older woman turned to face her in surprise, holding some herbs she had been picking for dinner. "Do you remember when I was attacked by that man...." and she shuddered with the pain of being forced to talk of it.

"Of course child, what of it? Are you quite well?" asked the housekeeper and her eye roved over Amelia, and stopped on her slightly swelling stomach. "You're not.... with child are you dear?" Amelia nodded and broke down in tears, the kind woman holding her in her arms and stroking her hair maternally.

"I have been so ill recently, I didn't want to tell you because I was hoping I might lose it," Amelia wept, "but it appears not, as I am four months along now."

Mrs Gaunt thought for a moment and then said. "I'll have to tell the mistress o' course, but I wonder, if there's a way..." she stopped and regarded the pregnant woman with affection. "Go on now, Amelia. I will let you when I know what is to be done." She turned back to her herb basket with a sad shake of her head.

The housekeeper called Amelia to speak to her later that evening in her sitting room. "Amelia, I have discussed your situation with Mrs Smith, and she...er... said you will have to go back to the factory," she said, her voice quavering slightly. "I suggested there may be a way of you staying, having the child and keeping it here, but she says not. I'm so sorry Amelia, I wish I could do something more but..." Her voice tailed off, and Amelia could see how upset the poor woman was.

"It's all right Mrs Gaunt, I expected this. There is nothing that you, or anyone, can do to help me," she said quietly, her head bowed. "When am I leaving?"

"Tomorrow, when the lad goes to Green Ponds, he will take you that far, and the magistrate will organise your return to Hobart Town," replied the distraught woman. "It is not fair that you should suffer a second time by the actions of that monster. As if the attack was not enough! Sometimes I wonder how God could let these things happen."

"Yes, I wonder too. Thank you Mrs Gaunt." Without another word, Amelia went to her room to prepare her belongings, as she now owned several dresses that Mrs Smith had provided for her. She could not help but think on Mrs Gaunt's final words. "It is easy to explain it," she spoke loudly and bitterly in the privacy of her room. "There is no God!"

The time came to depart, and Amelia climbed into the cart without a word. She hugged Mrs Gaunt but could not trust herself to speak without breaking down. Amelia looked back once but saw Siobhan waving, visibly tearful, so she faced the road again, pressing her lips together resolutely, and hardening herself for the ordeal ahead.

Enduring the bleak winter in the Female Factory that year seemed to be harder than ever before. The winds seemed icier, the days darker and Amelia's constant stomach-clawing hunger never abated. She spent most of her days trying to keep warm, and although Mrs Winters had made some allowances for her pregnancy, Amelia forced herself to keep moving, as it was the best way to keep the numbing cold at bay. No new ships were due to arrive until Spring, so the women could not even look forward to the spark of life that new acquaintances inspired.

A sickness swept through the convict population late in the season as the promise of warmer weather drew nearer, and infants died on a weekly basis. Two women in the assignment yard also succumbed and others developed symptoms, and the women became frightened, anticipating that every small cough or fever would develop into the fatal malady.

They spoke of little else, and many became quite desperate to escape the disease as most of them regarded it as a death sentence. The matron and doctor were kept busy caring for those new cases of the illness and organising the burials for those that did not survive. It was a dreadful time for all.

Amelia gave birth in early December, and the labour pains took her by surprise, as they started several weeks early. She left the weaving she was doing and went to walk around the yard for a short time, hoping that the pains would stop. The guard on duty in the yards observed her, but surprisingly did not order her back to work, and Amelia did not notice that he passed through several times while she was there.

She went into the privies, and while there had a sudden surge of pain, and her birth waters broke. The labour intensified instantly, so she was unable to call for help, and Amelia found herself on the dirt floor in the full throes of childbirth. The child was expelled quickly, yet she was blue, and had the birth cord wrapped tightly around her neck.

Amelia must have cried out, as suddenly the door opened, and the guard swiftly entered carrying a blanket. He saw the baby was not breathing and miraculously removed the cord, holding her upside down, and tapping her sharply. The child elicited a weak cry and audibly sucked in air. "There now, let me wrap the bairn in this," he said kindly, and wrapped the baby securely in the woollen cloth.

"Thank you, Sir," said Amelia weakly, propping herself against the wall. The man handed the child to her.

"My wife just had her second baby a month past," he said, by way of an explanation, "and I knew your time had come when you were walking about in the yard. If you will excuse me, I will go and fetch Matron," and he hurried away.

Mrs Winters returned with the guard, and she checked the baby while he looked on.

"I expected number eighty six to go to the nursery, but when she did not, I went lookin' for her, and then I heard her call out," he said. "I grew up on a farm before I joined the convict corps, and I knew what to do from delivering calves and foals."

"We are lucky that you happened to be on duty today, Mr Petrie," nodded Mrs Winters in gratitude. "This one was not expected until the end of the month, so I'm afraid I was not aware as perhaps I should have been." She glanced at Amelia apologetically.

Amelia did not blame her. "I understand, Matron," she said. "It took me by surprise too and I am very grateful to Mr Petrie for his help."

"Right let us get you to the nursery with the child then," decided the woman in charge, helping to lift poor Amelia from the dirt. "Do you think you can walk?"

Amelia could not stand, so putting another blanket right around them, Mr Petrie lifted mother and baby, and with Mrs Winters supervising, carried them both to the nursery.

She remained in the filth of the nursery building with the child for several days before returning to work. The baby, who was named Jane, bore the features of her father and it was difficult for Amelia to regard her without abhorrence, let alone develop any affection for her. It was also obvious from very early in the child's life that she was not normal, as she lay flaccid and unresponsive, and crying only rarely. As the months went on, the lack of improvement became even more pronounced.

"Look, Matron, she cannot even hold her head up," Amelia said. "By this age she should be much stronger." Mrs Winters examined her and agreed that her weak neck and lack of bodily strength seemed odd, so the doctor was summoned.

"It seems that the child is severely affected with a retardation of development," reported the man. "I am surprised she has survived this long Amelia. How old is she now?"

"Five months Sir, but I've been suspecting that something was wrong for a while now. I've had six children, so I know how they usually develop."

"Well, another month till she is weaned," said the doctor morosely, "then it will become apparent whether she will live or die. It is in God's hands." and he left with a shake of his head. Twelve babies had already died in the Female Factory last month alone, and they had all been normal healthy children at the same age, so he did not hold out much hope for this one.

Amelia secretly thought that it would be for the best if Jane did not survive. How could she ever endure the child's presence? If Amelia was ever to be granted her freedom would she be prepared to spend her life caring for her, when she was not only abnormal, but provided a daily reminder of the man she hated, and the manner in which she was conceived?

The baby was duly weaned onto the diet of sugar, water and bread a few weeks later, and Amelia was sent to crime class for the mandatory six month punishment for the crime of becoming pregnant.

Chapter 22.

Morag and Elsie were almost constant occupants of crime class. They were notorious for their disregard for the rules, disdain for the guards, and their physical intimidation of the other women. Since the death of Sarah, the sisters had become even more unmanageable, and despite the constant punishments of hard labour, they had found ways to improve their lives.

There were trusted convict women who acted as turnkeys, and they had free movement around the facility. Some of these were in the pay of the Scottish sisters, and a smuggling ring operated freely in the prison. Food, clothing, tobacco and other items were provided by outsiders, brought in by the turnkeys and delivered to Morag and Elsie. Amelia had plenty of time to observe the racket in operation, but hesitated to get supplies in this manner herself, for fear of putting herself under the control of the dangerous women.

Amelia alternated between periods working at the washtubs and unravelling ropes in the cells. Six months was much longer than she had spent in crime class before, and time seemed to drag interminably. She was asked at the end of a particularly long boring day to collect the baskets of unravelled rope from each of the cells and deliver them to the gate for collection. Amelia went from cell to cell collecting the baskets from the weary women, but when she got to the cell that Morag should have been in, the door was open and Morag was nowhere to be seen.

Amelia lingered indecisively, as she didn't want to leave the cell opened in case she was blamed for Morag's absence. She looked up the corridor to the area containing the dark cells, and a small sound prompted her to take a lantern from the wall and investigate.

Around the corner and at the very furthest end of the corridor, one of the cells stood open and a faint light glowed. The sounds became louder and it put Amelia in mind of the snarling and hissing of an animal. She hurried to the door and the sight that she beheld was one that she would never forget.

A woman was against the wall, backed into the furthest corner of the cell. She was naked, her body was covered in red marks and she was biting, scratching and snarling like a cat. One of the officers, a truncheon in his hand and his trousers around his ankles, was obviously attempting to rape her. He wielded the truncheon and it thumped into bare flesh. His bare backside gleamed white in the dim light, and the man panted heavily, putting down the cudgel as he fought to control his victim with both hands.

Frozen with shock at first, it was the smell that eventually drove Amelia to action. A sour, sweaty smell, mixed faintly with rum, oozed from the man's pores, and the familiar stench took a moment to register in her brain. It was then that Amelia lost her senses completely.

She picked up the discarded club and swung it at the man's head, clouting him firmly above the ear. He fell to the side and Amelia rained blow after blow on his head and body, exerting all her strength as she was driven to a madness that she never knew she possessed. But suddenly she was grabbed from behind, her arms pinioned to her sides.

"Amelia, Amelia, for the loov of God, stop! Ye'll be killin' 'im if ye doon't stop and ye'll be 'anged for murder!" Amelia looked at the stick in her hand, and then down to the man lying at her feet. The red haze in her head receded, and she turned, dropping the club to the ground. It was Morag, who was speaking urgently.

"Look a' me! Doon't kill 'im, or ye'll suffer for it. I 'ave a better way to poonish 'im for what he has done." She picked up her dress and quickly donned it and her pinafore as well. Amelia just stood and stared at the man lying unconscious before her - had she really done that?

Morag spoke again. "'Ere Amelia, 'elp me off with 'is troosers," and she began to struggle with the guard's clothing. Amelia, spurred into action, helped her immediately, kneeling beside his legs and tugging at his boots.

"Are you sure he's not dead?" she ventured fearfully to the other woman.

"Noo, 'e's still breathin', more's the pity, it's more than 'e deserves, the bastard!" she said vehemently.

"Morag, are you all right?" asked Amelia, "I could see he'd been beating you. Did I stop him before he...before he...?"

"Mebbe this time ye did. This was no' the only time though. 'E used to rape Sarah in the dark cells, but after she died, 'e started on me, an' 'e's been doin' this for moonths. I just couldn't stop him, and no one would believe me if I told. I'd probably ge' the iron collar meself!"

Amelia cast her mind back. He must be the officer that the women had attacked in the laundry yard, the incident that had resulted in Sarah having the iron collar. "You mean, all this time, he has been...?" The other woman nodded curtly. "Oh Morag, I could not stand by, I had to stop him! I thought for a moment he was... a...a man I once knew." She paused and put her hand to the scar on her cheek. She decided not to elaborate. "What will we do now?"

"I don't knoo if this'll stop 'im. Boot it's is me best chance, thanks to ye, Amelia. I thank ye for coomin' to me rescue." They looked at each, and although Amelia had been frightened of Morag in the past, a common bond of understanding had taken a tenuous hold. "Poot oot the lantern and close the door," Morag instructed. "When the puir laddie wakes oop with noo troosers, 'e'll be forced to come oot to ge' 'em, won' 'e? Then everyone will knoo wha' 'es been oop to!" She laughed and the two women, carrying the trousers, departed cautiously and retreated down the corridor.

"Amelia, ye lock me in, and take me basket. Take the troosers and put 'em.... in a place where everyone can see 'em. Go!" Morag went into her cell and Amelia, locking the door, left with the trousers safely hidden in the basket.

She decided to make them hard to reach, so the horrid man would not be able to retrieve his clothes quickly. After delivering the baskets of rope fibre, Amelia had the opportunity in the dim light to decide what to do with them. She stood in the corner of the yard near the chapel looking up at the wall. If only there was a way she could get them up there...

First tying the legs in knots, each one containing a rock to weight them, she swung the trousers back and forth a few times to get the feel of the weight and threw...not hard enough and the trousers landed back in front of her feet.

Amelia looked around furtively to ensure no one had heard the thud as they landed. She was afraid to throw them too hard and have them disappear over the wall entirely. On the second attempt the trousers flew higher and caught, not on the top of the wall, but on the large wooden cross mounted on the top of the chapel and hung there, swinging to and fro.

A wry smile came to her face. "Thou shalt not..." whispered Amelia to herself and left quickly, well satisfied.

It wasn't until the next day that the dazed officer staggered out of the cells into the yard, looking vulnerable without his trousers. He emerged to find two other guards and Mrs Winters standing there staring skywards, and he looked up. There they were, mounted on the chapel crucifix, and Matron lowered her gaze to stare accusingly at him.

Unbeknown to them, a large group of women watched avidly through the door to the laundry yard. By now of course, they had all been apprised of the events. They could hear angry voices but not make out what was being said until Matron shouted.

"This is not the first time, Sir! Don't you think I know what was behind all that business with the washtubs and Sarah who attacked you before! You have no business working in this place. Get out at once, you will be charged for this! And for God's sake and mine, put some trousers on!" and she watched in disgust as he followed the other guards out of the yard, his genitals drooping and wobbling pathetically. His progress was accompanied by a rousing cheer from behind the wall of the laundry yard, and Matron turned, hands on hips, exasperated. "Get back to work, you lot!"

Amelia was forced to tell the story seven times to the women working unravelling ropes in their cells, as she collected their baskets that evening, and they all treated her like a hero. For a moment Amelia could have sworn that she saw a tear in Morag's eye when the tale was told, but the tough woman shook off her feelings in a determined fashion.

"How ye ever got 'em oop there, I'll never noo. The chapel cross – now tha' was a stroke of genius!" and in typical Morag fashion she laughed coarsely and added. "I wish now tha' ye'd rammed tha' damned truncheon up 'is arse too, Amelia!"

Crime Class was a slightly more peaceful place for the next few weeks, as all the women, especially Morag, were subdued. Amelia guessed that the Scot suffered with constant aches from her injuries, but, accustomed to pain, she bore it stoically and never spoke of the incident again. One way or another, thought Amelia, past events had made them all who they were. She had to admit that this included herself. She had often dreamed of killing her husband, but had never considered herself genuinely capable of it, until now.

One day, Matron came to fetch Amelia from the laundry yard. "Amelia, you are going to probation. Follow me!" and she paused at the door, waiting. Amelia wearily dried her hands and followed. She turned at the door and looked back at the wretched women who slaved away at the tubs.

She would not be sorry to leave them, but Amelia now had a better understanding of those women who were considered irredeemable. No longer afraid of them, she wished that she could help relieve their suffering.

Morag looked at the small, dark woman who had risked everything to save her, and briefly lifted one hand in acknowledgment, her face expressionless. Amelia nodded, and turned away.

John Skinner hated the damned stone around him and he fought his confinement unceasingly. His knuckles were bloody from bashing the heavy blocks, and his forehead was grazed where he had been beating it against them. He had been put into solitary again, for fighting with another convict.

"Here!" he screamed, "let me out you dogs! You bloody dogs!" and he collapsed onto the hard bench. His head ached and he could feel the blood pounding in his temples. Pieces of sandstone and dirt fell onto his face, and he spluttered and shook his head violently.

The food slot opened. "Shut up Skinner! The guv'na says if you don't shut up, you'll get another week." It was Bradley, the old lifer, who brought his bread and water.

"Who's gonna make me?" Skinner roared, "You Bradley? Are you gonna make me?" The small door slammed shut hurriedly. "Come on you bastards, come and make me!"

There was movement at the door and the heavy wooden barrier opened, and Skinner charged, flailing his fists and screaming with the last of his energy. "Come on! If I'm going to hell, you're comin' with me!" His crazed attempts were cut off by the crack of a heavy truncheon. Two guards, swinging the weapons with strength, forced him back, until the man fell, and the blows continued to land until his ranting was silenced.

"There, that should shut the crazy devil up for a bit!" said one in satisfaction. "I'll go report to the Governor about this one again. He's causing unrest among the other men - they can 'ear 'im goin' on ya know!" They went out, slamming and locking the door, leaving the injured man lying in the dirt with blood oozing from wounds on his head and face.

Putting Skinner in solitary repeatedly had not worked, thought Major Horsham, the governor of the coal mine facility. He looked out over the thick window sill at the blue water glinting in the bay. The man was a menace, and in the two years he had been here, labouring on the site preparing the accommodation for the convict mine workers and building the jetty to load the ships, Skinner had spent half the time in solitary confinement on bread and water. He had also received two sentences of lashes.

The punishment only seemed to make the man worse, and now with the first shipment of coal almost ready to send to Hobart in June, Horsham had many headaches to deal with and no time for this. Perhaps the solution may lie with working the man so hard that he had no stomach for fighting. The Governor considered sending him down underground, although he had no mining experience like the Welsh, Irish and Cornish convicts. He could not afford the operations of the mine to be interrupted at this stage, as he had a deadline to meet for the first shipment. If there was any more bad behaviour, fifty lashes at a time should dampen his spirits! Thus resolved, he gave the order to the guard. "When Skinner comes to, send him up to the mine crew. Tell them if there is any trouble, to report to me immediately."

"Yes Guv," responded the man at the door, saluting, and went to report to the guard in charge of the solitary cells. Sometime during the night Skinner came out of his oblivion, as groaning was heard by the guard. Nevertheless, with complete disregard for his injuries, at dawn he was bundled out of his cell at gunpoint, and sent staggering down to the muster station where the other convicts were wearily gathering before walking up the hill to the mineshaft for another day's toil.

The work in the mine was hard and dangerous, performed in almost total darkness. The men worked from dawn until dusk chopping out coal from the walls with pickaxes and loading it into buckets to be raised up the shaft to be loaded into the small railway trucks.

They worked by the light of gas lanterns or candles, and emerged black with coal dust each evening, completely spent from their exertions. The loaded trucks would be sent hurtling down the inclined plane on rails, the downward momentum easily producing enough force to pull several empty carts up to the top of the hill on the opposing track. At the bay, the rail tracks went right along the jetty, where the coal was loaded into the hull of the ship, ready for transport to Hobart Town. The lucky ones worked on the jetty. Skinner was sent underground.

Skinner refused to work with any effort, and the men on his shift were resentful of his lack of contribution, as they themselves had to labour harder to get their quota finished. One of the members of this group was Trevor Martin, a tough miner from Wales, and he stood up to the troublemaker.

"Look 'ere, ye 'ave to do more, the rest of us are already doin' extra, as we've go' the young laddie, and 'e can't do as much as a man," and he pointed to Freddie, who was little more than a boy. He was small and weak looking, about fourteen years of age.

"'S not my worry," retorted Skinner. "I've got me work cut out just survivin' this place, an' me plan don't include babysittin' some brat!"

Martin turned away, breathing deeply, trying to control himself. "God help yer then if y' ever need a hand yerself then, John Skinner!"

They continued to struggle to fill buckets one man short, as Skinner did as little as possible, especially when there was no guard watching. The other men were disgruntled, and when it was decided to allow John Skinner back in the barracks with the other men for the night, most of them deliberately ignored him, but another fellow from his team came and sat down beside him.

"Warren James." And he put out his hand in a friendly gesture. Skinner shook it reluctantly.

"How long 'ave you been here then James?" he asked, in an effort to gain an ally.

"Four years now," sighed the other man, staring at the rough ceiling. "I got seven, but it may as well be life, if you're down the mine."

"What do you mean?" asked Skinner curiously.

"Well, I've worked hard, got into no trouble, and I've got three years to go, but me lungs are shot already. If I do get out after seven years, I may as well be dead anyway," he said morosely.

"What did you do to ge' transpor'ed then?" asked Skinner, feeling a little less hostile.

"I organised a protest, *a protest*, mind you, at the Forest of Dean. They were supposed to open up the forests to grazing again, we'd been fighting the ruling for years, but they never did. The foresters had nowhere to graze their cattle, we were starving and our traditional way of life had been taken away." He paused in disgust.

"How did that end up with ya bein' arrested?" asked the other man.

"We were just removing fences to let our cattle into the banned areas. The officials came along with some troops, read the riot act and declared us a dangerous mob. We had to all escape into the forest and hide, but eventually someone told them where we were, and as the instigator, I was put on trial for inciting a riot!" Warren James hung his head looking defeated. "I was an educated man compared to some of my fellow foresters; I'd never done anything against the law in my life!"

"The bastards! That's why I hate 'em so much," said Skinner with venom, "you do somethin' completely within your rights," he thought of his wife with a vicious leer, "and they arrest you for it!" He decided to try and get James on his side, he didn't want to be the only one causing trouble, but between them, they could give the authorities here a big problem and it would serve them right! He mentioned his plan to James.

The forester was not a rebel though, and was not keen to participate. "Look, I understand your need to stand up to them Skinner, but it's no good, they'll get you one way or the other, and you're only making it harder for the rest of us."

John Skinner felt a familiar surge of anger at this attempt to convince him to conform. He would just have to create trouble on his own then, he decided bitterly, the devil take them all! So over the next few weeks, the man from Worcester made sure he got under everyone's skin. He already had a reputation as a troublemaker within the labourer's mob, but now he had a whole new group of men to influence.

He would manipulate bad feeling between Trevor Martin and the other team members by telling lies and placing blame. Creating a conflict was simple, and once he did, telling the guards that it was one of the other men to blame for the situation, usually earned them a jab in the head with the butt of a rifle. He was stirring up discontent, and John Skinner loved it. One way or another, it took the focus of the guards away from him, and he enjoyed watching the dissatisfaction and anger develop between the other men.

One shift, three full buckets of coal were 'accidentally' tipped over on the way up the shaft, wasting hours of work. The supervising guards were furious. Skinner told Freddie who, true to form, went and told Martin that Warren James was responsible, whilst he complained to James that Martin had deliberately tipped the buckets to get him into trouble with the guards. Martin and James ended up in a fistfight, and both were sentenced to twenty five lashes. John Skinner did not realise it, but the simmering situation he had created was about to explode.

Major Horsham looked at the records of the men. In the last two months, four of the six men in the shift had been sentenced to lashes and two of them had felt the cuts twice each. He hesitated to put the men in solitary, as he needed numbers to make up the shifts down the mine. The guards had complained about the group several times as they were struggling to keep the situation under control. Productivity was being affected and his deadline for the coal delivery was approaching.

He called in a guard. "When the men come down this evening, fetch me Trevor Martin." Following his discussion with Martin, Horsham called for Warren James, who until recently, had been a model prisoner. He then spoke to the lad, Freddie, and at last, he had got to the bottom of it. One name kept coming up, one name at the bottom of all the strife, it was that damned John Skinner again!

"Keep a close eye on that Skinner today," he said to the guards the next morning, before the men departed. "It is he causing all the trouble you are having up there." They nodded, and saluted before setting off up the hill as usual.

The mine shafts were constantly filling up with ground water, and two men would be removing bucket loads regularly. As well as the buckets of coal being lifted up, the winch, manned by convicts on winding wheels at the top of the shaft, also transported about one hundred gallons of water per hour.

The winch ceased to operate about midday, and the six men were working down in the shaft, unaware that anything was wrong. They continued working loading the coal and water into buckets for a time, then realised that the winch was not lifting the buckets up or lowering empty ones down. Freddie, who was at the bottom of the shaft attaching the buckets to the rope, went to Martin, as Trevor Martin was the most experienced miner in the group and acted as the group leader.

The Welshman called up the shaft. "Wha's the trouble with the winch?"

"Rope's broken in two places. They've gone to get another one!" called a voice faintly from ground level.

"Better 'urry lad, the water level seems to be risin' faster than usual," called up Martin again.

"All right, I hear you." And the person with the disembodied voice at the top presumably went to pass on the message about the water level.

After about two more hours, the men down the shaft, over three hundred feet deep, knew they were in trouble. Excess ground water was seeping in at a rapid rate, and the lower tunnels were already full of water. They waited at the highest point, nervously looking at the rising surge.

"I've got to get out. of 'ere!" exclaimed John Skinner, anxiously looking for an escape route. "I can't swim, and we'll all be swimmin' in 'alf an hour!"

"Swimming or drowning," added Warren James morbidly, as if he didn't care whether he lived or not.

"Mebbe we should ge' them to throw down the old rope knotted together, and we'll try and climb oot one man at a time," said Martin eventually. He called out to the top, and eventually the rope was lowered, knotted together in two places, but it would only take the weight of one man at a time. He directed one of the crew to go up first, and being strong and light, he swarmed up the rope like a monkey.

"That's 'ow i's done!" said Martin. "Nothing to it." Another team member was sent up, and he took much longer, having more trouble climbing. Skinner was cursing and spitting at Martin as he had wanted to go up next, and he felt valuable time was being wasted.

"Ye're bloody scum, Martin!" ranted Skinner, "you should let me go next, then."

"I'm no' of a mind to do that." said the laconic Welshman, deliberately avoiding Skinner's direct glare. The guard had taken him aside and indicated that it was Skinner causing all the unrest with the men, and Martin was angry about the trouble he had been in. He had suffered two lots of lashes as a result of the conflict and this was, as Martin understood now, directly attributable to the man in front of him. "James, ye next."

Warren James climbed up the rope with great difficulty as he was a strongly built man, and weighed heavier than the others. Having to rest propped against the shaft wall several times on the way, it took what seemed a very long time for him to reach the top. Young Freddie was then due to climb, and Skinner was incensed, as he could feel the water lapping at his boots, and he was terrified of being trapped down the shaft.

Freddie was only a slight lad, but of poor health and not very strong. He got about halfway up the rope and started to slip down again, wailing that he could not go any higher. He struggled and strained to lift himself but slid down and fell back to the bottom of the hole.

"Let me go, Martin! Leave 'im, he ain't gonna make it!" said Skinner, but the Welshman would not stand for it.

"I'll climb with 'im, I'm strongest, and I can lift him oop as well as meself. Ye wait and come last. It's the only way we'll all make it."

"No Martin, no!" and Skinner threw a punch in desperation, as he and Martin scrambled for the rope and fought to hold onto it. The water was around their knees now, and rising rapidly. The situation was fraught with danger. John Skinner thought quickly. Under the water, he could feel a good sized rock with his foot and he pretended to bend over, exhausted. Then he rose up like a demon from hell, the rock in his hand and madness in his eyes. He struck Trevor Martin in the head, and as the man fell back with a splash Freddie grabbed him and held his head above the water, his accusing eyes fixed on the culprit.

Leaving them to their fate, Skinner grabbed the rope and climbed as fast as he was able, desperate to escape the tide of water that was threatening to engulf them. Hand over hand, he strove and strained and finally he clambered over the lip of the hole, pulled the rope up after him and lay on the ground exhausted.

"Quick, lower it down again," said Warren James, "there's still Martin and Freddie to come up."

"No," lied the man from Worcester. "They're gone, the water was over our 'eads, I just managed to grab it before bein' swept away like them!" and he put his head in his hands, as if he were distressed.

The men were preparing to leave the shaft site having accepted with regret the loss of the two men, as no new rope had arrived from the barracks and nothing more could be done that day. They all stood and began the trek down the hill, when a sudden shout from one of the men stopped them in their tracks. A man was heaving himself over the edge of the mine shaft, a man back from the dead. It was Trevor Martin!

With an almost superhuman effort, he had climbed up the side of the mineshaft, with nothing to hold onto except bare rock and on his back was tied the limp body of the boy, Freddie. The exhausted man's head lifted and his eyes met the one he was looking for. His accusing stare bored into John Skinner.

"I know what ye did. I know what ye did you cowardly devil!" and he fell back in fatigue. The other men ran over, along with the guards, to untie the boy and help Trevor Martin to his feet. John Skinner furtively started down the incline plane on the rail line for the coal trucks. He didn't want to hang around while Martin spilled the beans. He hurried down, with no particular plan in mind but to escape.

"That man Skinner, Freddie told me 'e took a rock and 'it me over the 'ead with it to stop me climbin' the rope to help the boy! 'E 'ad time to come oop after us, but 'e just left us for dead and saved 'imself! I woke oop, and the water was already oop to me neck, but Freddie had saved me from drownin'. Didn't you Freddie?" He paused as he looked at the boy, who was lying lifeless on the ground. "Freddie?"

The men looked down, not wanting to meet the Welshman's eyes. He dropped to his knees next to the body. The boy was dead, probably drowned before Martin had managed to climb above water level.

"Skinner! Where's Skinner?" cried Martin. "If it's the last thing I ever do, I will get tha' bastard!" and he looked amongst the men but he could not see him. They all scattered, trying to catch sight of the offender and Trevor Martin ran over to tracks down the incline plane.

"There 'e is!" and he jabbed his finger towards the guilty man. Sure enough, the fugitive was a hundred yards away down the tracks, on the run as fast as he could. Martin glanced at the laden coal truck next to him, waiting to run down to the harbour, then back down at the fleeing man. He put out his hand and before anyone could stop him, simultaneously let off the brake, and unhitched the line holding the truck at the top of the hill.

The vehicle started moving down the tracks, and with only a slight rattle of the well-greased wheels, it rapidly gained speed. Skinner seemed not to hear anything until the vehicle was almost upon him, and then he turned his head suddenly as if aware that death was on his heels. His mouth opened, but he had no time to cry out. The heavily laden wagon struck him with immense force, snapping his head back and almost cutting his body in half even as the impact drove him onto the lines under the steel wheels. The truck continued on its merry way down the hill and slowed obediently at the bottom of the hill, gently rolling towards the jetty to be unloaded.

Twenty men stood spellbound at the top, shock silencing them, until one guard recovered his wits and said to the other. "It's a good thing that we managed to stop that convict from escaping is it not?"

"A lucky outcome really," agreed the other, nodding vigorously. "All right men, we had better go and make our report to the Governor and take young Freddie's body down. Skinner can stay there until the Gov'na wants to send a body retrieval team. I don't think he is going anywhere! Let's go men." They all tore their eyes away from the carnage on the slope and started down the bush track to the barracks, Trevor Martin carrying Freddie, as he was inconsolable and would let no one else help him.

Martin was not to know that his actions that day would become legendary amongst the convicts at the coal mine. The feat of strength that they had witnessed would never be forgotten, climbing all the way up the shaft with the boy already dead on his back. Even the guards regarded him with awe.

In stark contrast, John Skinner was reviled by all, and the torn pieces of his body were scraped up and thrown into the sea for the sharks.

Over one hundred and fifty years later, the Port Arthur Coal Mine long since abandoned, the relentless wind and washing of the rain gradually obliterates the cells and stone buildings, but the silent heaviness of the misery and hardship remains.

The stone steps are worn down from the repetition of long suffering footsteps trudging in weary procession, reflecting the gradual erosion of the spirits of the convict men. More suffering and ugliness was endured there in those few short decades than in the entire preceding six hundred million years and nature has begun the process of erasing it all, as if removing an insult to her perfection.

It was June, and winter had hit hard and early at the Female Factory. Snow fell on the mountain, and the cold winds swept down the foothills and onward to Hobart Town. The female convicts at the Factory felt the cold more than usual, although hardship was a way of life for them.

But there seemed to be no sun day in, day out, not even to warm the walls in the corner of the yard, where Amelia had so often sought a familiar refuge. Her favourite slabs of stone were growing moss for the first time in the four years since she had arrived, and moisture ran down the surface, giving off a mouldy, decaying smell.

Jane had survived despite her affliction, and had surprised everybody by clinging to life, when other healthy infants died of disease or lack of nourishment. The child had grown to look more and more like John Skinner and in the eighteen months after her weaning, her mother had spent little time with her.

She had been sent to the orphan school the previous December when she turned two years old, though she could not walk or speak like a normal two year old. One of the guards had to carry Jane to the coach and although her mother was aware that she was leaving, did not see her off. Amelia tried hard not to think about her daughter, and busied herself with whatever task she was given.

None of the men that came with their wives seeking domestic servants ever chose Amelia again since the ill-fated period at Mr and Mrs Smith's farm and she felt despondent, as if she had nothing more to live for. It was Lucy Hurst that gave Amelia hope again.

"Amelia, Amelia! I've go' a letter!" waved Lucy excitedly as she rushed across the yard. "Can you read i' for me?"

"Of course I can Lucy, but you should be able to read most of it yourself now, shouldn't you?" asked Amelia in surprise.

"Well yes," said Lucy uncertainly, "you did teach me to read and write on the ship, Amelia, but I haven't 'ad much practise of recent times and I'm so excited to ge' a letter, that I couldn't make head or tail of it!"

Amelia laughed at the girl, with her flushed cheeks and sparkling eyes. It was a lonely existence indeed, when the arrival of one letter could be the cause of so much anticipation. She read it out loud.

"Dear Lucy,

as you know, the last time I saw you, several years ago, I was assigned to a gentleman who was a publican."

"Oh, it must be from Ann! Yes, that's right! I told you I thought he had an inn or pub. Go on!" Lucy said.

"I started helping Mr Ford, for that is his name, in his public house, waiting on tables and suchlike. We got along very well, and a short time ago, Mr Ford asked me to marry him!"

"Oh, Amelia, marry 'im! I'm so 'appy that Ann has been so fortunate!" Lucy exclaimed.

"So I am now Ann Ford," Amelia went on, *"and Mr Ford and I are very happy. I am to have our first child very soon, and we have decided that we need more help in our establishment. I have told Mr Ford much about you, my friend, and also about*

Amelia, who I hold in very high regard. I hope that you may know Amelia's whereabouts."

"Well, o' course I do, you are readin' the letter! But Ann does not know tha' o' course," Lucy said hastily.

"Shall I continue?" asked Amelia.

"O' course, Amelia, I'm sorry for interruptin', I'm just so excited!"

"Mr Ford says that the two of you sound ideal as new staff for us, if you would consider coming to us for employment, and he says that if this is acceptable to you, he will write immediately to the convict office to offer places for your assignment."

"Maybe Mr Ford can 'elp us apply for our Tickets of Leave!" said Lucy wistfully, "then we could be paid employees."

"I'm not sure Lucy, it may be that Mr Ford could not afford to pay us." Amelia sounded calm, but her heart leapt with long lost hope. "But even assignment would get us out of this place away from the sickness that is present here, and some good food," she said thoughtfully. Amelia looked down at the letter once more.

"Please answer this letter without delay, and Mr Ford will organise the correct paperwork. I do hope you can get a message to Amelia, and ask her too.

Your friend,

Ann Ford (Henry).

The Hope and Anchor Tavern, Macquarie Street, Hobart Town."

"Oh Amelia you must write back now!" exclaimed Lucy. "You want to come with me, don't you?"

"Of course I do Lucy! I was just thinking of what a beautiful hand the letter was written in. Mr Ford must be a decent man, as he has obviously allowed Ann to continue her education. That settles it. I am determined that working for such a man cannot be unpleasant, and we shall start a life away from this place for the first time in years!"

"Yes Amelia, and perhaps a ticket soon also!" squealed Lucy, clapping her hands.

"Before I answer the letter, I must speak to Matron and tell her what is proposed," and Amelia hurried off to see the woman in charge.

After satisfying herself that the assignment was in order and Matron would also support the plan, Amelia wrote back to Ann and accepted the invitation on behalf of Lucy and herself, pending their release from the factory. A few days later Lucy and Amelia collected their meagre belongings and stood in the receiving area, waiting for Matron and Mr Ford.

"I never thought that this day would come, Lucy," said Amelia, "I was giving up hope of ever getting out of this place."

"It's times li'e those," said Lucy wisely, "that you need a friend, and I can' believe i' that Ann had no' forgotten me! I knew she would never forge' you, Amelia, as you were such a help to us both when we were burnt so badly on the ship."

"Well, I never expected that the simple service of treating people in the ship's hospital would ever be reciprocated in such a thoughtful way," said Amelia, surprised.

"What's 'ciprocated mean, Amelia? asked the girl, as Lucy had been transported at eighteen and had little education.

"It means given back," explained Amelia. "Here comes Matron now."

Mrs Winter introduced Mr Ford, who welcomed them like long lost sisters, and then she wished the two women good luck and indicated to the guards that they should open the gates. The matron efficiently marked in her ledger the time and date of their release, and waved once as they stepped out onto the road with the huge stone wall behind them. Amelia glanced back at the wall once before they walked down the road to where Mr Ford's horse and cart was waiting.

"How different it seems now, to be walking away, not like the first time we walked up here from the ship - do you remember Lucy? I was carrying Evan, and he was so heavy." She fell silent, memories of her son flooding back. "Do you know that he would be six years old now, Mr Ford? I wonder if he is well and happy."

"I've no doubt he is Amelia," answered the kind gentleman, "I hope he is learning how to read and write!"

"Matron said that all the children are educated at the orphan school," said Amelia. "That is one of my comforts. But the other is that one day, when I have the means and the situation to do it; I will go there and take Evan home with me." Her voice broke and Amelia was silent for a time, thinking of her son.

Mr Ford helped them up into the cart. "Wha' about your daugh'er?" asked Lucy curiously. "Won't you take 'er home too?"

"I fear I may never be able to claim her, Lucy," said Amelia carefully, "she had a retardation of development, and needs special care." She did not mention the child's other affliction. Her resemblance to John Skinner was a far worse misfortune in her mother's eyes.

The horse trotted smartly, and soon reached the Hope and Anchor Tavern that was on the main street in town. Mr Ford took them to Ann directly, who was heavily pregnant and resting.

"Ann, we are so happy to see you!" declared Amelia, and Lucy nodded. The younger girl was quite overwhelmed at seeing her good friend again, and simply knelt next to Ann's chair, holding tightly to her hand.

"Lucy, Amelia, it has all worked out well!" Ann said. "I have been so fortunate, and I want to share my good fortune with someone else and I cannot think of anyone else I would rather share it with than the two of you!" and they all laughed. "Of course you have just met my husband, Mr Ford."

"Mr Ford, we are so grateful. Sir, you must let me thank you on behalf of Lucy and myself, for your assistance." said Amelia, and curtseyed in sincerest respect and gratitude.

"I can see that you are a lady of education, Amelia, and I will be very happy to have your help in many ways, as my lovely wife will be so busy with other things." His eyes twinkled and he turned to Lucy. "I have been told, Lucy, that you are a bright, personable girl, and would do very well serving my customers in the bar. Do you think you could do that?"

"Oh I would, Sir, I love talkin' to people bu' I'm no' so good a' figures, or writin', like Amelia... although she 'as been teachin' me, but I will work hard, Sir!" This spontaneous bubbly outpouring drew a chuckle from Mr Ford.

"You are going to be just what we need, both of you. Now, if you will come with me, I will show you the rooms I have ready for you."

Ann bid them goodbye till the evening, when they were to eat supper together, and the women followed Mr Ford upstairs. The rooms were comfortable with a small, shared parlour between and they were to eat in the tavern. The arrangement was most convenient. A surprise followed, as Hannah, another old shipmate and her friend Sarah, were in the tavern; they were lodging in the adjacent building and the women had a pleasant hour catching up with all their news.

The work in the tavern was reliable and constant. The women were kept busy at all times, Lucy in the bar and waiting on tables, and Mr Ford taught Amelia to do the ordering of stock, and how to organise the cellars and store rooms which kept her occupied during the day. Amelia also waited on tables in the evenings.

The customers were mostly respectful, and kind Mr Ford was there to sort out any unpleasantness if any of the men stepped over the line of acceptable behaviour. The two women were glad to have a good situation and worked well so that Mr Ford was very pleased with them. They each got one day off per week, when they were allowed to go about the town, which was a welcome treat.

Ann's child had been born, and she was most taken up with caring for her healthy baby girl. Sometimes she allowed Amelia to take the child on to her lap, and Amelia would rock her, silently reliving the days when her own children had been babies.

Hannah had her Ticket of Leave and had gone back to her previous employment as a prostitute. She cheerfully told Amelia that she was doing well as her services were in demand and paid well and encouraged her to apply for a Ticket of Leave also. Amelia broached the subject with Mr Ford.

"Mr Ford, I am very eager to obtain my Ticket of Leave, so that I can earn my own money and begin a new life," she explained to him late one evening, as they were washing glasses behind the bar just before closing. "Would it be possible for you to sponsor me? I would be ever so grateful."

"Of course I could Amelia," he said, "but there is only one problem with that plan. You see, I could not afford to pay you full time. I may be able to offer you several evenings work in the tavern each week, though," he added, putting his glass down and hanging the cloth on a peg.

"I hadn't thought of that," admitted Amelia. "But perhaps that would be enough, and I could get extra work elsewhere."

"Perhaps you could," said Mr Ford doubtfully, "would you like me to send in the application?"

Amelia was filled with gratitude for the kindness shown to her by this man. Ann was lucky to have found him. She smiled, "why yes, Mr Ford, if you please!"

The application was successful, and in a little over a week, Amelia was a Ticket of Leave holder and could work for a wage. Mr Ford offered her three nights per week working in the tavern, plus her meals, so although she would not have money to spare, she would not go hungry. Amelia was confident she could manage.

Hannah's friend Sarah had moved on, so there was a vacancy in their rooms next door, and she agreed to lodge there for the rent of one shilling per week. Amelia was eager to begin saving money, and looked for other work, but paid work for women in the new colony was scarce.

When a gentleman in the tavern propositioned her one evening, Amelia suddenly became aware that she could earn a whole shilling from providing the service that he required. It was not an easy decision for her to make, to resort to prostitution, but she determined that it was necessary in the circumstances. Amelia began a discreet sideline business, providing an essential service to a few select clients.

Chapter 25.

Amelia had been working for the Fords and illicitly 'on the town' for several months when she met a most interesting person. One evening she was helping in the bar, waiting at tables and taking orders for drinks. A man sitting in the corner caught her attention, holding up his mug to indicate that he wanted ale. Amelia nodded to him, and as soon as she had delivered her tray of glasses to the kitchen, went to take his order.

He was dark haired and attractive in a masculine way, with a few days growth on his chin and intense eyes. Something stirred inside Amelia as she regarded him. "Yes Sir? Another ale for you Sir?"

"Thank you, yes," he murmured, gazing at Amelia. She felt uncomfortable under his intense look, and she bobbed a curtsey and fled to fetch his drink. She paused at the bar, waiting for Lucy to fill the mug, and leaned against it for a moment, her cheeks flushed. What was wrong with her? Lucy noticed something too, and addressed her.

"Are you well, Amelia?" she asked in a raised voice to be heard over the noise.

"Yes, yes, thank you kindly Lucy, I'm just hot, that is all," and she took the mug onto her tray, making her way back across the room. Lucy's eyes followed her suspiciously. The gentleman in the corner was watching her as she approached. As he had taken off his coat, Amelia noticed he was muscular in a way that indicated great physical strength, and she could not tear her eyes away as he reached for his ale. Finally she turned to escape his regard, but a strong hand suddenly grabbed her wrist, preventing her from walking away. At the unexpected touch Amelia started and looked back.

"Just one moment! You must tell me your name, and why such a pretty woman as you is working in a tavern!" the man said, leaning forward to hear her response.

"My name is Amelia Sir, and I am working for Mr Ford, who has been most kind to me. Now if you will excuse me Sir, I must attend to those tables."

"Well Amelia, I am Richard Barton. Thank you for the drink," he said seriously, and he leaned back against the wall, not taking his eyes off her.

"Mr Barton." she curtseyed and hurried over to some other patrons who were trying to get her attention. Amelia worked for several more hours and was conscious of Mr Barton's intense dark eyes following her about the room. Just before closing, she noticed that he had gone.

Lucy commented on the man as they cleaned the tables. "Amelia, that gentleman, you know tha' one in the corner? Well I don't know if 'e was a gentleman, but 'e was watching you all night! What do you suppose 'e meant by it?"

"I'm sure I don't know, Lucy," Amelia replied, "but there was something about him wasn't there?" Lucy made no more comment but eyed her speculatively.

Richard made up his mind he would go to the tavern again that night. He could not get the small, dark haired woman out of his mind; Amelia, she had said her name was. She was educated, he could tell by her speech, but there was something that drew him to her. She was pretty, of course, but it was a certain dignified elegance in her movement that most attracted him. He must see her again!

He went about his business that day acquiring some new brick-making equipment, but all the while held the evening in great anticipation, and at dusk he made his way to the place, meaning to have a meal there.

Amelia was again working on the tables and Richard saw her immediately, moving about in her quiet, efficient manner, giving the customers a smile and kind word as she went. His heart unexpectedly started pounding, and he moved to a table quickly, taking deep breaths to quieten his heart. His reaction to the lady was quite unusual. He made up his mind to catch her in conversation and find out more about her. She saw him as he took his place and gave him a nod and a shy smile, showing her recognition. Richard was elated, she remembered him!

During the evening, the two chatted about this and that as Amelia came and went with food and drink, but this was most unsatisfactory as the tavern was busy, and Amelia could not talk for longer than a minute at a time. He needed to see her again, she had bewitched him! Richard spoke to her before he left for the evening.

"Amelia, would you allow me to escort you home after work?" he asked.

"Thank you Sir, but I lodge right next door, so there is no need," she replied, and then continued. "If you be thinking of coming back tomorrow Sir, I won't be here. I do not work on Tuesdays."

"I have to go back to Bothwell on Friday," said Richard hesitantly, "but may I be so bold...would you consent to having lunch with me tomorrow?"

Amelia answered cautiously. "I am most flattered Sir, but please don't be spending your hard earned money on me." Barton's face fell, and Amelia could sense his disappointment. She went on hurriedly, "I could make us up a picnic basket, the weather is better now that it is spring, and we could eat by the river."

"Yes! Amelia, a picnic would be most enjoyable. Shall I come by your lodgings at eleven?"

"Come by here, Mr Barton, as I will prepare our repast in the kitchen. I'm sure Mr Ford won't mind." She looked up at him as he stood. "Good night Mr Barton."

"Goodnight Amelia, until tomorrow then!" and he flashed a quick grin. Donning his hat, he opened the door and stepped out into the night.

Amelia was both excited and nervous about her outing. She had not had a relationship with any man for some years and, on reflection, she had not had good luck with men at all. Still, Mr Barton seemed kind, and they would be in public, so she felt there would be no untoward expectations.

Lucy was most decided in her reaction to Amelia's news, and her mouth dropped open. "'E wants to see you again! I knew i'! I saw him watching you tha' first nigh' and I knew 'e fancied you! Oh, but you must grab 'im Amelia, 'e's a good one!"

"Lucy, how do you know that?" Amelia admonished. "You have never even met the man!"

"I can just tell, Amelia," said Lucy mysteriously, "an' e's such a fine figure of a man too!" and she raised her eyebrows at Amelia in mischief.

"Lucy!" exclaimed Amelia, pretending to be shocked. "That's enough of that if you please." Lucy knew nothing of Amelia's other form of employment, and the feigned offence was in part an attempt to avoid any kind of suspicion. "Now, what shall I make for our picnic?" and the two of them spent an enjoyable hour planning the feast. Mr Ford had said he didn't mind in the least if Amelia made a picnic in the kitchen, and wished her a pleasant day.

The next day dawned fine with warm sunshine, and Amelia sang as she packed a basket, including a bottle of ale that Mr Ford most kindly gave her to take. Ready early, Amelia called upon Ann for half an hour before she left. Ann's child, named Hilary, was a joy, and starting to take notice of things in her world. Ann was very happy, and her domestic bliss was obvious to everyone.

"Amelia, I wish you could find a good man and settle down," she said, "it is so hard here in the colonies if one has to survive on one's own, as there are so few jobs for women!"

"I'm not sure if I want to settle down, Ann," Amelia replied quietly, holding Hilary on her lap. "The presence of men in my life seems to attract only grief."

"But Amelia, you are too young to be alone for the rest of your life!" exclaimed Ann. "Let this Mr Barton be the one, you are a good enough judge of people by now to tell if he is a kind man!"

"We will see, Ann, but I must tell you it is something I did not expect. Seeing you with Hilary, though, does give me pangs for my own home, and... children." She did not elaborate but stood up, handing the child to her mother so that her movements distracted her from the sudden emotions that were stirring. Ann, knowing how much Amelia missed her children, kept silent.

"But who can tell what the future will bring!" said Amelia brightly, "I already have my ticket, and employment here with you, so life is already looking better is it not?" and she collected her wrap, preparing to go downstairs. Kissing Ann on the cheek and giving Hilary one last cuddle, Amelia descended to collect her basket and wait for Mr Barton.

He arrived punctually on the hour, and Amelia gave him a quick curtsey. "Mr Barton."

"Good morning Amelia!" he said, bowing his head politely, "please let me take your basket." It was strange, Amelia reflected, how they were nervous and overly polite in each other's company, as if they were two young people in their first courtship. She handed the heavy basket to him with a smile and he took it seeming not to notice any weight at all, and they set off walking slowly, Amelia pulling her shawl closer against the cool breeze.

Amelia could not remember such an enjoyable day. Mr Barton, or Richard, as he asked her to call him, was good company, and gave her such a feeling of strength and safety that she relaxed in his presence, and the two learned much about each other.

It was a surprise to find that Richard was on a Ticket of Leave, as he seemed far too much the gentleman to be a convict. But admitting to him that she too, had come to Van Diemen's Land as a convict was now easier, although he was equally astonished, and they laughed over their mutual surprise.

Richard told Amelia that he was living in Bothwell, and as he was a bricklayer, he had come to Hobart to visit Mr Shoobridge's quarries in West Hobart, to learn about the process of adding lime to clay to improve the quality of bricks. He also needed equipment for his work in Bothwell that he could only acquire in Hobart Town.

"How does adding lime improve the bricks, Richard?" asked Amelia, interested.

"Well," he explained, pouring ale from the bottle into a mug for her. "The lime stops the raw bricks from shrinking and drying out, and in the firing process, it causes some components to melt and bind the brick together."

"So the brick is harder, more like stone!" she said thoughtfully.

"I didn't know you were interested in such things, Amelia," Richard commented.

"I always lived in a stone house, but I think these new bricks you are talking of would be just as good," Amelia said. "I always wanted to have my own stone dwelling one day, where I would feel safe."

"Well, you never know, I might build one for you someday." Richard looked at Amelia with a smile, his eyes crinkling at the corners, but his smile faded as something unsaid passed between them. Each now understood that the other

209

hoped for a future together, but it was too early to be discussing such things yet.

Richard came to the Tavern again the next night, the evening before he left for Bothwell. He had to return in time for the monthly muster of the Ticket of Leave men at his registered place of residence.

He promised Amelia that he would be back in the town in a month, and he took her hand in his and regarded her with his intense, burning gaze before they parted. Her long dark hair which was swept up on top of her head shone in the candlelight. Amelia's high cheekbones and straight backed stance gave her the elegance of a lady, and he raised her hand to his lips. A shiver of anticipation went down the back of Amelia's neck. "Goodbye Amelia, until we meet again." He abruptly dropped her hand and strode out, bowing his head as he ducked out the door.

Amelia, still holding the hand up that he had kissed, looked around and saw Lucy staring at her unashamedly with her mouth open. How could any man be so strong, and yet so gentle? Amelia wondered. She did not know how she would bear the month apart before Richard returned.

The only answer was to keep herself busy, and shaking her head to the girl behind the bar, she resumed her duties. Amelia could no longer bring clients to her room, as she could think only of Mr Barton, and felt that it would be disloyal to do so.

Richard did return in October, and the affection between the two grew into a passionate affair in a matter of days. The physical attraction between them could not be ignored, and throwing caution to the wind, he stayed the nights in Amelia's room, although being very careful not to be seen. When Richard Barton declared his undying love for her, Amelia told him that she returned his feelings, and was upset beyond reason when Richard informed her that he would not be able to return to her until the New Year.

"On my return, if you will wait for me my love, we will make more permanent plans," consoled Richard, and he held her in his arms, stroking her beautiful hair. "I cannot live without you Amelia, but I am compelled to be back for Muster and to complete the next project that I have been engaged for." And with that she had to be satisfied.

Amelia wrote her love a letter in December, although she was not certain that he could read. As he may have to engage someone to read it for him, she avoided any personal content in the missive. Several weeks after writing the letter, Amelia discovered with mixed feelings of joy and fear that she was pregnant with Richard's child, and waited impatiently for Richard to arrive in Hobart Town. She was eager to share her news with her lover, but hoped that he would not be angry.

Mid-January brought Barton south again, and Amelia flung herself on him as he arrived at her lodgings. The austere surroundings were forgotten, as the two were swept up in their feelings for each other. They embraced and kissed hungrily as though they were starving waifs thrown a loaf of bread, and then Richard tore himself from her lips with regret.

"Amelia, oh, Amelia!" Richard said tenderly, and he knelt on one knee on the wooden floor of her room. "Will you marry me? Please say yes, as I cannot imagine life without you, and I wish to take you back to Bothwell where we can make a life together."

Amelia felt the tears about to overflow, and as she held Richard's hand, and looked down at this man, she knew she loved him with all her heart, and all her fear and grief would be of the past. "Richard, I would love to be your wife, but I hope you will be happy when I tell you that...I am with child. Your child."

He did not answer directly, and Amelia felt a sudden wave of fear as they remained immobile, their gazes locked, until Richard suddenly leapt to his feet.

Catching Amelia in a great bear hug, and grinning in excitement and happiness, he swung her around. "Amelia, really? Our child?" and he stopped, reverently lifting her hand to his lips. "Amelia, I love you, and I never want to be without you!" Then he gently embraced her, and they sat talking all night, making plans and speaking of the future, two people who at one time thought that they would have no future at all beyond prison walls.

Richard planned to apply to the convict office for marriage permission, and within days, he made the necessary application. While waiting for the result, Amelia, although having to work at the tavern some evenings, spent all her remaining time with Richard. The permission seemed to take longer than expected, and several weeks went by as they waited. Richard was so occupied with Amelia that he completely forgot that the day for the monthly muster at Bothwell had come and gone.

When they discovered that the couple were engaged, there was a celebration in the tavern. Ann and Mr Ford, Lucy and Hannah all raised a glass that night wishing the happy couple joy in their lives together in Bothwell. Lucy said that she was content to remain assigned to Mr Ford for the time being, as she was worried about finding paid work and hoped in time that she too, could meet a man and marry.

After consuming a good deal of ale, Amelia and Richard retired to bed making rather a lot of noise in their departure, and failing to notice the police constable who was watching from the corner of the room. An hour later, the door of Amelia's room was flung open, and three officers leapt through, brandishing their pistols. The couple had no time to move, and sat up, befuddled with drink and love. They were told briskly to don their clothes, and doing so, they were both hauled off to the jail to be held overnight before facing the magistrate.

Chapter 26.

"Amelia Hobbs, as you were found to have taken a man into your room from the public house, and you are living with another woman known to be 'on the town', you are therefore found guilty of running a disorderly house, and your Ticket of Leave will be revoked. You are to serve six months hard labour at the female factory."

Amelia was angry at the charge, but although she tried to protest the sentence by drawing the magistrate's attention to their marriage application, he refused to allow her to speak and would not vary in his opinion. The fact that Amelia had previously been working as a prostitute some months ago, she considered no longer relevant, as now she was engaged to be married. She felt harshly treated by the authorities, but yet again, she was powerless in the face of the system that controlled her. The sentence would remain, and Amelia was taken back to the factory without delay.

"Richard Barton, you have failed to report for muster at your designated place of residence, and have been living in Hobart Town, so you are found guilty of being absent from your registered residence, and you will serve three days solitary confinement. Your Ticket of Leave will not be revoked as long as you are of good behaviour hereafter."

Richard was full of anger and resentment when he heard of Amelia's plight, but during his three days confinement his fury calmed, knowing that it was futile. He formulated a plan, composing a letter in his mind that he resolved to have written and sent to his beloved as soon as he was released. Amelia received the letter at the end of the week.

Amelia, My Love.

Do not despair at the situation, as I know that is what you are doing! My love for you is undiminished, and I detest the thought of you being in that place. Do not fear that I will stop loving you, as I will go back to Bothwell and continue to work to save coin for our future. As soon as your sentence is finished, I will apply to have you assigned to me here at Bothwell and I shall remove you from Hobart Town. We will then make a plan to re-apply for your Ticket of Leave, but at least we shall be together.

I am much distressed of the thought of our child being born in the female factory, and hope that you and the child will be well. Please think of me and be happy for our future is assured, although we will have to wait a little longer.

Your loving fiancé,
Richard.

The first person Amelia laid eyes on when she entered the gates of the Female Factory was her old friend Molly. Molly was delighted to see her.

"Amelia, I 'aven't seen ya for so long! I 'ave so much to tell ya!"

"Molly! I am very happy to see you are well. But you have not been back here these last four years, so things must have gone well for you?" Amelia hugged Molly and the two women exchanged news.

"Amelia, ya'll never guess! I'm going to be married!" gushed the younger girl. "I was assigned to tha' gentleman tha' you saw the very first day. 'E an 'is wife, Mr and Mrs Goodman, 'ave a large property in a town called Richmond. 'E is a successful businessman there. They've been so good to me Amelia, givin' me clothes and helpin' me go on with my learnin'."

"That is wonderful, Molly. So what has changed?"

"Well tha's just i' Amelia," she explained as the two women walked slowly across the yard. "I me' a lovely young man in Richmond, an' we've applied to marry! 'Is name is William Mitchell, and 'e's ever so nice, and 'e wants to open a saddler's shop!" Molly spoke excitedly.

"So where will you live, Molly?" asked Amelia, they had reached the dormitory building, and paused outside facing each other.

"Will 'as a 'ouse already, and 'es been workin' makin' things out o' leather. 'E 'as sold them through Mr Goodman's depot till now, and buildin' up the business for a few years. We can ge' our own shop though, as Will go' 'is free certificate last year. I'll be assigned to 'im first 'till me Ticket of Leave comes through, and I'm going to 'elp Will in the shop!" Molly looked very satisfied with her situation.

"Oh Molly, I'm so glad to hear this wonderful news. But why are you back here at the factory?" asked Amelia curiously.

She explained further. "Mr and Mrs Goodman, the people I was assigned to, they've 'ad to travel up North for a month for business, so I have to stay 'ere for a few days until me assignment and marriage permission come through, and then I can go back to Richmond with Will. They will 'elp me apply for me Ticket o' Leave soon, they said."

Amelia was thrilled at the news, and filled Molly in with some of the events that had occurred, but she decided to omit any mention of John Skinner or her baby Jane. She did not want to spoil Molly's happiness, and told her instead of her blossoming relationship with Richard Barton, and the events of the past few days.

"I have never felt this way about any man Molly! I love him and I want to marry him. We already had applied for marriage permission when we were arrested! I am also having a baby, Molly," Amelia said. She felt slightly embarrassed to have to tell Molly that for the second time fate had interfered with her marriage plans, leaving her unmarried and with child. "I can't believe this has happened on the eve of our happy day, and do so hope that Richard will wait for me!"

"Amelia, if 'e don' wait for you, then e's not worth 'avin'," said Molly emphatically, completely without judgement. "I'm sure 'e will, jus ya wait an' see." She kissed her friend on the cheek before they entered the building.

Sure enough, on Friday, as Molly was preparing to leave the factory, Richard's letter arrived for Amelia. When she read it, Amelia wept with relief and knew that she could now hope again. She showed the letter to the young woman, who was in the reception area waiting to depart and noted with satisfaction that Molly could now read it herself. Smiling through tears, the two women hugged each other tightly, and Amelia whispered.

"I wish you all the best of everything and happiness for your future, my dear. I'm going to call the baby 'Molly' if she's a girl!" and stood back to watch her friend leave. Molly was now weeping with sadness at the parting, but after looking back at Amelia with a wave, she happily stepped through the doors in the stone wall for the last time. Her fiancé was waiting in a carriage to bear her away to her new life in Richmond, but Molly knew that she owed it all to her dear friend, Amelia.

July came, and in the cold, snowy weather, another child was born to Amelia, and the little girl was duly named Molly. She was healthy and vigorous, and was born in the nursery. Amelia wrote to Richard and her friend Molly, now that she had her address, to tell them of the happy event.

Matron had allowed Amelia to work off her six months labour at the wash tubs partly before the birth, and partly after while still nursing her child, so that her release would come sooner. As it was, a full twelve months passed before Amelia's release was approved, and in January 1837, with the assignment to Richard Barton arranged, she left the female factory, vowing never to return.

In the shadow of the mountain, the great wall of the Hobart Female Factory still remains as a testament to the endurance of the women who lived there. The rivulet even now rushes down from the peaks, through the foothills, past the imposing Cascade Brewery and the wall, its icy torrent striving to cleanse away the bleak legacy of deprivation.

The ancient sandstone edifice casts a gloom over the site, creating a permanent chill where moisture and moss give off a damp, decaying smell. Yet faint scoring on the stone blocks in the sunny corner of the old yard, signify the irrepressible desire of the downtrodden to reach the light, and our very presence here is confirmation that they succeeded.

Chapter 27.

Richard was waiting for her outside, twisting his hat nervously in his hands, and Amelia flew into his arms, the child between them and the weary months of toil at the tubs forgotten.

"Amelia, Amelia, I thought the time would never pass until we were together again!" exclaimed Richard. "I kept thinking of the two of you constantly, and could hardly concentrate on my work." He stopped and took the little girl carefully from her mother. "And who do we have here?" he asked, cuddling her and making her giggle.

"Richard, I would like you to meet your daughter, Molly!" said Amelia proudly. The child was blooming, as she had been properly nursed by her mother and would not have to endure the early weaning that was the practise of the institution.

"Well good day to you Molly!" said Richard gently, holding his daughter close. The baby smiled, and a father's love for his child began to grow from that very moment.

They walked the distance to Hobart Town, Richard carrying Molly, and Amelia, a hessian sack with her few belongings. Richard had hired a carriage to take them to Bothwell the next morning.

"I have asked Mr and Mrs Ford whether we can stay at the tavern tonight, and set off in the morning," said Richard, as they strolled blissfully towards the town.

"Oh what a wonderful idea," said Amelia with delight. "I hope they are not angry with me for departing so abruptly."

"No, they are not," Richard answered, "Ann received your letter, and they were very angry at the authorities for their unjust treatment of you. I suppose I did miss muster, but you - to have to bear another year of imprisonment! The charges were false!" He paused, trying to compose himself, then muttered, "disorderly house indeed!" Amelia closed her mouth firmly and nodded in agreement. She thought it best not to mention her nocturnal activities prior to meeting him as it would all be put behind them now.

It turned out that Lucy was still working for the Fords, and it was a wonderful reunion, filled with hope and expectation for the future.

"Do you have to apply for marriage permission again, Mr Barton?" asked Ann.

"That is already done, Mrs Ford," answered Richard. "I have this very day submitted the necessary form, as I want to marry this beautiful woman as soon as possible!" He looked at Amelia fondly, and she smiled with relief.

During the evening a man sitting near them raised his glass and wished the couple well. Amelia felt sorry for him, as he looked in ill health and she approached him. "Thank you Sir, but are you well?" The man's unhealthy pallor and wracking cough indicated that he may well need a doctor.

"Thank you kindly, Ma'am, and no, I am not well, but a doctor cannot help me." A fit of coughing then ensued and Amelia waited anxiously, instinctively wanting to help him.

"But Sir, how is it that a doctor cannot help? Have you consulted one?"

"The cough, Ma'am, has resulted from many years working in a coal mine. It is a particular affliction from which miners suffer, I am told, and it shortens one's life rather."

"A coal mine, you say?" A memory stirred in Amelia's brain, and she went on. "Sir, could I be so bold as to ask your name?" she asked.

"Warren James, at your service, Ma'am," he replied politely, and bowed his head briefly.

"Mr James," said Amelia hesitantly, and she looked around to ensure no one of her party was nearby. "My name is Amelia. Would it be possible that you have been working at the Port Arthur Coal Mine?"

"Why yes, that is correct, I was there since thirty one but I have a Ticket of Leave now. Why do you ask?" he rasped.

"I knew of a man who was sent there, by the name of Skinner, John Skinner."

"Skinner!" he exclaimed in a loud voice, then conscious of the stares of other patrons, he lowered his voice. "I knew him. I knew that man," he said bitterly.

Amelia, afraid that their conversation would be interrupted, asked Mr James what had happened to him, pretending that he was simply an acquaintance. Mr James informed her in blunt terms that John Skinner had been a troublemaker of the worst kind, and that the man was now dead, and he had witnessed his death himself.

Amelia stood up, suddenly feeling faint. She closed her eyes, grabbing at the side of the table for support. John Skinner was dead! That evil man had departed this earth, and it was the last piece of news that she expected to hear on this night. She opened her eyes, saw Richard hurrying over to her with a look of concern on his face, and she turned to the man urgently, still holding on to the table. "Please do not mention our conversation to my fiancé, as here he comes!"

"Amelia! Are you quite well?" asked Richard, "I looked over and you looked white in the face, as if you were about to faint away. Come and sit with me, I fear the excitement is too much for you. Excuse us Sir." Nodding to Warren James he gently propelled Amelia away.

She said to the man in parting, "I thank you Sir, and from the bottom of my heart, I hope your health improves." As Amelia made her way toward her friends, she thought regretfully that Warren James looked as if he did not have long to live either.

Warren James bowed politely and watched the woman walk away. Somehow, he could not form an opinion on her reaction to Skinner's death - she did not seem at all sad at the news, but it had certainly shocked her nonetheless.

Early the next morning the couple took leave of their friends and climbed into the carriage, promising to come and stay whenever they happened to visit Hobart Town. A two day journey was ahead but Amelia did not mind, as the long hours in the coach gave her time to think. She thought a great deal about her son, Evan, waiting for her at the orphan school. Amelia remembered with a lurch of guilt that she had not told her husband about Evan or her previous marriage and other children in England. When she got her Ticket of Leave would be time enough to tell Richard, and they could go and fetch the boy then.

She reflected upon the years of suffering at the hands of John Skinner, and felt that justice had been served in a strange way. As they journeyed, she tried to put the memories of her first husband from her mind, and a strange sense of peace began to steal over her. Amelia knew with finality this time, that never again would he be able to hurt her, and she turned her thoughts to pleasanter things. She was on her way to Bothwell with Richard!

They stopped at the Royal Oak Inn at Green Ponds to change horses and sleep overnight and Amelia felt like a queen in the comfortable rooms. She had never stayed in such a place in all her life! Mrs Ransom, their hostess, was very helpful, and on the second day, after the horses laboured over the steep hills and down onto the dry plains of Bothwell in summer time, they arrived.

Richard had the use of a wooden hut in the town, on land belonging to Mr Patterson. He was to maintain and improve the building in return for its use. He settled Amelia and little Molly there, making sure they had an adequate supply of wood for a cooking fire, and all the water they needed. It was only one large room, with hard packed dirt floors and a large fireplace at one end. Richard himself insisted that he would stay temporarily at Hunterston until they married. Amelia hoped it would not be too long and set about making the place as comfortable as possible. The house was not grand, but Amelia did not mind, as long as she was with Richard, she was happy.

The permission to marry came in February, but as Richard was very busy building a new brick barn at 'Ratho', they could not arrange the wedding until June. The cold weather came, and Amelia was surprised at the snowy chill of Bothwell, but when Richard explained how elevated the place was, and very nearly in the highland country, Amelia understood why it was so much colder than Hobart Town.

St Luke's Church had been finished five years before, and was a centre of activity in the town, as several denominations shared the same building. She stood before it, staring in wonder at the chiselled sandstone walls and the clock tower majestically rising above the tall arched door. The lintel over the door was decorated at each end by a carved stone head, one male and one female, looking down from lofty positions over the congregation. The outer door of the building was open, and the inner door was studded with brass and had a fancy brass handle. Amelia was suddenly nervous at the prospect of walking into such a magnificent place of worship, but the door opened and someone gestured for her to enter.

A picture of the Mother Mary holding her baby Jesus and a dove, was depicted in a huge glass window, and the light shone through, intensifying the richness of the vivid colours. Amelia looked down and noticed that there were little doors giving access to each wooden pew, where some of Richard's friends and the Patterson family were standing for her entrance.

Mrs Patterson had offered to hold Molly during the ceremony. Amelia had met the kind woman and her husband in the months after arriving in Bothwell, and the older lady smiled at her and spoke to the little girl, who was pointing at her mother.

The aisle itself was made of great stone flags that Amelia stepped on as she made her way to the altar where he stood;

Richard, the man she would grow old with. Amelia radiated happiness as she regarded him. So strong, so gentle, and best of all, he loved her. It was an unfamiliar, but precious sensation.

Richard watched Amelia, his love, walk towards him. Her simple dress and jacket did not diminish her elegant poise, and his heart was filled with pride for this woman who had endured so much, but was willing to spend her life with him.

After the ceremony was over, they all walked down to the Castle Inn which was just down the main street, and celebrated with some glasses of ale and dancing. Amelia danced with her husband, looking up at him with shining eyes, while he held her safely in his strong arms and contemplated how splendid their lives would now be.

The happy couple, at last husband and wife, were delivered home by Paddy in Mr Patterson's farm dray, the family having driven back to Hunterston earlier in the evening in their carriage. Richard climbed down with care, holding little Molly, who had fallen asleep.

Paddy waved goodnight and they went inside, putting their daughter carefully in her sleeping place in the corner. The hut was now very homely, thanks to Amelia's efforts, and she lit some candles, the light throwing dancing shadows on the plank walls.

Richard put a match to the fire that had been left already set in the hearth, and he pulled his wife's hand so that she sat down with him on the soft sheepskin rugs that Mr Patterson had given them for a wedding present.

Amelia put her head on her husband's shoulder and watched the leaping flames. "My love, can you believe that we are finally married? Truly husband and wife at last, after waiting so long."

Richard's jaw clenched with emotion and he held her tightly, the shadows emphasizing the angles of his face. "If you had asked me that question some years ago, I would never have imagined being so happy at this moment. In fact, I would not have expected even to survive until now!"

Amelia raised her lips to his, and they kissed tenderly. She helped her man lift his shirt over his head, and he lay back with his head on her lap, muscles rippling in the firelight. Amelia ran her hands over her husband, feeling the warmth generated by the friction of their skin. His huge shoulders finally relaxed and she pushed him over so that he lay on his stomach in front of her.

Although Amelia had seen his scarred back before, the sight of it was always shocking, and she traced her fingers over the upraised criss cross patterns, imagining the pain that Richard must have suffered. Growing impatient, the big man grabbed his wife and pulled her down beside him and began to caress her, kissing her with increasing ardour. He gently eased her jacket from her shoulders and unlaced the front of her dress. The sight of her breasts, still swollen with milk, filled Richard with an urgent need, and he rose and pulled off his clothes, flinging them away to the far corners of the room. It was all he could do to pull Amelia's dressed off with care, but it was the best she had, and had looked so beautiful wearing it that it would be a shame to tear it.

They lay skin to skin, Richard's arm around her slender waist, as he stroked her body, and their passion mounted. He took her then, in a moment of triumph and joy, as the years of heartache and pain receded, leaving only the glorious present, where no worry or sadness existed.

Their immediate need sated, the couple basked in the warmth of the fire and spoke of their hopes and dreams for the future and their love for one another. They made love again before going to the cosy bed together, and lying in each other's arms, they finally slept.

Chapter 28.

Amelia hummed to herself as she walked to Wentworth House holding Molly, who was growing heavy, on her hip. It was the very grand residence of the presiding magistrate of the Bothwell district, Mr Charles Schaw, who had not only taken over duties from Capt Wentworth several years previously, but had also purchased his house.

Mr Schaw was a fair man, but meticulous, and took his duties very seriously indeed, never letting a misdemeanour go unpunished. Indeed, earlier that year, before the wedding, Richard had been charged and fined five shillings for failing to attend church. Of course Richard could not explain to the magistrate that despite his best intentions, he had been unable to stay away from his love *every* night until they were married.

Amelia smiled to herself as she remembered their long night and morning of lovemaking, which had made the requirement to go to church seem insignificant. But the smile faded when her thoughts turned to the hefty fine that poor Richard had to pay from his hard earned savings.

It was almost two months since Amelia and Richard had become husband and wife, and they were still adjusting to living together and getting to know one other. Amelia was on her way to submit the application for the reinstatement of her Ticket of Leave, and this was an important step for the couple, as it meant that Amelia could seek paid employment, take in washing, or whatever else she could to help earn something to add to their savings.

Richard had promised to build Amelia a brick house once they had saved enough to buy their own plot of land, as he knew that was what she wanted more dearly than anything. But as saving was so slow, the project remained in the distant future.

In the meantime, Richard built an extra room at the back of their hut, containing a laundry area for Amelia to work in, so that she would not have to have the tub out in the yard. Little Molly was a year old now, and trying to walk. Watching children while working was always difficult, and this would help Amelia keep the child safe while she was busy. She delivered her application to the Magistrate and went on her way, calling to buy some eggs and milk on her way back home.

Later in the month, Amelia received notification that her Ticket of Leave had once more been granted. Joyfully, she began her plan of doing extra work for a little coin; Richard continued with his work as a bricklayer about the town and little by little, their savings grew.

The following year, in July, it was Molly's second birthday, and Amelia had baked a cake for the little family to share. Richard arrived home in the dark, cold and tired from his day, and gratefully sat down to eat the hot mutton and vegetable stew that Amelia had prepared for their supper. It was later while they were eating a piece of cake and watching Molly enjoying hers that Amelia, feeling nostalgic, mentioned Evan for the first time.

"I remember when poor little Evan was two, he had never known a happy home like this," said Amelia, forgetting that Richard knew nothing of the boy. "He had known nothing but hardship and prison walls." She stopped suddenly, and reddened at her mistake.

"Who?" asked Richard at once, sitting up. "Of whom are you talking?"

Amelia thought quickly, she did not want to lie to her husband. Perhaps it was time he knew the truth, or some of it anyway. "Richard, Evan is..." she paused, and took a deep breath, "my son. I brought him with me on the ship from England." She watched her husband warily, not knowing how he would react to the news.

"Your son! You did not tell me of this!" exclaimed Richard.

"Yes Richard, it should not surprise you to know that I was once married, before I left Worcester, as I was thirty years old by then, and I brought my son with me."

"Married? But to whom? Was this...fellow called Hobbs then?" stuttered Richard, uncomprehendingly.

"No, my love," said Amelia gently, "Hobbs was my father's name. His name was Skinner, and he is dead now." She could not bear to think that Richard was angry with her. She deliberately did not mention her other poor children left behind, for the moment. She had not decided whether she could face telling him.

Richard stood up abruptly, scowling. Amelia was alarmed and she also stood, putting her hand on his arm in supplication. "My dear, do not be angry. I...I should have told you, I know, but it makes no difference to our love!"

"Of course it makes a difference!" Richard stated emphatically, his voice raised. "You have kept this from me.

231

What other secrets do you keep?" Molly started crying loudly, distressed at the angry voice of her father.

"Richard, I love you," said Amelia quietly, "I implore you, do not upset yourself!" But Richard, his face dark with fury, stomped out of the house, and Amelia could hear the sound of his boots receding down the lane. She considered running after her husband, but decided that it may be best to leave him to reflect on the news until he calmed down a little. Then she would broach the subject again.

Amelia tidied up and put Molly to bed. Oh dear, she thought, that did not go at all well. She had not seen Richard's anger surface until that night, but she was aware that he possessed a temper, as he had told her that in the past, his hasty reactions had occasionally got him into trouble. Richard did not return that night, and Amelia could not sleep, worrying about him.

Richard Barton stalked down the street, his hot resentment swirling and mixing with phrases of the conversation between himself and his wife. While the argument continued to repeat in his head, Richard walked without any destination in mind. Finding himself outside his familiar haunt, The Castle Inn, he went into the bar. A tot of rum would help him calm down, he thought.

Paddy was there, and now that he had a Ticket of Leave also, the two men often enjoyed a drink together at the local inn. Richard, usually a taciturn character, after a rum or two told his friend of what Amelia had said. "I cannot understand why

Amelia kept this from me!" said Richard sadly, his anger now evaporated.

"Maybe she t'ought ye'd be angry!" answered Paddy brightly. "Look, Richard. Is it loikely that a woman of t'irty would never have been married? Oi'm surprised she only had one choild, really."

Richard considered this. "Maybe you're right Paddy, I should not have raised my voice to her. But she is my wife, she should trust me."

"Well, ye did get angry, so maybe she was roight to worry about telling ye." Paddy said frankly. "She's had a rough toime of it, Richard. Trust doesn't come easily after somet'ing loike dat." He went on with his wise words. "Mebbe it isn't ideal, ye know- her being married before, but he's dead anyway. So what does it matter?"

"Perhaps you're right, Paddy."

"Where's the choild now?" asked Paddy curiously.

"I don't know, I didn't ask her," replied Richard, hesitating. "But I don't want to know, anyway." He suddenly looked anxious.

"You'll probably foind out soon enough," said Paddy yawning. "What is it?" noticing Richard's expression.

"I haven't told her something either, as it happens," said Barton, cautiously. "I was married once, too."

"What!" exclaimed the other man. "Back in England?"

"Yes. I was married in Lancashire when I moved there from Jersey. We had... a child, too, a little girl called Emma." As he spoke his daughter's name, Richard struggled to prevent his voice breaking. He had pushed the memories of his other wife

233

and child to the back of his mind, as he was afraid of thinking about them, lest he should break down. He would never see them again, and it was as if they had died, along with his son.

His wife had come to him with child, and Richard had taken the boy as his own. The birth of his daughter had completed their happiness, until that dreadful night. The illness had not seemed too serious, and so Richard had foolishly stayed overnight in the next village, too drunk after a night of revelry with some acquaintances to return home. In his absence, the fever had taken a rapid turn for the worse, and his wife, stranded with the two children, had no way of calling for help.

She had blamed Richard for the death of her son, and their marriage was mortally wounded. Richard had never before mentioned his family in conversation in the thirteen years he had been in Van Diemen's Land, but carried the burden of his guilt in secret. Even now, he could not speak of the boy.

Paddy was regarding his friend with his mouth open. "Were ye planning on telling Amelia then?" he asked, "Oi mean, you have just walked out on her because she told you of her past marriage, and ye've done exactly the same t'ing?"

Richard looked slightly embarrassed. "Well, it's different for me," he tried to explain, but he could not tell Paddy of his shame.

"Different moi eye!" said Paddy, but he did not berate his friend further and the pair sat in silence, thinking about their lives and drinking rum. Both of the men proceeded to get thoroughly drunk, Richard not wanting to go back and face his wife, and Paddy not having one to go home to at all.

At closing, the publican tried to get the men to go home, but they would not. They could barely stand, and the owner of 'The Castle' was hesitant in pushing the issue on his own. In frustration, he was forced to call on the police constable, who made the men go to the cells overnight. Richard was charged by the magistrate the following day for drunkenness and duly fined yet another five shillings.

Amelia was not happy about the fine, as it was so difficult to save money, and to lose another five shillings in one like that was devastating. She was so happy to have her husband back the next day though, that she decided to say nothing about it. Richard did not mention the incident again, and Amelia hoped that she was forgiven.

More than a year passed, and Amelia thought constantly of her son. Now that Richard knew about Evan, surely she could fetch him. Richard had not asked her where Evan was, and Amelia simply did not know how to broach the subject with him without risking his ire. Finally in November of 1839, Amelia took advantage of Richard's benign mood with the onset of the warmer weather and talked to him one evening. Little Molly was in bed, and Richard and Amelia enjoyed a cup of tea alone in their cosy little hut.

"Richard, my dear, I want to talk to you about something," said Amelia hesitantly, clutching her cup nervously.

"Oh?" said Richard suspiciously, narrowing his eyes.

"Well, it's about, my son...Evan."

"Amelia, I told you, I don't want to talk about it," he said stubbornly.

"Please, Richard."

"What is it woman?" he said somewhat impatiently.

"Evan was...taken from me and put into the orphan school at New Town."

"You mean, he is still alive then?" Richard asked.

"Yes, I believe so," replied Amelia, and she spoke quickly. "I have long wanted to get poor Evan and bring him home to me... he's been in that place for so long, he would be ten years old now." She looked at her husband hopefully, not daring to move.

"No, Amelia." Richard's voice was ominously final.

"But Richard, he would be a son to you, and a brother to Molly. He has been there since he was four years old...."

"I said no!" Richard stood up, and his face had darkened.

"But Richard!"

"That child is not, and will never be my son! You are not to bring him here!" and he went to walk out the door.

Amelia could not understand why her husband, her kind, loving husband, was acting this way. She grabbed his arm beseechingly. "Richard stop!" But he continued out the door, practically dragging Amelia by his arm.

"Richard you cannot keep doing this!" Amelia shouted, and in frustration, she slapped him, trying to get him to stop and listen. Her husband wrenched her hand from his arm and flung her away from him, and shouted at the top of his voice.

"I...will never... have... some other man's... brat... in my house!"

Amelia responded hysterically, screaming at the top of her lungs and beating ineffectually at the strong man. He cursed and shouted and shook his wife by the arms then threw her down onto the road. By now, the neighbours had come outdoors and were trying to placate the pair. One of the sons ran for the constable, as it looked likely that the woman would be hurt. The lawman galloped up the street on his horse, as the melee continued and Richard gave his wife a sharp slap on the cheek, trying to bring her to her senses.

With the help of the neighbour, the constable pulled the two apart, and the man slumped against a post, breathing heavily. Richard was taken to the lockup to cool down, and the neighbour's wife took Amelia, who was sobbing into her apron, inside and made her a cup of tea.

Richard's charge of disorderly conduct against his wife only came with an admonishment by the magistrate rather than a fine, but was duly recorded, and then he was sent back home. He arrived to find Amelia sitting with three year old Molly in the yard, watching her play with some sticks, and he approached her nervously.

"Amelia?"

"Oh Richard!" she said, standing up quickly.

"I am so sorry, my love, I don't know what came over me." Richard opened his arms and Amelia ran to him in relief.

"I'm sorry too, Richard, I just couldn't bear...the thought..." she stopped, tears threatening.

"Of what, my love?" Richard said gently, and he lifted her chin to look at her dear face. "Don't be frightened, I have had time to think, and... I know you have been afraid to talk to me about it. I do not want you to feel that way anymore, my dear one; we have had too many years of fear and regret."

Amelia looked at him with a silent plea in her eyes, and Richard's heart lurched. "Come, let us go inside and talk about it now." He picked up their daughter, took her hand and they went in.

"I could not bear the thought that I might never see Evan again," Amelia told her husband. "You see..." She let it all spill out, about her husband John Skinner, of her father's death, of her tormented life in England and of her five beautiful children. She told of the dreadful day she was informed that her children would stay behind, and of her fears for their survival.

She spoke softly, her head on Richard's shoulder, and for the first time for many years, felt her soul unburdened of much grief. Amelia told Richard that she had heard of her husband's death, but did not dare disclose the events of that night when Jane was conceived. Jane, Amelia decided, would remain a secret, known only unto her, as the knowledge would surely be too much for her husband to bear.

Richard felt a familiar shame surge up to fill him, as he understood the extent of his wife's pain and suffering, and he held her fiercely, allowing her to tell him all. He realised why Amelia was so desperate to fetch her son from Hobart, as she had lost so much, but he was terrified that his wife would find out what an unworthy husband he was. The presence of her son would only remind him constantly of his past failure to protect his adopted son, and if she ever found out his secret, Amelia would leave him.

Amelia finally finished her story, and they sat silent, warm in each other's love. She lifted her head and regarded her husband solemnly, her face tear stained. "So, husband, will you allow me to bring my son home?"

"No," said Richard, his hand stroking her scarred face. "I understand you have suffered very much, but I cannot have that man's child here in my home."

Amelia and Richard were happy together but for this one unresolved point between them. Amelia knew that there was something behind Richard's stubbornness, something unsaid, but she knew not what it could be. They loved each other, and worked hard to save money and provide a good life for little Molly, and it was in the new year of 1840 that Amelia became aware that she was again, with child. Richard was thrilled, as he loved Molly, and looked forward to providing a brother or sister for her.

Paddy had got to know Richard's wife well over the last few years, and had grown fond of her. Sometimes he called by their cottage with produce from the farm he worked at, and Amelia was grateful for his friendship.

One day late in January, the kind Irishman stopped the farm dray outside the house and gave Amelia a bag of potatoes, and she asked him to sit out of the heat, and take a cool glass of water. Paddy was in fine spirits and talked of this and that, making Amelia laugh. Suddenly he stopped and leaned forward.

"Amelia, I know about your son. I was wit' Richard when he came to de pub dat night when ye first told him. I just wondered, when are ye going to bring him here? Oi'm surprised ye haven't done it yet."

"Oh Paddy, I am trying to understand, truly I am, but Richard will not have him. I think he cannot stand the thought of me having been another man's wife, and Evan would be a daily reminder of that. I am just hoping that time will bring a change in his opinion."

"Ye mean, Richard is refusing to have de boy, even dough he was married before too and had a choild himself? Dat does not make sense to me, Amelia; surely he must know what it would mean to ye." Paddy fell silent.

"What do you mean, Paddy?" Amelia said quickly. "What do you mean he was married before too?" She felt the blood rising to her cheeks and raised her hand to her face.

"Ye mean, he never told ye?" Amelia shook her head in alarm.

Paddy asked her again, he couldn't believe what he was hearing. "He never told ye he was married in England and had a choild too? A girl oi believe."

Amelia sat back, her face frozen except for the red flush that was working its way from her neck and up her face. "No, Paddy, he didn't."

"Amelia, I t'ought he told ye!" and the Irishman blanched. Oh no! he thought, what have I done?

She said quietly. "If you will excuse me Paddy, I have some work to do now," and stood up.

Paddy got to his feet too, very worried about the consequences that his revelation would bring. He liked the couple and did not want to cause trouble, but it was too late for that now, he thought in dismay. "Oi'm off to the pub, den. Good day, Amelia," and he left abruptly.

240

Amelia confronted her husband with her knowledge of the truth when he came home. She told him of her disgust when Paddy had told her that he, too, had a history, and remembered how he blamed her so severely for hers! Her indignation was such that she could scarcely believe it even then. Amelia would not allow Richard to touch her when he pleaded with her to listen, and she turned her back, displaying a cold aversion to his entreaty.

Richard eventually left the cottage and went to The Castle Inn and downed three tots of rum in quick succession. On seeing Paddy there, he then flew into a rage and the two men got into such a violent fight that Richard in his frenzy of anger also struck the two police constables who came to break up the ruckus.

When the constables finally overcame his terrible fury, his shirt had been torn off, and Richard's powerful torso was exposed, rippling with muscle and dripping with sweat. Paddy, who was leaning against the bar, his eyebrow dripping blood, caught sight of Richard's mutilated back.

"Mary, Modder of God!" he whispered.

Richard was once again thrown in the lockup. It took several days for the magistrate to hear his case. Unfortunately the string of small charges on Richard's record stood against him, and he was dismayed to find that for fighting, drunkenness and resisting a constable in the course of his duties, he was sentenced to three months hard labour on a road gang at Green Ponds. Richard and Amelia were to be separated once again.

Chapter 29.

Life was a challenge for Amelia while Richard was away. Pregnant, and with an active little girl to tend, she struggled to earn enough coin just to buy food. Her laundry work did bring in a little, so they endured in the hope that Richard would be back soon.

Paddy was her saviour. One day, he arrived with a wooden box, and inside were two fat brown chickens. He helped her make a pen to keep them in, and turned the box into a nest for them to lay their eggs. At least they would have two eggs most days, which was a huge help when to buy meat was impossible.

Her friend also continued his habit of dropping in with a bucket of vegetables or milk every week or so, and occasionally, he was able to procure a leg of mutton. He felt somewhat responsible for the situation in that the couple now found themselves, and wanted to help however he could.

"Amelia, I do hope dat ye can forgive me," implored Paddy. "When oi spoke to Richard on dat first noight and he told me of his woife, oi felt sure he would have gone home and told ye."

"It's all right, Paddy," consoled Amelia. "You were not to know, and it is better that our past lives are now out in the open, even if it takes us a while to become accustomed to the idea." She hung her head. "I was so cold towards Richard the night you told me, before he left to go to the inn. I was not so much shocked or angry that he had been married or had a child, but I could scarce believe that he had reacted so when I told him that I had. He seems to believe that it is acceptable for him, but not for me!"

"It's only because he's an Englishman Amelia, an Oirishman would never have t'ought loike dat! He's a fool, Amelia, to risk losin' ye, and oi told him so." He grinned. "Oi also told him, while he was doing his best to knock me down, dat he should have told ye about his woife. Oi hope he remembers dat."

"I hope he forgives me too," said Amelia sadly. There was nothing that she wanted more, than to have her husband back home, so she could tell him that she loved him still.

Richard was having a difficult time on the road gang. Having had his relative freedom on his ticket for so long, he resented his treatment at the hands of the soldiers, and could not bow easily to their authority. He contemplated the events leading to his arrest constantly and berated himself for leaving his pregnant wife in such a position. How could he abandon his wife again? Was he destined to be a poor husband and father forever?

The big man was filled with self-loathing and took it out on his shovel, hoping that by punishing himself he would be worthy of forgiveness. In his guilt, he convinced himself that his wife would leave Bothwell and take their daughter away from him.

One day, while feeling irrational with anger and exhaustion, Richard was allowed to walk a short way to the creek to have a drink of water and relieve himself. He looked back, and seeing no soldier within sight, began to run. He must get back to Amelia. Amelia, my love, I'm coming!

The soldiers recaptured Richard within the hour. They had discovered him in such a state of desperation and extreme anxiety that one of them had to knock him unconscious with his rifle to subdue him. He was held in the lockup at Green Ponds for two nights and could be heard calling out for his wife. Richard's sentence working on the road gang was extended for a further three months.

Amelia, on hearing this news, broke down in tears. Her child was due to be born in August, and Richard must not do wrong at all if he were to be home by then. Amelia thought of the pain in her back and legs as she washed at the tub, and how she must now continue to endure it until the month before the birth. This was now Amelia's eighth pregnancy, and her body was tired.

She wrote an impassioned letter to her hot tempered husband, pleading with him to work well until the end of his sentence so that he could come back to her. She assured him that her love for him remained, and that he had her forgiveness for the past.

Mr Schaw welcomed Amelia into his office, and she sat down with her daughter on her knee before him.

"Mr Schaw, thank you for seeing me, Sir."

"Pray, what can I do for you, Mrs Barton?" he enquired politely.

"My husband, Richard Barton, as you know, is in Green Ponds, working on a road gang," Amelia began, and Mr Schaw raised his eyebrows.

"Yes, of course."

"I know that he has been some...trouble, and I have written him a letter that I hope you may have delivered to him there. It may help."

"Why would I, Mrs Barton, and I am sorry to say this to you, assist this man who has been a constant source of irritation to myself, the law, and other citizens?" Mr Schaw did look a little sympathetic, however, so she continued.

"Sir, my husband and I hold each other in very high regard, but it has been difficult, adapting to our new life here. We had some... harsh words to each other, and I think he is afraid that I will leave him."

"Well?" Mr Schaw asked a little impatiently, shifting in his chair. "What is this letter you mentioned?"

"Mr Schaw, I have written to Mr Barton, assuring him that I wait for him, and entreating him to work well and give no more trouble so that he may be home in time for the birth of our child in August," Amelia explained. "I hope this will also help your officers in their duties, as he will be more... cooperative," she concluded, looking at him hopefully.

The magistrate considered for a moment, then held out his hand. "Very well, Mrs Barton, give me the letter. I am visiting Green Ponds the day after tomorrow and I shall ensure that he gets it. You see, I am not without compassion," he said, taking the folded paper and rising elegantly to his feet. "Good Day, Mrs Barton."

"Thank you, Sir, and good day to you," said Amelia smiling with relief. Holding Molly by the hand, she left Wentworth House with a lighter step.

July came and with it, the joyous occasion of their reunion. Richard was not sure of his reception, but he made his way to the house and cautiously called out. "Amelia?"

A scuffle from the laundry room was accompanied by a squeal of delight, and Amelia opened the door into the yard, and extended her arms to receive her beloved husband.

"Amelia, oh Amelia, I am so sorry my love, so sorry for everything! Do you forgive me, truly?" said Richard in wonder, his arms around her and his chin resting on her hair.

"Of course it is true. I will always love you Richard," said Amelia, her voice breaking and the tears starting to flow. "Didn't you get my letter?"

"Yes I did, Mr Schaw delivered it to me personally. He asked me if I could read, and when I said I could not, he read it out loud. I was determined from that day to return to you, my dear wife, as it must have been so difficult for you." He held Amelia away from him and regarded her fully pregnant figure. "You must rest, my love, I will care for you now."

Richard took his wife's arm and led her into the house to lie down. The repentant husband finished the tub of washing with his own hands, and vowed that from this day, he would be a better man. He also resolved to make his peace with Paddy, and had the opportunity to do so several days later.

Lucy was born a month later, and the couple regarded each other with great affection over the head of the sleeping babe. "Here is your daughter, Richard," Amelia said softly, and she placed the child in his hands. He was a man of immense strength, but held the delicate girl gently, and showed her to her sister.

"There Molly, you have a little sister, and you can help your mother take care of her," he said. Molly nodded solemnly, and stroked Lucy's head.

"Having a child is such a gift of love," ventured Amelia, cautiously, taking advantage of Richard's gentle mood. "Perhaps you might consider, now that you have had time to think, that I could bring Evan home soon? You must know the love that a mother feels for her children, and that it is agony to be separated from them." She dared not hope to dream, but Richard nodded, regarding his two daughters fondly.

"That feeling is not reserved only for mothers." Richard spoke with a catch in his voice, and rose abruptly. "I will think about it," he said curtly, and leaving Amelia to rest, he went to make her a cup of tea. Amelia's eyes sparkled and the colour mounted in her cheeks.

"Did you hear that, my girls?" she murmured quietly. "Soon you may also have a big brother!"

It wasn't until January of 1842 that Richard reluctantly agreed to have Amelia's son live with them and they travelled to Hobart to collect Evan. It was the year of his thirteenth birthday, and Amelia was afraid that he might not remember her. Richard sat with the two girls in their hired cart holding the horse, while Amelia went into the orphan school to inquire after her son. Her heart was beating so hard, that she was amazed that it did not burst from her chest, but she tried to maintain a look of calm.

The matron of the school completed some paperwork, noted that Evan was to be released into the care of his mother, and then got up from her position behind the desk.

"I will fetch the boy, Mrs Barton, if you would be so kind as to wait here?"

Amelia waited and waited, and to pass the time, she looked from the window, where several children were being given the air in pushchairs. "Come on Jane, let's go inside now," said the nurse to an older child, a girl of around eight or nine years. The girl, obviously unable to run like other children, lay back in her chair with a dull, uncomprehending look on her face, a face that strongly resembled a man that Amelia would rather forget! She knew in that instant, that the child was her daughter.

She turned abruptly from the window as Matron returned with a boy. It was Evan. He looked just the same, but had lost the baby roundness from his face. It was leaner, more grownup. Amelia and he looked at each other intently and she spoke gently.

"Hello, Evan, do you remember me?" and she waited hopefully.

A flash of recognition crossed Evan's face, and he approached Amelia with his cap in his hand. "Good afternoon Mother," he said formally, and allowed Amelia to hug him carefully. She did not want to overwhelm the poor boy all at once. After they had chatted for a few minutes, Evan recalled some events from before their parting. He remembered the

Female Factory, and also recalled Molly, although he had not seen the cheeky cockney girl since he was two and a half years of age.

"Evan, you have a sister called Molly now," Amelia said, "and a baby sister called Lucy. I am hoping that you would like to come and live with us now." She held her breath, trying not to cry for fear of making Evan feel awkward.

"Yes, Mother, I would like to come with you," he said politely, and Amelia laughed and hugged her son, but tighter this time.

"Hobbs, Hobbs..." the Matron was saying to herself. "Don't we have another child of that name here?"

"No Matron," said Amelia decisively, picking up Evan's hessian drawstring bag, and moving towards the door. "I have no other children here. Good day, Matron, and thank you." She nodded to her son and they left the room, descended the steps and headed for the conveyance that Amelia pointed out to Evan.

"Mother, am I really going to ride on a horse and cart?" the boy breathed, his eyes round.

"Oh yes, my son, you are," Amelia answered, tears threatening once more, "come and meet your new family!"

Chapter 30.

Despite Richard's misgivings, he quickly came to accept that Evan was a wonderful addition to the family. The lad was respectful and grateful to learn anything that he could. He could read and write, but had no experience with practical tasks, and under Richard's tutorage learned to chop wood for the fire, look after the chickens, and drive a horse and cart.

With Evan's help, Richard built another room onto their little wooden hut, as a sleeping place for the children, and as a result of sharing so much time together the two grew to like and respect each other. Amelia was also very happy that her husband and son were getting along so well.

The boy particularly loved to work with animals. When he was outdoors he was happiest, and Richard decided to take him to Ratho and introduce him to Mr Reid, the owner. Sheep shearing was about to take place, and Mr Reid offered Evan a job in the shed, sorting wool and sweeping the floor, and he was thrilled in his quiet, reserved way. Evan's work at Ratho was so reliable that he was soon learning wool classing and other duties and Mr Reid decided to take him on full time.

In this way, extra income was generated, and Amelia and Richard's savings finally grew after years of setbacks. Richard managed to control his temper, and family unity and teamwork produced a feeling of security that the two had never known before.

Bothwell, 1845

Evan had just arrived home from work, and Amelia was preparing the evening meal for the family. It was a fine, nutritious meal of mutton, potatoes and vegetables, and she had also made a pudding for dessert. She was hoping that there might be a reason to celebrate, and she was right. After six o'clock, Richard dropped his boots outside with a clatter, and threw open the door with a bang.

"It has come, Amelia, it has come!" and he waved a folded paper at them with a flourish. The girls stared in wonder, then five year old Lucy ran to her father and put her hands up to be cuddled. Richard picked her up, and with his wife and eldest daughter also clamouring for a hug, and Evan grinning with delight, the family laughed and talked all at once. Evan approached Richard quietly and held out his hand.

"Congratulations, Sir," he said with a pleased smile, and they shook hands. Richard put Lucy down and announced.

"Now that my Certificate of Pardon has come through, I am pleased to announce that I am officially a free man!" His voice broke slightly and he coughed, trying to regain control. "It has taken twenty years, but it has finally happened, and I am very glad to share this happy day with you all, my beloved family." He went on, clapping his hand on Evan's shoulder. "To continue our celebrations after this excellent dinner, as he is now a man with full time employment, I would like... my son to share a glass of ale with Paddy and me at The Castle Inn!"

"Yes Sir," said Evan, in wonder. "I would like that very much Sir."

Molly was now fourteen years of age, and was hoping to secure a position in Mrs Lord's drapery shop. It was 1850, and Mrs Lord had been in the district for two years. As the wife of a very wealthy businessman, she had been responsible for the running of his businesses for many years while her husband was away for periods of time in England. Mrs Lord was the talk of the district, and it was said that she came to Van Diemen's Land as a convict, and had attracted the attention of Mr Lord, whom she had subsequently married.

It seemed that Mr Lord no longer visited Bothwell, where he had run livestock since the settlement of the area, but his wife acquired a newly built house just out of town, 'The Priory', and had settled there for her retirement. It was a very grand building indeed, and Molly felt intimidated by the powerful lady. She had never spoken to her directly, and she hoped that her courage would not fail her when in the woman's presence.

As Molly approached the store, Mrs Lord's conveyance stopped out the front and a young man assisted the lady to alight from the high-set carriage.

"Wait for me, if you please, James," instructed Mrs Lord. "I must speak to my store manager and I have some other business that should take me about an hour."

"Very good, Mrs Lord," replied the young man obediently, and he turned to see to the two horses who were harnessed in front of the phaeton. Molly was early for her appointment, so she stopped next to the horses hoping to stroke them.

"Good morning, miss," said the man politely, and he tipped his hat. Molly blushed to be treated with such consideration, and she noticed how very pleasing to the eye he truly was.

"Good morning, Sir," she said shyly. "Am I permitted to stroke the horses, Sir?"

"Of course," he replied, smiling. "They are very fine animals are they not?"

"They are indeed," she murmured, patting their soft noses and admiring their gleaming coats. "Do you take care of the horses for Mrs Lord, Sir? They are so beautifully kept!"

"I do, my name is James Derrick, Miss, and I work as a groom and driver for Mrs Lord."

"Oh! Then they are a credit to you, Mr Derrick," and she turned reluctantly to go inside to see about her employment.

"Just a minute, Miss!" the driver said, and Molly turned back. "I have told you my name but you have not told me yours!"

Molly blushed again, and looked down in confusion. "Molly Barton, Sir," and she glanced up at him through her lashes. He was regarding her with admiration, and she bobbed a curtsey before hurrying indoors.

Mrs Lord was very kind, and asked after Molly's family. She said that she knew her father as he had worked for her the previous year, building a large barn to house pigs and sheep at the rear of 'The Priory'. As Mrs Lord knew Mr Barton to be a hard worker, and Molly was well presented and polite, the girl was offered the position. Molly was to help in the store, tidying shelves and assisting customers. If she wished, there may be an opportunity to learn dressmaking. Molly was excited and optimistic for her future, and could not wait to return home and tell her mother.

She accompanied Mrs Lord outside to her carriage and watched as the helpful Mr Derrick handed her up. He nodded at Molly and said, "Miss Barton," with a smile, before mounting the driver's seat and taking the reins. The horses started off and sprang into a lively trot, looking very smart as they went. Molly waited, watching the carriage for a moment, before hurrying home.

James Derrick stopped off at the shop whenever he was in town, and one day on his afternoon off, he walked Molly home after work. After that he became a regular visitor to the modest home of the Barton family.

James had been transported aboard *'Kinnear1'* eight years before as a boy of fourteen, and had been assigned directly to Mrs Lord. He was now 'free by servitude' and continued in his position as a paid employee.

He was a person who was interested in a wide range of subjects, and enjoyed sitting with Richard and Evan at the table after dinner to discuss all manner of things while the women cleared up. Amelia liked James very much, particularly the courtesy he showed to their eldest daughter, and it was obvious that the young couple were growing very close indeed.

Chapter 31.

One Sunday after church, as the family walked home from St Luke's together, Richard and Amelia were in deep discussion.

"Amelia, I think we may have enough money to build a better house. There is a plot of land available on Patrick Street that is a reasonable price, and now, with the two of them working, nodding at Evan and Molly, we have saved quite a good sum."

"Oh, Richard! Could it be true?" Amelia was stunned at the thought of having reached their goal. "Oh my dear, I thought this day would never come!"

"Let us go home and make some plans, Amelia. Then we can perhaps go and look at the land." They all hurried home, chattering excitedly about the house, and how many rooms it might have.

Molly saw James waving at her and waited to walk with him. Evan was quiet, as usual, but he did not participate in the discussion as he normally would. Amelia stepped aside from the others and spoke to him.

"Evan, you do not seem as optimistic as the rest of us," said Amelia, concerned. "Do you not think that building a new house is a good idea?"

"Oh yes, Mother, I do. I know it is something that you have long wished for, and I hope you will be very happy." They reached the house, and went inside. Amelia, as was their custom on Sundays, put on the kettle for a cup of tea with cake.

"What is wrong then, Son?"

"I have been awaiting a good time to tell you," Evan turned and spoke to his family. He smiled at Lucy, who sat next to him, her eyes regarding her brother with adoration. "Some time ago I applied for a position as the sheep manager of a large property south of Launceston, and Mr Reid supplied me with an excellent reference. Yesterday I received a letter offering me the full time employment."

Richard was the first to speak. "Well done, my boy, well done!" and he and Evan shook hands.

"I suppose this means you will be leaving us soon, Evan," said Amelia regretfully, hugging her son. "I am proud of you and wish you well of course, but I will miss having you with us!" and she suddenly turned away, busying herself with the tea, so that Evan would not see her tears.

Lucy said nothing but sat very close to her brother and listened, not quite sure what was going on. She was eleven years old that year, and Evan was her favourite person in the world.

Just then Molly and James came in, their faces shining with love. It was obvious that there was a growing regard between them. They were constantly laughing and touching each other's hands.

"You did not hear Evan's announcement," said Amelia to her daughter. "He has a position as manager on a big farm, and will soon be leaving us."

"Well," said Molly, "you are a man now, Evan, and I am sure that you wish to meet a young lady and have a family one day. It is a good time to settle in a more permanent situation.

Congratulations!" and she smiled at Evan brightly, though she would miss him very much also.

Evan was not one for speaking to a group, as his shy reserve usually prevented him, but compelled to speak, he stood up. "The last seven years have been the happiest of my life, living here in Bothwell. I have to thank you all, as if I had never lived here, I would not have found myself in this happy position. I wish to thank my mother, for never failing to love me, and never forgetting me, even when life was hard for her." He looked around the room and his eyes settled on his step-father.

"But most of all, I owe my success to Richard, who I have come to know as my father. He taught me everything I know and helped me to develop my love of animals and farming. So, with all my heart, Sir, thank you!" Evan put out his hand and shook Richard's, their hands clasping for a prolonged moment and then he sat down with a thump, his face flushed.

Amelia leaned against the table, her hands clasped together in pride for her son, and tearful that he would soon be gone. She glanced at her husband, who had not spoken, and was startled to see the tears running freely down his weathered face.

They waved Evan off a few days later, and the girls were in tears, sad to lose their brother. Lucy in particular, was inconsolable. Amelia hugged her daughters, understanding their pain but feeling proud of what her son had achieved. She was glad that she had been able to provide Evan with some years of stability, enabling him to find the path to his future life.

Richard had been particularly silent, wrestling with his feelings and the urge to clear his conscience. As they went back inside their hut, he looked at his wife.

"My dear, there are certain matters I need to share with you, things I should have told you long ago. It concerns my family in Lancashire."

Amelia took his hand and sat down. "I am so happy you are ready to tell me," and she waited patiently for her husband to speak, knowing that Evan's departure had been very difficult for him. They sat comfortably together, staring into the fire for hours that night. Richard finally acknowledged the wife and child that he would never see again, and their son, dead but for his own negligence. He was a tortured soul seeking solace, and found it in his loving wife.

Chapter 32.

One evening, a few days after Evan had made his departure, a knock on the door startled Amelia, and James and Molly came in, the young man waving a piece of paper urgently. "Gold! There's gold been found! Have you heard?" There was a moment's silence, then they all started clamouring for information. James held up his hands, and when they had all quietened, he explained.

"Mrs Lord gets all the newspapers from Victoria, and she lets me have them when she is finished with them," James went on breathlessly. "I was reading this copy of 'The Argus' and there is a story there that a German, Dr Herman Bruhn, has been rewarded for finding gold at Clunes." He handed the paper to Amelia, as Richard still struggled with reading.

She noted that the page was dated the first of April, 1851, and the report did indeed confirm a gold discovery, and mention a number of other locations in Victoria where it was rumoured that there may be rich deposits. She handed the page back to James. "James, what does this mean? Are you thinking of going there yourself?"

James took a deep breath and looked around. "There have been whispers of gold there for some months now, but now that a substantial find has been recorded, things have changed." He glanced at Molly, and she nodded reassuringly. "Mr Barton Sir, Molly and I have been talking and... we want to get married. We want to go to Victoria to find gold!" He looked at Richard expectantly.

Richard stared at James, and then his gaze travelled to his daughter's face, glowing with love and pride. He took a deep breath. "There is nothing more to be said, but congratulations James, to you and my daughter! I have known and respected you for some time, and I know you will take care of her."

Amelia interjected. "But you are only fifteen, Molly, are you not too young to be marrying yet?"

"Mother, James and I know what we are doing!" Molly insisted. "We want to marry and start our life's adventure together. He will take care of me, as father says. Please be happy for us Mother!"

"Of course I'm happy for you," said Amelia, gently. "It just would be a big change for us all, with Evan leaving too."

Amelia was also worried about her daughter moving away from them at such a young age, and into a strange place with no family to support her. She and Richard talked of it all afternoon and into the night. Finally, Richard came up with a solution, and he broached it with his wife.

"Amelia, there is but one course of action that will make you easy. We must go to the goldfields also. Perhaps we can make our fortune there at long last, and you can be there for Molly."

Amelia thought for a moment. "There is only one thing stopping us doing that, my dear."

"What is it?" and he regarded his wife quizzically. Richard could not think of any reason that they might not go.

"I am not yet free. I remain a Ticket of Leave convict and I am not allowed to go to the goldfields!" she exclaimed with frustration.

Richard spoke with urgency. "Then we will apply for your Certificate of Freedom at once. If we get it, we will follow the young ones to Victoria!" His eyes were shining with the thought of embarking on this adventure, and Amelia could not dissuade him.

"But Richard, what about the new house?" Amelia protested, all their plans now seemingly discarded.

"We will use some of the money to pay for our passage and settle there. If things go well, we shall find enough gold to build a brick house in Victoria!" Richard spoke with great anticipation. Amelia could think of no other argument, and her desire to protect her daughter was the deciding factor.

There was a blur of activity in the following weeks. James applied to marry Molly. Amelia granted official permission as her daughter was not yet sixteen, and the couple were married at St Luke's only three weeks later. The newlyweds departed for Victoria immediately, promising to send word of their location.

There was still an obstacle remaining in their path, and Amelia, having been to lodge her application with Mr Schaw, waited eagerly for the result. Amelia and Richard were to follow her daughter and son-in-law as soon as they were able, and Lucy of course would accompany them.

The week after the marriage ceremony it happened. Amelia had walked to the main street with her daughter to buy some fresh meat. She paused outside the butcher shop, placing the paper wrapped parcel into her basket, when a voice called to her.

"Mrs Barton, there is a letter for you!" It was Mrs Finch at the mail office. Amelia waved across the street, and they crossed to collect it. The envelope was large, with official stamps on the back, and Amelia dared not hope that it may be the certificate she had awaited for so long.

She stood in the street and ripped the envelope open, Lucy clamouring to see what it was about. Her mother stayed very still for a moment, until Lucy realised that she was crying, and she patted her mother on the shoulder.

"What is wrong, Mother?" she enquired, concerned.

"Oh my dear, there is nothing wrong. Nothing wrong at all!" and Amelia threw her arms around her daughter. "Let us walk by where your father is working on the way home!" she said excitedly. "We shall soon be seeing your sister again, Lucy!" And they set off gaily, swinging the basket between them.

As they approached Richard's work site and she could see her husband in the distance, she broke into a run. Amelia Barton had received her Certificate of Freedom. A full twenty years after she had first stepped onto Van Diemen's Land, Amelia was free. She ran feeling as light as a bird, the burden of her convict past lifting with every step and blowing away into the wind.

The icy stream of the Clyde River, born in the highland lakes, flows swiftly through the property of 'Ratho', and past the grandeur of 'The Priory' and 'Wentworth House' on its way south. The old homesteads stoically survive as the decades drift inexorably by into history, taking with them the memories of the original settlers and their convict workers who established the town.

St Luke's Church endures proudly. The uneven flagstones in the aisle are patterned with coloured light cast down from the stained glass windows, just as they were when they bore Amelia to the alter at her wedding.

Just down the street The Castle Inn is still, after so many years past, filled with the familiar sounds of friends talking and laughing over a pint. But outside its thick walls, the air resonates with an echo of the Big River People who resided there long before and the sounds of their last corroboree.

Chapter 33.   Victoria, 1851.

Amelia, Richard and Lucy boarded 'The Shamrock' at Port Dalrymple in June. They were bound for Port Phillip, and Molly and James had travelled on the same ship several weeks earlier, already having found lodgings in Melbourne for them all. Amelia had received a letter from her daughter, with the address and directions.

As the ship set sail and travelled up the Tamar River, Amelia and Richard held hands and bade goodbye to Van Diemen's Land, the land beyond the seas. They both felt that to leave now that they were both free would constitute a fresh start, and they could leave their respective years as convicts behind. They were both sad to leave Bothwell however, as they were part of the small community there, and Richard had lived and worked there for twenty years.

Mr Patterson had bid him a fond goodbye, wishing him all the best of luck for his life ahead, and Paddy threw his arms around both of them with tears in his eyes, proclaiming that they were the best friends he had ever had.

In Melbourne, the family reunited and moved into the rented house that Molly and James had arranged. The women set about making the place a temporary home, while the two men began buying the equipment they needed. James had met up with his friend Edward Young, who had already been working at gold diggings for several months, and he advised them on the items to acquire.

They had to purchase a horse and cart, gold cradles, tools, water barrels and buckets, and also two canvas tents for accommodation, which could be set up or dismantled with ease. Amelia was worried about the amount of their savings that was spent on all of this, but Richard and James assured her that it was an investment in their new business, which would pay off when they struck gold.

When gold was discovered at Andersons Creek near Melbourne in July, Richard and James went there with Edward to learn about the business and try out their method, while leaving the women at the house. They were only working there for two months, when the newspaper reported a rich source of gold struck at Mount Alexander, near Castlemaine. Richard and James hastened to get their possessions packed, and a stock of food to take.

Leaving their lodgings behind, the two men sitting up in front driving the horse, and the mother and two daughters riding in the cart with their belongings, the family set off for the goldfields. They were going to meet up with Edward along the way, and the three men planned to work together and share profits.

It was spring in Victoria, and the area east of Melbourne had received a good fall of rain over the winter. As they travelled further from Melbourne, the cart tracks became muddier, and the horse struggled over the soft earth. Many times the family got down and helped to push the cart through the wet ground.

The way became a succession of quagmires, and here and there they came across a cow or horse, which had fallen from exhaustion and been left behind, dead on the roadside. Mile after mile, their destination grew nearer, and the amount of rubbish on the roadsides mounted.

Amelia slowly became aware of a strange humming noise that steadily got louder until it filled the air. The road had become almost impassable when finally their horse and cart, accompanied by Edward on his own riding horse, mounted the crest of a hill to begin the final descent to the strike area near Castlemaine. The horse was allowed to come to a standstill to rest, and the family paused to gape in wonder at the extraordinary spectacle which confronted them.

The entire valley before them was crawling with men, like ants on a nest. There were no trees remaining, and the hillsides were covered in canvas tents. The creek beds were crowded with wooden gold cradles, and men hurried around doing all manner of activities, digging, loading buckets and cradles, and carrying things here and there. An incredible din filled the air, like a loud roaring sound, which Edward said was from the gold cradles, clacking back and forth.

Amelia and her daughters stared at each other in horror. "Twenty years!" she exclaimed to Richard.

"What do you mean dearest?" Richard raised his voice to be heard over the racket.

"I have survived twenty years of my life as a convict, and the very moment I am free, we come to live in...this?" she gestured with her hand despairingly.

Richard took her hand and pressed it to his lips reassuringly. "This is our salvation, my love. You will see."

With trepidation, they began their descent, and before long, they were in the thick of the throng. Edward took James to find the commissioners tent to purchase a licence, and find out where they could peg their claim. Richard waited with the women, he did not like to leave them unguarded in such a place, as there were filthy, rough looking characters everywhere, and it was obvious to him that keeping themselves and their possessions safe would be a very great challenge indeed.

The area was called Specimen Gully, Barker's Creek, and it was south of Mount Alexander. Once a site had been identified, and the men had pegged out the claim, they unloaded their equipment, erected the large tents on higher ground not too far from the creek and set to work almost immediately, leaving the women to organise their belongings and cook some food for the evening meal.

It was eleven year old Lucy's job to look after Edward's horse as well as their own, and she fed both of them some hay and grain that they brought with them. But from that day on and every day, she would have to walk the horses to grazing and water, as the supplies they had would not last.

It would be dangerous for her, and for all of them, going about their tasks, but there was no time to worry or complain, as there was much to be done. Amelia and Molly took turns either operating the gold cradle, or the household chores of acquiring and preparing the food, and washing clothes.

The method that the men employed to find gold was simple. They had a nine foot square claim, and they went about systematically digging up buckets of the coarse, quartz gravel

267

and loading it into a barrow, which was taken down to the creek where the cradle stood. The gravel was tipped into the cradle, along with a quantity of water, and the rocking action of the implement washed away the dirt and fine pieces, leaving any heavy gold deposits behind.

One of the women, grasping the handle, would rock the cradle back and forth until the load was done, and inspect it for any gold that may be found. The men did the heavy digging and shovelling of the gravel, and transported the loaded barrow down to the creek.

Edward had been friends with James since he had been in Bothwell with his father the year before, visiting relatives while on their way to Victoria. His few months of experience and willingness to help his new found friends had been invaluable in getting the men started on their venture quickly and with the most efficient method.

The three men got on well together, sharing the work, and in exchange he lodged with James and Molly in their tent, ate with the group, and they all shared the expenses. It was an arrangement that was to prove convenient to both parties as within a month or two, none of the family could imagine life without Edward and he seemed to fill the hole left by Evan's absence.

The gunshot signalling the end to the day's work sounded, and it made Amelia jump, as it did almost every day. The cradles fell silent, and Molly, who had been operating their cradle that day, together with the weary men, trooped back to the tents, bringing with them a barrow of unwashed gravel to store inside their living space.

They all gathered in Amelia and Richard's tent, where Lucy and her mother served up the standard daily fare of damper and mutton soup for their supper. Vegetables were very hard to come by, and generally they purchased some for Sunday only, and made do without for the rest of the week. James filled them in on the goldfields gossip that he had picked up during the day.

"I heard that O'Donnelly down the hill had a big find today!" he said excitedly. "It was said that he dug one bucket load of gravel that contained twenty pounds of small nuggets!"

"Twenty pounds!" exclaimed Richard, accepting a bowl of soup from his wife. "That would keep us in gold licences for years!"

"Father!" said Molly in exasperation. "Twenty pounds of gold would pay enough for us all to be rich! You would not stay here, surely!"

"Well, that is true, Molly, twenty pounds of gold would yield almost a thousand pounds. What would we do with that if we found it?" If Richard's calculations were correct, thought Amelia, divided between the three men, over three hundred pounds each would make them very wealthy indeed.

"I think I would leave this godforsaken place and live in peace and comfort," commented Amelia.

"But Amelia, if you put up with the discomfort a little longer, you could find another twenty pounds of gold!" exclaimed Richard. "You would not give up after the first find, would you my dear?" Amelia was sure that she could quite easily abandon this hard way of life, but it was clear that Richard had been taken with the gold fever that had swept through the men, and stories of these huge finds of gold only fuelled his desire.

There were mad drunken celebrations in the Irish camp that night, but after midnight, when all the exhausted miners had fallen asleep, there was surreptitious activity nearby. A shadowy figure moving cautiously crawled up next to the tent of the man named O'Donnelly. He was armed with a sharp blade and he wielded it skilfully. No person awoke to hear the deed done.

At daybreak, a chorus of loud yelling and cursing could be heard, rousing the men from their beds. They all pulled on trousers and rushed out to find out what the uproar was about. When Richard returned, he brought bad news. "It seems that O'Donnelly was not too careful who knew about his good fortune. All that remains of the canvas bag containing the twenty pounds of gold is a neat cut in the side of the man's tent. The gold has simply disappeared into thin air!"

The first time Amelia found gold in the cradle she let out a squeal of delight, although it was only a few tiny fragments. Richard admonished her for her careless lack of thought.

"My dear, you must not announce our finds to the world! We will become prey to every thief in the area, and the dear Lord knows that there are many of them. Hide the gold safely in a pouch, and tell us quietly when you can do so while attracting no attention."

Amelia felt embarrassed at her outburst, and kept her elation well in hand after that. The licence to prospect for gold was costly. Thirty shillings per month allowed them a claim, and although the first few months took up some of their savings, they did find some alluvial gold that allowed them to keep up the licence payments.

The stories continued to come thick and fast, men were finding huge quantities of gold in a day, and some were working quite close to them. The men were infected with the excitement, and doubled their efforts, coming in exhausted at the end of every day. This continued for several weeks, until Richard reported that the man in the next claim to theirs had hit a large quantity of gold at a depth of six feet.

The next day Amelia looked up and could see the men with their heads together on the claim, and while she continued the back breaking work at the cradle, kept glancing up at them to see when the next load would be delivered. It was James who brought the barrow, and he stopped next to Amelia.

"Amelia, keep a calm countenance, but I know that this barrow contains some good finds. I could see the gold as I dug, and the load seems heavy." Amelia stared at him, then quickly resumed the rocking, speaking quietly.

"What will we do if there is a lot?" I will need to hide the gold until tonight. We have to continue until the gunshot as if nothing has happened!" she said.

"I will shovel this load in very slowly," said James, "and if there are any nuggets, you can put them in the pouch and give it to me to take back up the hill. I will keep it safe, and you can continue washing the rest as usual for any small pieces."

Amelia felt her heartbeat in her chest, and they proceeded to load and wash a shovel load at a time, watching for the glint of gold. As the third shovel poured in, they both

271

saw it, and washing carefully, Amelia exposed a rough nugget of gold! She unobtrusively threw the pouch down next to it, then pushed the piece into it, being very careful to keep her movements slow and unhurried.

James picked it up before loading another shovel of gravel and some water. Another two, slightly smaller nuggets lay there, glistening wet with promise. Amelia took the heavy pieces and passed them to James, who put them into the pouch. Surely there would be more in the next load!

There were no more nuggets in the load, and once James had ascertained this, he left to go back to the claim with the barrow, and Amelia continued to wash the last of the gravel. There was only time to wash one more barrow load before the gunshot signalled the end of the days digging, and they all hurried to the tents without a word, impatient to be able to weigh the find.

"About fourteen ounces, wouldn't you say?" asked James, and he hefted the pouch and passed it to Edward, who in turn passed it to Richard.

"At three pounds two shillings per ounce, that will give us around...forty three pounds and eight shillings total. Around fifteen pounds each when we split it three ways!" Richard was exultant.

Amelia was amazed at how quickly her Richard could do figures in his head. For a man who could not read, it was interesting how quickly one learned to calculate when gold finds were involved! She took the three nuggets in her hands, and felt the heavy richness of them. Lucy and Molly wanted to hold them also, and they all savoured the moment. Fifteen pounds would not make them rich, but ensure that food would be available and gold licences and equipment could be procured for some months to come.

"Richard, we cannot keep the gold in here! Remember what happened to Mr O'Donnelly? You must take it to the commissioner's tent for safekeeping!" Amelia urged.

"You are right, as always, dear wife!" said Richard. "Edward, you come with me and we will deposit this under armed guard. James, you stay with the women and finish your supper." The two departed, Edward carrying a heavy mattock as a weapon. They reached the guarded tent and placed the gold in a tin box kept for the purpose. After weighing the gold and issuing a receipt, the Commissioner informed Richard that the next armed run to Melbourne was in three days' time, and they would receive payment when it returned.

"Let us just hope that the armed guards stay awake at night!" whispered Edward as they walked back to their tent. "I'm sure that some thieves would not hesitate to shoot them if they could."

The following night, the family awoke to the sound of gunshots and men's shouts, and could not sleep for the rest of the night. The story was quickly circulated the next morning that thieves had been spotted dragging bags of unwashed gravel away from claims during the night. When they had been shot at, they had escaped, abandoning the washdirt.

It was decided that the men would stand guard with a pistol over the claim in the hours of darkness, taking turns so that they were on watch till midnight, then midnight till dawn and have every third night off. It would be hard on them as they laboured so hard in daylight hours, but necessary.

Another thief was shot trying to steal gold from a tent the very next evening and panic set in amongst the miners and their families. Gunshots would ring out at intervals in the darkness, as the men on watch would fire at anything that moved. It became so dangerous that the patrolling police constables refused to move about the diggings at night for fear of being shot themselves. The gold was taken to Melbourne without incident, however, and the men were duly paid in full.

After months of back breaking labour, the full heat of summer was upon them, and the valley had a constant haze of dust that hung in the air, filling everything with grit, and invading the lungs. They sweltered during the day, and tried to defend themselves against clouds of mosquitoes at night. Clean water was impossible to find anywhere within walking distance, and when the three men decided to abandon the claim and move to Pennyweight Flats, where new gold finds had triggered a rush, the women were relieved. They pulled up their tents, loaded all onto the cart, and set off.

During the next six months, the family had some small finds and moved twice more to Reid's Creek and Woolshed Gully with limited success. Amelia and Lucy walked to the butcher's tent one day to try and buy some fresh mutton, and found the storekeeper packing his belongings.

The butcher relayed the most extraordinary tale that they hurried back to the men immediately. The story was about 'Peg Leg gold', large pockets of gold that were being discovered in Peg Leg Gully near Bendigo. It was said that men were pulling up single buckets laden with forty and fifty pounds of gold, and one claim alone had yielded two hundred and eight pounds of the precious metal. Within hours the six of them had struck camp and were bound for Bendigo.

It was a journey of about forty miles to the area north of Bendigo. It was May, and the weather was still good and the ground firm, making the going easy. The horse could not pull the cart the whole distance up and down hill with such a load in one day, however, so it was decided to stop halfway and camp overnight to allow the poor beast to rest. Edward's horse had an easier time of it; just carrying one rider, but Edward often rode on ahead to find the best route to take, and then back, and so travelled more miles.

A likely spot was found to camp with a creek nearby and a stand of bush that provided some shelter from the wind. The night time chill reminded them that winter was on the way soon, and the fire provided some welcome warmth while they ate a meagre meal of tea and damper. Edward felt uneasy, and hearing the horses whinny, got up from the fire to check on them.

Suddenly, the sound of pounding hooves was heard, and a horse thundered into their camp and skidded to a stop, the dust swirling about it. Before any of them could move, a man vaulted from his mount, and approached, pistol in his hand. He was filthy dirty, as many who worked on the diggings were, but there was an aura of desperation about him. His clothes were rags and he looked hungrily at the damper.

"Your bag of gold, if you please!" the bushranger demanded. "Quickly now, and you'll not be harmed."

"Begging your pardon, Sir, but we have no gold," said Richard politely, trying to delay the man. "We are on our way to the diggings near Bendigo, and we hoped to find some there." He did have a money bag containing a few pounds, but that was precious little to set them to rights at the new camp, and he was not about to give it up easily. He looked at the three women and James, hoping they would follow his lead.

The bushranger raised the pistol threateningly. "You speak as if I cared where you are going. Hand over your money bag now or I'll blow a hole in you and then take it anyway!"

Richard did not know how he could delay things further without putting the women in danger. Where the devil was Edward?

Amelia spoke quickly. "We would happily share our meal with you, if you wish," and she held out a shaking hand offering a loaf of damper. The hungry man reached for the food, and for a few seconds his attention wavered.

In an instant Edward was at the man's side, pistol raised to his temple. "Stand down man! Leave these people alone. They have nothing for you!" For a moment nobody moved. Suddenly the bushranger grabbed Edward's gun, the two men struggled hand to hand, and they fell heavily to the ground together. A pistol shot tore through the night silence and the ragged man gained his feet, ran to his horse and leapt on, galloping away into the darkness.

Richard jumped up and ran swiftly to Edward, who was lying very still on his back in the dirt. "My dear Edward, are you hurt?"

"No Richard, thank you Sir, I am well," their saviour answered, and he stood up slowly. "His pistol shot went into the air, thank the Lord," he said nonchalantly, brushing down his coat.

"Edward!" cried Amelia, hastening to him right behind her husband. "You saved us from that dreadful man! But why did you not shoot him?"

"No Amelia, I could not do that," he replied, and for a moment she thought his compassion for the man had prevented him from doing so, but he continued. "My pistol was not loaded! I had time to pull it from my belt, but that was all!"

They all stared at each other and then the tension was broken by James, who was doubled over with laughter. Richard turned and stared at him, not amused. "Well, I would have thought that an unloaded pistol was not a very effective weapon, but it saved us, regardless. It's not that funny, James, if you please. Edward might have been killed. He saved us all, and our money!"

"It is not Edward that I laugh at..." James chortled. "When the thief ran off, did you not notice? He held on to that loaf of damper as if it were gold itself! He even kept it while they fought, and still had it in his hand as he galloped away!"

They all laughed heartily, even the women, who had been badly frightened. Edward vowed to load his pistol and stand guard that night in case the brigand returned. James thought that with his belly full of damper, the poor fellow would be more likely to sleep, but good naturedly offered to take his turn. Lucy told Edward that he was a hero, and the brave man blushed.

The next morning, after having travelled a good distance, Edward riding by their side with loaded pistol in his belt, the group met a young gentleman by the name of Gordon Hawkins. He had been at Eaglehawk Gully, north of Bendigo. Those at the strike site considered that the mother lode had been found, and some diggers were shovelling gold from between each other's feet. He told them to go to a place called Red Hills, and they would be sure to make their fortune.

Mr Hawkins was on his way to Melbourne, and by the bulging bags on his saddle, he had gold to deliver. The group did not ask about it, but warned the gentleman about the bushranger they had encountered, and begged him to be on his guard. Richard suggested that he wait and travel through the area alongside others, and have safety in numbers. Mr Hawkins was anxious to travel quickly, however, and thanked them for their concern before riding swiftly southward.

The number of people making for Eaglehawk Gully mounted as the day went on, and there was a veritable crowd with them by the time they arrived that afternoon. Amelia was used to the frenzy of the goldfields by this time, but still drew her breath at the sheer numbers of people amassing in the area. Red Hills had twenty thousand people descend upon it overnight with the first reports of rich gold, and five or six thousand people were arriving every week.

Once the claim was staked and the tents were up, the three men went to the grog shop for ale while the women prepared their repast. It was dusk and the gunshot to cease the day's activities had already sounded, so nothing more could be done that day. Work would begin in the morn and they all wondered if this would be where their fortune was made.

One evening, a few days later, Molly was helping prepare some dough, and she spoke quietly to her mother. The men were walking over the diggings, to assess the surrounding area, and Lucy was tidying the bedding and belongings at the other end of the tent.

"Mother, James and I are very happy together."

"Yes," said Amelia, "he is a fine young man, and he loves you."

"How long do you think we will be travelling around like this, living in tents?" There was a longing in her voice that Amelia sympathized with.

"My love, I do not know. Until the men have satisfied their gold fever, until we have made enough money to settle somewhere permanent, until..." she stopped and sighed. "Why do you ask dear?"

Molly looked down, her hands covered in flour, resting on the table. "Because I am going to have a child, Mother," she said, but tears started to fall. The older woman held her head upon her shoulder, stroking her long hair.

"Why so sad, Molly, do you not want a child? I know James would."

"Oh yes, Mother, but here? In this filth and tumult? I do not want my baby to hear blasphemy and cursing every day and think that gunshots, stabbings and thievery are normal life!" she spoke in an impassioned voice. "I want to feel safe, and have a stable home, where it is easier to care for the little one. I don't want anything fancy, just a home!"

Amelia understood only too well the feelings that her daughter suffered, all she herself had ever wanted was a home of her own, with a little vegetable garden and some chickens. The closest she had come to this was the planned house at Bothwell and that had been cancelled to travel to Victoria.

Although life together with Richard had been difficult at first, the family had been happy at Bothwell, and not for the first time Amelia wondered if they had made a mistake embarking on this mad and dangerous journey. They would have had that home by now if they had stayed, and Richard would have had a constant source of work.

"Mother," Molly spoke again, interrupting her thoughts. "Don't mention this to James just now. I'm sure it is early days yet."

"Of course, my dear, if that is what you want." And they continued to make their rough dough in silence. Amelia promised Molly she would try and acquire some meat and vegetables as soon as she could, as she and the baby would need proper nourishment.

She went in search of the butcher's tent the very next morning and the smell led her to the right location. There were carcasses hanging, piles of offal and skins to the side, and bones covered in scraps of meat. The rotten stench was overpowering, and Amelia could not hide her disgust when she approached. What would it be like when summer came? She purchased a leg of mutton, and from the grocer, potatoes and some cabbage.

Looking around while making her way back to their tents, Amelia took in the surroundings. Molly was right; it was obvious that this was not the place to have a child. Besides the rotten carcasses at the butchers, there were dead horses that had fallen from exhaustion, garbage everywhere and latrine pits for human waste. The din was incredible, and the stink was unbelievable. Whores were not out at this time of the day, but Amelia knew that they plied their trade around the grog shops at night, and there were drunkards everywhere one looked, lying about or vomiting onto the ground.

The butcher had wrapped the meat in some sheets of newspaper; it was several pages of the 'Bendigo Advertiser' of the day. As she went to store the joint in their little meat safe, an article on the page caught her eye. A familiar name stood out in the printing, the name of Gordon Hawkins. She read the article quickly, then putting down the meat, Amelia ran to where the men were working, shovelling dirt into buckets.

"Richard, Richard, I read something in the paper. I think it is bad news, at least bad news for that nice Mr Hawkins we met on the road!"

"What is it Amelia?" Richard stopped what he was doing, and wearily leant on his shovel. James and Edward came over to hear.

"Do you remember the gentleman we met on the way here who gave us helpful information? The one we met the night after we had been held up by that dreadful bushranger?" She paused, panting for breath.

"Yes, of course, what of him?" Richard asked.

"I bought some meat from the butcher, and it was wrapped in some sheets of today's paper. It seems that Mr Hawkins never turned up in Melbourne where he was expected, and has not been seen since! The article says that it is feared he may have met with foul play at the hands of bushrangers!"

Richard rubbed his dirty hands across his forehead, wiping the sweat from his brow and leaving a brown smear. "Oh no! We did warn him to be careful! Do you think Mr Hawkins became a victim of that desperate fellow there at the creek?" He turned to the other men.

James agreed that he may well have been held up at the same place as they had. "The poor devil is probably dead and thrown in a mine shaft somewhere, and his horse and those large bags of gold in the hands of that rogue, who I think was capable of anything! And you, my friend," he turned to face Edward, "probably saved us from the same fate."

Amelia shuddered when she now understood how close they had come to being murdered, and putting her hand on Edward's arm in silent thanks, she walked to the creek to tell Molly, shaking her head with sorrow. She relayed all that had been said.

"When will all of this madness end?" she asked of her daughter.

Molly answered with a matter-of-fact tone. "Why Mother, when all of the blessed gold is taken from Victoria!"

Richard spent some time building stone fireplaces at the ends of both tents, to keep them warm at night, and the men grew thick beards as winter approached, to ward off frostbite. Inland areas in Victoria were exceedingly cold in winter, and the worst of the bitter weather lay ahead before the warmer weather relieved them.

James and Edward had made a promising start to their prospecting, finding small quantities of gold that would help them all last on the goldfields a little longer. Their reserves had dwindled and it was getting harder and harder to find the thirty shillings each and every month to pay the gold licence, as a pound and a half was a lot of money. As the months went by, it became less and less about making a fortune and more about surviving the next month, and then the next.

It was Amelia's turn to work on the cradle one morning at sunrise, but she did not want to go outside. The temperature had been well below freezing overnight, and now, in the first light of day, was no better. Even inside the tents with the fire going, it was appallingly cold, and the women wore blankets wrapped around them over all the clothes they possessed, but could not achieve any semblance of warmth.

Sighing with misery and resentment, Amelia threw off the blanket and stepped out from the canvas flap. Icicles hung from everything and each step caused a crackling of the frozen ground. Winding her woollen shawl around her lower face and over her mouth to lessen the impact of the frost on her exposed skin, she walked stiffly to the creek. She managed to grasp the handle and begin work by wrapping her hand in the end of the shawl. After several hours of toil, the body would at least be warm and looser, but the face and hands remained numb.

Out on the diggings, the police constables had thrown a man to the ground and were standing over him with their weapons. "Where is your licence?" demanded one.

"Sir, I only just arrived, I have been meaning to go to the Commissioner and..."

"Lying dog!" shouted the other constable. "We have been watching you diggin' for gold all morning, and you've made no attempt to get a licence!"

"Please, I haven't got any money left, I will give you some as soon as I find some gold!" pleaded the fallen miner.

"What do you think, constable?" asked one of the other. "Will we let this gent find us some gold?"

"'Ow much money do you 'ave?" asked the other lawman. "Come on, out wiv it."

"I've got ten shillings, that is all!" the man held up a small bag. The officers grabbed it and allowed him to stand. Pushing him towards the Commissioner's tent, they prodded him with their guns.

"You can 'ave a week to find some gold and pay a proper licence or you'll go to jail," said one, "and you'd better bring the money to us, 'cause we'll get 'alf of it. Come on, let's take this li'le lot to the Commissioner."

"But, that leaves me no money for food or water!" objected the poor miner. "I can't dig for a week when I have nothing to eat!"

The bigger of the two constables struck him in the head with his rifle butt, causing the man to stagger forward. "Don't tell me ya problems!" and they were lost to sight as the three went downstream. The constables, often ex-convicts, were attracted to the job because of the fifty percent reward they earned if they arrested unlicensed miners and got them to pay.

"Poor man," said Amelia to herself, as she watched the altercation from her position down by the fouled creek. But she could do nothing, as they too, were almost out of money, had seen no sign of the riches they were promised, and might be the next ones feeling the rifle butt on the side of the head.

The freezing winter had become a sweltering hot summer, and the flies were almost unbearable. They stuck to the face, the eyes and the ears, clung in dozens on sweaty backs, and swarmed over the rotten meat and bones. The tired woman forced herself to push the handle back and forth, back and forth.

There was no glint of gold in the cradle, and Amelia bent to scoop up a handful of dirty water to rub over her face. She resisted the urge to drink it though, as there was disease in the goldfields and they were trying to drink only the clean water from the bucket in the tent. They had to acquire it from a water wagon as the creek water was putrid. She spoke of her fears to Richard.

"My love, Eaglehawk Gully will be the death of us! We have little water left to drink, and no money to pay our gold licence this month. It is due at the end of this week! The only food we have left now is flour for damper, so we will have to last on that."

"Amelia, my dearest." Richard took her hand and sighed. "I'm afraid that our savings are almost gone. With the stories of the finds here - who would have thought we would get nothing?" The two sat in mutual affection and sympathy, their love for each other had not diminished with the hard existence.

"Richard, as long as I am free, and I have you, I want for nothing. Things could not get much worse, so I'm sure we will find gold soon!" Amelia spoke emphatically, trying to keep their spirits up. Richard gave her a grateful look, but then a loud scream interrupted them, and they ran to the next door tent.

Molly was lying upon her bed, white faced, her hands clutched to her stomach, and poor James was beside himself with worry. Edward stood anxiously in the corner, not knowing what to do. "Amelia, do something, please do something. I think Molly is dying!"

Amelia pushed James out of the way and lifted the blanket. Molly was drenched in blood, and she turned to the men. "I hope she will not die, James, if I can stop the bleeding, but she has lost your child that she was carrying. Get me some water." She pushed the palm of her hand down into Molly's belly and kept the pressure on firmly. Richard and James looked at each other. The bucket by the door only contained a few cups full of clean water. "Richard," Amelia insisted, "I cannot wash her in that filthy creek, or she will certainly die then!"

Richard strode to his tent and came back with three shillings, which he thrust at James. "Here is our last three shillings, go and buy a bucketful from the wagon." James ran out the door, no doubt grateful for something useful to do, as he could not bear seeing his wife in pain.

It was futile. A few grains of gold here and there was just enough to pay the licence, but within several months, a new strike was made at McIntyre. Molly, having recovered well, was fit to travel, and so to everyone's relief, Eaglehawk Gully and its so-called riches was left behind forever.

Edward was on guard, mounted by the side of the cart, both pistols loaded. The talk of holdups and bushrangers was rife, and murders were becoming an everyday occurrence. The road to McIntyre was packed with wagons, carts, horses and wheelbarrows, with many on foot. The place was not so far to travel, and only the day had passed before they reached the site. The strike had been reported only two days previously, but a horde of Chinese diggers had already descended on the township, pegging out three hundred claims overnight.

Amelia and her family had nothing against the strange gentlemen from the east, but many miners felt resentful towards them, as they came in great numbers and took away gold that the residents of the colony felt was theirs by right. The feelings against the Chinese grew so that they had to appoint guards to protect themselves in the night-time hours.

Prize fighting was very popular on the goldfields. The men involved made large sums of money from the purses offered, and gambling on the result was another way to earn a fortune in wagers. These fights attracted huge crowds, and the longer a champion went undefeated, the more frenzied the challengers fought to become the next one crowned. The audience indulged in large quantities of liquor, and often became involved in fights themselves, triggering brawls involving hundreds. The women felt unsafe at McIntyre, and Amelia expressed her concern to her husband.

"My dear, what are we to do with Lucy? I daren't send her out to take the horses to graze on her own, as it is becoming far too dangerous. How long will we remain here?"

"I will talk to the others," said Richard in answer, "I don't like it here either, perhaps we can move on soon, and in the meantime, you or Molly will have to go with Lucy and the horses."

One night, there was trouble in the camp. A group of Irishmen who called themselves 'The Tipperary Mob' were carousing and drinking late, picking fights with the other men. They were known for being troublemakers, and there had been a bare knuckle fight that evening, stirring up feeling with liquor and a lust for violence.

Some of the men from the camp banded together and challenged the Irishmen, and a skirmish developed. Shovels were swung, picks were wielded, and gunshots fired. The screaming and confusion was terrible to hear, and everyone at the Chinamen's Gully camp cowered in their tents, terrified. When the noise calmed down, three men were found dead, murdered by the Tipperary boys, but the Irishmen themselves had disappeared. The constables were called and a search began for the men responsible.

It didn't take long before the culprits were found drinking Guinness in one of the grog shops, and the constables surrounded the place. "Come out, you men, in the name of the law!" went up the shout. Shots were fired but the perpetrators were arrested without further bloodshed, and taken away to face trial. Tired miners and their families arose at daybreak and James and Edward came in with Molly, to break their fast.

"What a night!" exclaimed Richard. "I must say that I will be working with my eyes closed today, so I will not be able to see any gold even if it is there!"

"I can't believe," said James, as he often saw the funny side of otherwise serious situations, "that those men, the Tipperary Band, thought that nobody would find them in the grog shop! That would be the first place that I would look to find a bunch of Irish rogues!" They all laughed.

"I think we are in for more trouble here in McIntyre," commented Edward. "Many of the miners have banded together to get the Chinese thrown off the goldfields. They have even set a date to enact this expulsion of the poor fellows, and they will be using force!"

"When is this to happen?" asked Amelia, worried.

"July fourth," answered Edward, "and it is the first today. "Is it not unbelievable that we have been here almost a year already?"

Richard shook his head. "The eight ounces we found soon after we arrived here really has kept us going, but since then, not much luck. I propose we keep going to the end of the month and if we have not done better, let us move on."

The other two men nodded, and Amelia looked at Molly. Their words did not need to be spoken, they were both tired of this life and Molly had only revealed the night before that she was again, with child. Poor Lucy was so tired from her lack of sleep the previous night that she was still abed and took no part in the conversation. Although she was fourteen now and doing a woman's work, Amelia let her stay there for a few more hours.

Luckily the escalating situation with the Chinese was averted, as the deadline for their expulsion was called off. Simmering tensions remained, however, and in August, a big strike at White Hills, west of Maryborough, prompted them to pack up and move once more.

White Hills, 1854

Although many miners found nuggets of gold at White Hills and it was widely known that there was gold under the rock-hard outer layers, it was back-breaking work getting to it, and the conditions made it even more so. Fifty thousand men laboured over the diggings by the end of August. A thick cloud of dust hung over the area, and the constant dirt and gravel in the eyes caused many miners to develop a condition called 'Sandy Blight' which sometimes resulted in blindness.

"Amelia, can you look at Richard's eyes?" asked James, bringing the older man to her one day. "He seems to have something in his eye and cannot clean it out."

"Come and sit here, my dear, she said kindly, "let me see. I have some clean water here I will use some for your eyes."

"Oh no, Amelia, don't use the water for that! The price for a bucket is so high now, we can scarcely find enough to drink!" he objected.

"Hush now, Richard, sometimes you have to just... hush!" she said firmly, and patted the stool in front of her impatiently. He sat.

Amelia washed his eyes carefully with the water, but it made no difference, the irritation remained. "Richard, I am sure that you are developing the Sandy Blight," she confirmed. "You cannot continue to work in the dust."

He spoke with his eyes shut, but his body tense. "Amelia, I must work! I cannot do nothing!"

"Do you want to go blind, Richard? Then what would we do with Molly having a new baby and all?"

"A new baby?" James said quickly from behind her, and Amelia looked around, realising her mistake. "I'm so sorry James, Molly wanted me to keep quiet about the baby for now, until... well, you know what happened last time."

"Amelia, what will we do?" pleaded James in anguish.

She thought for a moment and answered. "Well, first we need to wash Richard's eyes every morning and night and bind them up while he is outside."

"But..." James started to protest but Amelia spoke over him.

"Quiet, let me finish James. I love you all dearly, and I am not about to let my husband go blind, for his sake and the sake of all of us. He could operate the gold cradle, you don't need to see to be able to do that. Molly and I can take turns at shovelling instead, that's all. And whoever brings the gravel can check the cradle for gold before they pour in the new load."

"Well, all right," agreed Richard reluctantly, "perhaps for a few days."

The two women toiled hard with the shovel, and as the days wore on, the water supply dwindled, and they started to buy water for washing gravel as well as drinking. The Simson Diggings, as it was known, was a dry place with absolutely no water at all in summer. Miners began to send their wash dirt nearly ten miles to Carisbrook, and some paid for water to be carted west.

Richards' eyes improved without the constant dust. One of his eyes seemed recovered completely, but the other now had limited vision and it appeared that he would never regain his sight fully. But soon he was able to resume working, when he had fashioned a mask for his eyes with only small slits to see through, giving protection from the majority of the dust. The others began wearing the masks too, in an attempt to avoid the cursed condition.

It was too late for poor Molly though. The terrible conditions and the hard work had done enough, and in November, she miscarried again.

The struggle to pay the miners' licence continued, and the situation was getting desperate for many. The long years of toil for little reward were taking their toll. One evening, the men brought a visitor to the tent, to share their modest supper of tea and damper.

"Amelia, this is John Chambers," said Richard, in introduction, "I knew you wouldn't mind, but we brought the poor fellow to eat with us."

"How do you do Mr Chambers?" said Amelia politely, and she separated the damper into seven pieces, rather than six.

"I am well, thank you Mrs Barton. It is very kind of you, when food is so scarce. I have been living on opossums that I hunted for the last month or two, but I can no longer pay my licence, so I have decided to return to England."

They all gathered around to hear Mr Chamber's story as they ate; he paid special attention to Lucy, and the girl hung on every word he spoke. He had arrived in Australia eight years before, and had spent a year in South Australia before hearing of the gold rush. Mr Chambers described how he had walked over five hundred miles on foot to Ballarat, and then worked on the goldfields for the last seven years. He had made only enough to pay his licence and a little food, and would return home with nothing but the shirt on his back.

"I am tired of digging for naught!" he said emphatically. "I have come to the conclusion that the only men who make their fortune from the goldfields, are those who supply equipment and other provisions to the poor devils who slave there."

After Mr Chambers had said his good nights and they had wished him well, the family trooped to bed, feeling a level of disillusionment that they never had felt before. Each of them asked themselves the question, but Amelia voiced it to her husband as they fell into bed.

"Do you really think we will ever find gold, or are we simply wasting our lives away in the quest for it?" The man had no answer to this question, but for the first time he was feeling old. He was approaching sixty, but had always been so strong. Now he could feel that inexorably, his strength too was fading, along with his dreams.

In December, the grim situation of the miners came to a head, and more than thirty poor souls were gunned down by the troopers in Ballarat while staging a riot protesting the miners licence fee. Most of them were starving, and had nothing but the rags they were dressed in, while the government officials grew fat on the proceeds of the taxes. This news threw a pall over the goldfields. Although there was talk of reform, any actual change seemed too far into the future to hope for.

Desperate situations bred desperate acts, however, and the thievery at the claims grew worse. One evening, after the shot had signalled day's end, a man tried to drag away some bags of gravel from the side of someone's claim, and suddenly, a pick handle started banging loudly in a gold pan. It was the signal that assistance was needed, so all the men ran from their tents to try and apprehend the man. An hour later, Richard returned with James and Edward following. They all gathered for a cup of tea and Richard explained the events.

"Well, you heard the call that someone was in trouble? Some filthy scum was trying to drag away two bags of gravel from right under the noses of the owner who wasn't armed. When he told him to stop, the scoundrel dared him to try and make him!"

James went on. "About a hundred of us all ran over, and before we even could see what was going on, there was a crowd of men around him, beating the man senseless with their bare hands!"

"Well, we didn't see it all really," said the older man, trying not to shock the women too much.

"Yes I did," interrupted James, "and they would have beaten him to death I think if the constable hadn't arrived to take him away, and well deserved too!"

"As it was, he may not survive," added Edward. "I was highly disturbed by the murderous frenzy, were you not James?"

"Well, yes," said James, tempering his enthusiasm. "But he was lucky the constable arrived promptly or he would have been slow roasted over the camp fire the same as that poor devil at Ararat."

"Speaking of Ararat," said Edward hurriedly, interrupting the gruesome tale. "Did you hear that the bushranger James Turner was hung yesterday?"

"No," said Molly, "was he that escaped convict who was finally arrested after shooting that soldier?"

"Yes, that is the man," confirmed Edward. "It turns out, I heard today, that he was responsible for over twenty holdups on that road, but he made a mistake when he shot and killed Sergeant McNally, as the whole regiment went after him! The other fellows who were caught with him got fifteen years hard labour."

"It is funny how it took the shooting of an officer of the law to get them to do something!" said Richard gloomily.

"Here, here!" said the other men in disgust.

Since the railway was put through to Ballarat the previous year, getting gold securely to Melbourne became easier, as did the transport of supplies to the goldfields area. The huge gold strike at Dunnolly had resulted in the formation of a permanent town there, and the richness of the surrounding diggings kept the town busy.

It was said that up to fifty thousand men were working on the various leads around the town, and the family could well believe it, as the main street was so busy that it was difficult to find a path to steer their horse and cart. It was still a tent town, but some permanent buildings were being erected. Business owners were paying over forty pounds for a position on the main street, as business was brisk, and the location of their shops were important in their success.

The news was brought by Edward soon after arriving at Dunnolly, and he burst into the tent saying, "they've done it, they've done it!"

"What is it Edward?" demanded Richard, standing up.

Edward was grinning from ear to ear. "The mining licences have been abolished! There will be no more monthly fee to pay!" They all jumped up and hugged each other in relief and joy.

"I've bought a casket of ale to share so that we can celebrate the good news," said Edward, and he produced a large flagon. Everyone was delighted, and as they had lived so frugally over the past years, it was a wonderful occasion to forget about their hardships. They all drank the ale, even Lucy, and laughed and told stories until after midnight.

From that moment on, their luck, so long absent, seemed to turn in their favour. The 'Miner's Right' which replaced the monthly fee, was a yearly token, and with the burden of the payment gone, everyone seemed to have a burst of energy. James and Richard came into the tent a few evenings later looking mysterious, and waited until they all sat down to eat before James looked at his father in law, who nodded.

"I have to show you all something that I found today at the junction of Wilson's Lead and Ironbark Gully," James said, casually dropping something with a thud on the small table. It was a nugget of gold!

"James!" screamed Molly in delight, then as everybody shushed her, she put her hand over her mouth, but stared wide eyed at the treasure. They all looked at each other, and Amelia chuckled softly.

She hefted it in her hand. "About half a pound, or eight ounces?" James nodded in confirmation, with a smug look of satisfaction.

"I was just walking over there to look for a new place to stake out, and I tripped over it, hurting my toe! I cursed, and went to kick the damned thing away. Good thing I didn't though," he said hastily. "I swung my leg, and just caught a glimpse of the gold before my boot connected with it. I was so desperate not to kick it in case I couldn't find it again, that I fell over, trying to pull my foot away in time!" Everyone laughed.

Richard, who had been waiting quietly, enjoying everyone's surprise, finally spoke. "Oh, and I dug this one out of the side of our shaft this afternoon." He slammed down a great chunk of the yellow metal before them, and looked around in satisfaction. Pandemonium broke loose, and with them all shushing each other, they hugged, dancing around the tent until they were breathless.

Amelia stood before her man, and their gazes met. "After all these years," she said softly, "I thought it would never happen." She put up her arms and the two stood, locked together, in relief and joy.

"I too, have some good news," interrupted Molly after the initial euphoria had passed, addressing them all. "James and I are having a child! As I think about four months has passed already, we hope that it is safe to tell you now." Everyone gathered around them in congratulations. They all felt that this was the best day in their lives.

The nugget weighed about twenty two ounces, and together with the other nugget that James had found, thirty ounces of gold would reap over a hundred pounds from the bank. Dividing the sum three ways, each of the three men got a share of about thirty five pounds. It was by no means a fortune, but with the abolition of the licence fee, this gave them all a sense of security that they had never known.

The men continued to dig over the following weeks, and added some small pieces of gold to their list of successes at Dunnolly. Stories were heard of several monster nuggets that had been found at Inglewood, twenty miles east, and some were convinced to relocate, but Richard, James and Edward decided to stay put for the time being. The women were relieved not to move again, but then disaster struck the area.

The rains hit with a vengeance. It was as if the skies simply opened, and torrent after torrent of water emptied onto the diggings. First the ground was slick and dangerous, then it became a quagmire, then a disaster zone, as mine shafts collapsed, burying miners under ten metres of wet clay. There were many deaths from people simply slipping and falling into water logged holes, and being unable to climb out, they drowned. Children disappeared, never to be seen again, presumed drowned, and the swollen creeks swept everything away that was in their path. It was completely impossible to continue any kind of mining in the conditions.

The rains finally ceased, and the Mayor of Ballarat arrived at Dunnolly to inspect the area. The women had taken the opportunity of the temporary cessation of digging to take the cart into town to collect some fresh food, and they watched the grand fellow walk the streets, talking to shopkeepers and miners. As the women stopped the cart, ready to alight, a young man appeared at their side and doffed his hat.

"Good morning Ma'ams and Miss," he said politely, but he addressed his warm smile to Lucy. "May I be of assistance in helping you down over the mud?"

"Why thank you Sir," answered Amelia, and she nodded at her daughter. Lucy immediately put her arms out to the gentleman, who carefully lifted her onto a less muddy section of the road, then immediately he turned and helped Molly and her mother.

"Thank you again, Sir," said Amelia, "and what, pray, is your name?"

"Tobias Bush, at your service," he said, with a flourish of his hat. "My father is here today to inspect the damage after the floods, and I have accompanied him."

"Will you be staying long at Dunnolly, Mr Bush?" enquired Amelia, as they began walking to the grocers.

"A few days I think, Ma'am," he answered. They arrived at the door of the shop and he took off his hat again. "Well, good day to you." He nodded at Amelia and Molly and taking Lucy's hand, he bowed over it. "And what is your name, if I may ask?"

"Miss Lucy Barton, Sir," she said shyly, "and thank you for your help."

"A pleasure, Miss Barton," and he gazed at her, enraptured. "If I might be so bold, when you finish your shopping, would you and your companions take tea with me?"

Lucy looked at her mother in confirmation and nodded. They finished their purchases, and spent an enjoyable half an hour with Mr Bush before heading back to Wilsons Lead, as the strike zone was known. The young man promised that he could call in a day or two when in that area with his father, the Mayor of Ballarat.

Tobias Bush convinced his father that he was needed in the town for several weeks to assist the magistrate with the inquests of those that had died in the floods, and so his father returned to Ballarat without him. Lucy and Tobias were often in each other's company, but Amelia was finding it difficult to go with her every time she went to town. She did not wish to deny her daughter the opportunity of forming a relationship with such a respectable person, so did allow her to drive in unaccompanied to meet Tobias for lunch on several occasions. Only two weeks after their meeting, Lucy Barton and Tobias Bush were engaged to be married.

The marriage was to be in Ballarat, and although Richard would have liked to go to the wedding of his youngest daughter, he felt that he needed to finish up operations at Dunnolly. If the truth be told, although Richard liked Tobias very much, he was not comfortable in the company of men such as the Mayor of Ballarat, and so Amelia, being aware of this, did not press the matter.

It was decided that the women would go on ahead to Ballarat in a coach and the three men would pull down their tents and pack everything to move to an area east of Maryborough near Flagstaff. A good strike had been made there, and it would be their new home. Richard bid his daughter an emotional farewell, kissing her tenderly, and promised to travel to Ballarat to visit once they were settled.

Lucy and Tobias were married in a big society ceremony in town. Amelia and Molly also felt slightly out of place associating with the family of the Mayor, however they were proud that Lucy would have a carefree and wonderful life with a wealthy family. The five years at the goldfields had been hard on poor Lucy, and she had little opportunity to make friends or continue her education. Tobias was interested in public affairs, and would in all likelihood succeed his father in the position of Mayor, so their future looked assured.

Leaving Lucy blissful with her handsome new husband to settle in Ballarat near his family, the two women took the coach transport toward Maryborough. Amelia wrote to Richard (via

James) that he was to meet them at Flagstaff, which was just a mile or two outside Maryborough, with the cart.

Richard had a surprise for his wife when they arrived. As the men were preparing to leave Dunnolly, he had met a person who owned a water wagon. The fellow needed to sell it as the heavy rains had meant there was no more work for him in Dunnolly for a while. Richard, thinking of the wise words of Mr Chambers, had remembered that those who made the best money were those who provided equipment or supplies.

The Maryborough diggings were dry, so he decided to spend five pounds from the proceeds of the gold nuggets to invest in the wagon, together with a strong horse to pull it. This business venture would add a new source of income for them all.

As soon as they settled, Richard began carting water from Deep Creek at Carisbrook, some two miles away. With his poor eyesight and advancing age, he was struggling with heavy digging and it would suit him better.

James and Edward used some of their money to invest in a puddling machine and other mining equipment. The puddling machine was a horse-drawn one, and it enabled many buckets of gravel to be hauled up from a greater depth. Consistently working to a deeper level kept the gold finds more consistent, and the company thrived.

Later that year, Molly had a baby boy, Dennis, and the family was thrilled that she could now leave the grief of her lost babies behind. Molly wrote to her sister to tell her the good news, as she too, was expecting her first child.

A forty pound nugget was found at Bluchers Gully, just nearby, by two Prussian men, and the rush of new people to the area had Richard's water wagon in great demand. Amelia convinced Richard it was time to build a more permanent dwelling as they had lived in tents now for five years, and could afford a more solid house.

The men set about building two timber huts. They split tree trunks to make thick slabs, and standing them on their ends around a framework, enclosed the large huts, each twice the size of the tents. The roof was made of overlapping lengths of bark, layered together snugly to form a waterproof cover, and to weatherproof the structure, clay was packed between all the slabs in the walls. Richard, being the bricklayer, built a permanent fireplace and chimney at the end of each one.

"Mother, we have so much room now!" said Molly, settling little Dennis into his wooden crib that James had made. "It is such a relief to stay in one place, I for one, will never move to another goldfield again!"

"I agree with you, Molly," said her mother, nodding emphatically. "I hope the gold fever has left Richard now, and with the success of the water business, we don't need to chase it any more. The other men can continue to mine this area for some time with their new equipment."

"I may not want to stay here forever, Mother, but for now, I am content," Molly added.

"Well, it isn't brick, but I am so pleased with my new hut that I feel for the first time since we left Bothwell, I have found a place I could settle permanently," Amelia said. "I am fifty six years old Molly, I don't want that nomadic life any more.

Maryborough is only a few miles away, and will supply all our needs."

At the end of the year, Lucy gave birth to the first of her children, a girl, whom they called Amelia. Richard and Amelia travelled to Ballarat to visit with their daughter and granddaughter, and found Lucy very happy with her situation. They had a lovely house in the town, and the Bush family had welcomed her into its fold. Tobias could not be happier or prouder, and he was already a prominent citizen in Ballarat, which was quickly growing in population to become a centre for the region.

The flats near Flagstaff were soon covered in holes and mounds, as thousands of men worked the surface for the elusive metal. The area was now denuded of all trees, and Amelia was glad they had taken some for their huts before they were all gone.

The vicinity had come to be known as Madman's Gully, and for good reason. Desperate men went mad with exhaustion, lack of water, or died from starvation. Theft, drunkenness, murder and suicide occurred regularly. Those looking for gold in the six feet of ground near the surface, found very little, and the lack of water became a huge problem for other miners.

Richard's water cartage business was booming. He felt better in himself now that long days of digging was no longer his chief occupation, and his wise investment in the wagon had been the best decision he had ever made. Of course their gold prospecting company had a supply of water for washing from Richard's wagon, so there was no shortage for washing gravel.

Drinking and washing water were no longer a problem either, and the women worked at the household duties in relative comfort. Richard was also able to bring a regular supply of firewood from out of the area, so the fires were warm, the food was adequate, and life was far better.

Edward still lived with Molly and James, and was regarded as a member of the family. The two huts often still combined resources for meals as had been their habit for so long and the evenings were pleasant, with everyone exchanging stories of the day. Edward's loyalty and friendship had been dependable over the years, and he had also taken on the role of chief protector. It was he who brought them the unwelcome news.

"I think we should take turns standing guard at night again," he said seriously to the other men.

"Why Edward, what has occurred?" asked James in alarm. He regarded their safety as being very important, especially as there was now little Dennis, his son, to consider.

Edward sat back in his seat, and sighed. "There is another madman on the loose. Two people have already been murdered for their possessions in the last two days, and there is no evidence to point to whom the criminal might be."

"Edward! Are you talking of the man who was found stabbed to death down near Bluchers Gully Track?" asked Richard, and when Edward nodded he went on. "Yes, I heard something of it today, but I thought they had caught the man."

"No, and since then, another poor fellow has been found dead, head first down his own mine shaft. All the miners are on high alert, and they will shoot anyone who moves at night. The authorities in Maryborough are sending more constables, as the situation here is getting beyond control." Just then, a pistol shot was heard, and then another, booming through the night, as if to emphasis what had been said.

Molly jumped, and looked over at Dennis to see if he had awoken, but he was impervious to the noise, sleeping fast as only a child could. The men organised watches for that night, so that none of them would have to stay awake too long. They hoped the man would be apprehended soon, as it would be a drain on them all.

Two days later, another victim was found, and it was confirmed that the murderer operated stealthily with a knife, as the miner was sliced to ribbons. The men increased their vigilance, and gunshots were heard throughout the hours of darkness. James was on guard that night, and as they were turning in to bed, a scuffle could be heard outside and James' voice shouting. "What the devil are you doing, creeping around our hut? Stand still Sir, or I will fire!"

Richard quickly wrenched open the door to help his son in law, who had a man standing at attention, the pistol at his head.

"Paddy? Paddy Aherne, is that you?"

"Richard, me old friend!" The man answered in relief. James looked back and forth between the two, then lowered the weapon uncertainly.

"James, you can put that down. This fellow is a rogue of course, but one of the best ones that ever lived!" The two older men embraced with delight.

"To be sure, that's a foine welcome for a poor Oirishman just off the boat from Van Diemen's Land!" exclaimed Paddy.

"Paddy, this is my son in law, James Derrick. James, I worked with Paddy at Bothwell for nigh on twenty years. We spent quite a bit of time drinking together at the Castle Inn too, of course," he admitted, laughing.

"My apologies for the manner of the welcome, Paddy," grinned James, "but we have a murderer on the loose in this area, and I am on guard at present. You were lucky someone did not shoot you, as we all have our fingers on the trigger!"

"How did you find me Paddy?" asked Richard, and he clapped him on the shoulder and stepped into the tent, the Irishman following.

"Oi was on moi way to Maryborough, and oi kept askin' at every place I came to if anyone knew of a big strong brute named Richard Barton!" He laughed. "Luckily, at Carisbrook, someone recognoised your description and remembered ye're name and ye're water cartin' business, and where to come to. Oi arrived a bit after dark, and so oi walked around lookin' for the water wagon. Never did oi expect to foind it next to the two best lookin' houses in the area!"

Amelia had put on a wrap and was surprised but very happy to see her old friend, Paddy. "Oh Paddy!" she exclaimed. "You are the last person in the world I expected to see. I thought we were all to be murdered in our beds!" She hugged the kind man and welcomed him. "Come in, Paddy, we were just going to bed, but I think I could find a cup of tea for a thirsty man!"

Paddy told them how he came to be in Victoria. "Oi worked in Bot'well until last mont'. But it was never de same after ye left. As I kept hearin' stories of de big nuggets to be found, I t'ought oi'd come over and troi me luck."

Over the next few days, Paddy, who Amelia invited to stay with them for the time being, had a bit of a look around Madman's Gully and Blucher's Gully, the neighbouring area. He was most impressed with the group's puddling operation on their claims at Madman's, and spent some time helping James and Edward, learning the basics of gold mining from them.

Everyone liked Paddy, he brought new life to the group, and kept the men laughing with his outrageous tales. There was yet another murder nearby shortly after Paddy's arrival, and the men continued to look to their personal safety with great caution.

A great rush to Emu, north of Maryborough, cleansed the area somewhat, as the vast majority of the diggers abandoned Madman's Gully in search of easier gold. Paddy was very keen to go there, as it was said that buckets full of gold were being unearthed by some lucky miners. Richard, his enthusiasm somewhat tempered by seven years of toil, had heard all the stories before, but Paddy's enthusiasm was infectious, and he spoke to Amelia about it.

"What do you think about trying our luck at Emu, dearest?" he asked tentatively. "Paddy is keen, and I thought that maybe we could go for a while."

Amelia absolutely refused. "Richard Barton, are you a single man with nothing to consider but yourself and Paddy's whim? How would we chase another rush without losing everything that we have here? As soon as we moved out, someone else would take our hut, and that would be that. Homeless again, and nothing to live for but a shovel and a bucket! We have the businesses here now, we are settled and I am not moving to follow another fruitless search for riches. Molly feels the same. We are not going, and that is that!" said Amelia emphatically.

Richard sat down, taken aback. He knew his wife did not want to go back to living in a tent, but the depth of her animosity towards the idea was a surprise. He spoke to Edward and James. Surprisingly, they too, felt the same as the women. They were operating their equipment successfully, and it was their opinion that there was still plenty of gold to be had in Madman's at a depth unreachable with a pick and a shovel. Now that many of the miners had moved on, they had a number of sites to choose from. James also felt it was unfair to Molly, who was trying to care for a child.

Richard reported the results of this conversation to Paddy. "She won't go," he said, with a shake of his head. "I talked to her and she is convinced that it is better to stay here, with the business and the huts."

"But Richard, me old friend, t' be sure she would be wantin' ye to foind her a big nugget of that yellow stuff would she not? The stories are that huge bucket loads are comin' from de ground and..."

"Paddy, we have heard those tales now for seven years! It does not matter what people say, when you get there, it is months of back-breaking work. If you are lucky, you find a small nugget or two, but we have never seen those buckets full of gold, and we have followed every rush from Castlemaine to Bendigo and back to Maryborough."

"But what if dis is de toime ye do foind it? Would ye be wantin' to give up dat chance? Oi came over here to foind gold, and oi'm not givin' up yet." The Irishman had the passion for the search for gold burning feverishly in his eyes, a look that Richard knew only too well.

"Look, Paddy," he said reasonably, "that is what the gold fever does to everyone. It catches him in its web of desire and he works and works for it. He finds a small bit here and there, and the sight of a glint of gold is enough to keep the fever burning. So he redoubles his efforts. He finds a larger nugget, and it is not enough to make him rich, but it is enough to keep him going for another year. This goes on until the life is sucked out of a man, and there is nothing left but an old timer with a sore back and no more money than when he started!"

"Oi know dat ye've got more experience dan me, Richard, but I want to go and troi. Oi will never know until oi do."

The big man shook his head. He was getting nowhere with his friend. The truth was, there was still a spark of gold fever left deep down inside that he was trying to stifle, and Paddy's excitement was fanning the flame of desire. But he had been through all of that. It was a waste of time to dig for gold, was it not?

Paddy finally convinced Richard to accompany him for a short time to Emu, and Amelia was furious. "You stupid, big ox of a man!" she cried in frustration. "How long can you keep digging holes in the ground? Until you drop down dead, or you get shot, murdered, or fall down a mine shaft?"

Her husband stared at his mild mannered wife in shock. He had only once her shout at him in all the years of their marriage, when he had refused to allow her son to come and live with them. Richard had to admit to himself that he had probably done plenty of ill-considered things since then that may have deserved his wife's wrath, but still she did not normally raise her voice. He opened his mouth to protest, but she interrupted.

"After all we have been through to get to where we are, Richard!"

"Where have we got to!" roared Richard in fury. "After all we have gone through, where are we?" His face was red, and his anger palpable. "In a bark hut, living on mutton stew! Is that your idea of the pinnacle of achievement, Amelia? Because it is with certainty that I know, it isn't mine!"

"You were the one who promised to build me a brick house, Richard!" cried Amelia, both hands out begging for an answer. "Well, where is it? Where?"

The couple stared at each other, the memory of all the years of futile struggle and striving fuelled their anger. Anger at themselves, their failure to reach the lives they wanted, and the years that were now slipping away, taking that dream from between their fingers.

"Get out of here then!" Amelia screamed. "Get out of here and go and dig holes in the dirt to find your precious gold! If you never come back, I won't be surprised. I have a water cartage business here that I will run by myself, and I will do well by it too, I'll wager!" And with that, Amelia stamped out of the door, leaving her husband alone.

And so it was that at aged sixty two, Richard set off for Emu with Paddy. His wife refused to see him off or say goodbye, and Richard, with his mouth set in an angry line, drove the cart away. Paddy was aware that the couple had fought over the plan, as he had heard the argument, but he reassured his friend that all would be well.

313

"Ah, she's mad now, but just wait till ye come home wit' a huge nugget of gold!" he wheedled, "enough t' buy her a stone mansion and two servants besoides!"

Richard Barton once more found himself living in a tent in freezing, filthy conditions, digging for gold all day for small reward. Emu was full of the worst kinds of vice and cruelty, gamblers, whores, criminals and murderers, all plying their trades. Women were abandoned on the diggings, and when it was discovered that they were defenceless, they were brutalised and used, and died quickly of starvation or disease.

No enquiries were ever held into the deaths of the many women whose lives ended in this fashion, and Richard could not bear to see the poor wretches begging or offering favours for a piece of bread. Some women even fought each other, stripped to waist, entertaining crowds of men for money to survive.

Attacks and murders were everyday occurrences, and the two men became exhausted from trying to work all day and taking watch half of the night. They found one small fragment of metal, but after several months, Richard could not take it anymore. He felt old and tired and he wanted to go home, but most of all, he missed his dear wife Amelia.

"Amelia was right. This is the game of a foolish man," he sighed to Paddy one night as they sat in front of their fire, exhausted, chewing some stale damper.

Paddy, for once, did not argue. He had been working as hard as he ever had in his life, even as a convict, and the process of disillusionment had begun. He stared into the flames as if the answer to his life's questions could be found there. "Oi cannot understand how we have found no gold after all dose stories," he pondered.

"But you see, Paddy, I told you before. We have heard those stories for years. Yes, some men have struck huge riches, but only one or two in fifty thousand. The rest of us poor devils make up the remainder, who find little or nothing. John Chambers was right, I often think of him, and what he told me."

"Who was dat, den?" Paddy had never heard of John Chambers.

"He was an Englishman I met at White Hills. He had mined for gold for seven years, and was leaving to go back across the sea with nothing to show for his work. He was wise enough to make that decision while he was still a young man, young enough to start again, doing something more rewarding that this fool's folly!"

Richard gestured around them to the hundreds of other fires, all with hungry, wretched men sitting before them. "He told me that the only people, besides the lucky few that struck it rich, that made good money in a gold rush, were those who provided goods and services to the diggers. That was when I bought the water wagon."

"Ah, 'tis a good business, dat," nodded Paddy.

The dawn came, and Richard stood with his pick and shovel in his hand and looked southwards. He glanced down at the tools in his big, calloused hands, and made a decision. Throwing the implements down, he shouted for Paddy.

Paddy agreed to give up and go home with him, home to Madman's Gully.

Molly had just given birth to a second child, a little girl, and they all celebrated. Paddy was still with them, and was talking about buying a share of the business. It was summer again, and water carting continued to equal gold mining in the income it provided. Richard thanked Mr Chambers and his wise words every day, for he never would have thought of it otherwise. The summer heat was fierce as always, but on that happy occasion, nobody could have predicted what was to happen two days later.

The hot northerly winds blew superheated gusts across the scorching, dusty goldfields of Madman's Gully. It was only ten o'clock in the morning, and already the heat was unbearable. It was hard to breathe, not only due to the dust, but the hot air carried smoke from bushfires, and the women could taste the acrid ash at the back of their throats. Molly was trying to keep the tiny baby girl cool by fanning her, and three and a half year old Dennis lay listlessly on his bed.

Amelia came in with a bucket of fresh water for her daughter. "I don't know how the men can keep working in this heat!" she exclaimed. "Surely they must come in soon. There is nothing to be done but rest today."

"Mother, thank you for the water, can you please pour some into this basin? Both the children need bathing to keep them cool, but it is baby I am most concerned for, she will not suckle, and has not had any drink or sustenance all morning," Molly said in a worried voice. "I think she is too hot, and now has no energy to try. Will the wind never turn?"

"We have had one day of this terrible wind now, and we have all had enough of it," said Amelia, "but if the bushfire grows, soon we will be engulfed in smoke too! Thank God we have our hut; there would be no shelter from the heat or the smoke at all in a tent." She was worried about the baby, and wondered if she should go and fetch James.

As the day went on, the heat climbed, well over one hundred degrees Fahrenheit, and the winds continued to blow, whipping up the bushfire, which was near Timor, to the north. Clouds of thick smoke enveloped the area, and the women began to cough, as it found its way into the huts through every crack and the chimney. They could not open the door to let air flow in, as the smoke was unbearable, and the oppressive heat climbed even further.

Molly put the baby into a bucket of water, to keep her cool, but there was nothing she could do about the air quality. The tiny baby still would not drink, and the young mother was frantic, watching her lying without any sign of movement other than a faint attempt to breathe.

"Mother, go and get James, please? I don't know what to do!" she cried, coughing, and glancing at Dennis. He seemed to be all right, and had drunk a good deal of water, but had also begun coughing.

Amelia ran out of the door closing it quickly, and struggled through the smoke. She was blown this way and that with the gale force gusts of wind, and smoke and dust invaded her lungs. Holding her apron over her mouth and nose, she stumbled on, and met the men coming back from the claim, who were dripping with sweat and exhausted. They had decided to give up trying to work and go back to the house. James ran on ahead when Amelia told him, and by the time they reached the huts, the smoke had worsened and they were all coughing and spluttering.

James met them at the door, distraught. "My daughter, my daughter has died! She would not drink and could not breathe...the heat...the smoke..."

Amelia, distraught, went inside with him, and the three other men decided to go inside Richard's hut, so that it was not too crowded. Poor Molly was wringing wet with sweat and sitting rigid on the end of the bed, holding the tiny dead infant in her arms. James sat beside his stricken wife, once more overwhelmed by grief, and Amelia wondered how much more loss they could endure.

When the weather conditions eased, it was discovered that dozens of babies and children had died that day in Madman's Gully and Maryborough. Many families did not have enough fresh water to drink, and the tents provided little protection from the billowing smoke and the beating sun.

The babe had died even before she was registered. They buried her there at Madman's Gully rather than take her to the cemetery, and erected a simple wooden cross. Molly would never again be the carefree girl she had once been, and Amelia felt her heart full of sorrow for her daughter.

Dennis survived, probably due to the plentiful water they had and extra protection provided by their wooden dwelling, and Amelia cherished her grandson. The vegetable patch had withered and died in that two terrible days, so food was scarce for a time, but the need for water was even greater, which luckily, Richard was able to provide to all in the area.

People from other mining companies often came to visit their operation at Madman's Gully, and after such a visit, James received a very good offer to go and work for a large business based in Maryborough. Molly was very keen to live in the town, near the doctor and the school. So it was that James accepted the position.

Paddy offered to buy out James' share in the company, and it was decided that as part of his share, he could live permanently in the second hut with Edward. James and Molly, along with their son, moved to Maryborough. It was only three miles away, so Amelia was able to visit her daughter often, and Molly was very happy in the first proper house she had ever lived in.

Amelia had, in a few short years, suddenly found herself to be the grandmother of twelve. Molly now had three children. Dennis was now nine, Amelia, who was three, and little Richard, who was nine months old. But Lucy had proven to be a prolific producer of offspring, and already had six children, Amelia, Susan, John, Richard, James and Evan.

Evan, Amelia's son, who kept in touch by letter, had married and had three children in Tasmania, as Van Diemen's Land was now known, and was doing very well. Amelia hoped that one day, Evan and his family might travel to Victoria to visit, but her son was kept very busy as he was now general manager of the northern midlands farm where he had worked for some years.

She was very proud of her family, and as the long years of toil were now behind them, Amelia could spend time travelling to see her grandchildren in Maryborough and Ballarat, although she could not bring herself to go back to Tasmania.

Edward had also married, and he and his wife still shared their hut with Paddy. The Irishman took over the water wagon, when needed in the summer season, so that Richard could work a little less. The gold mine had expanded and moved to a new site close by, and Edward now employed a large crew of men.

Richard had been negotiating to buy a plot of land in Flagstaff Lane, which led to Madman's Gully near where their present huts stood. Their savings finally substantial enough to purchase, the couple were very excited about the prospect. One day in March, Richard came running to his wife, holding some papers in his hand.

"Amelia, my dear! We have done it. We have it!" and he stopped breathlessly at the door. Amelia came out and stared at him in excitement.

"Are you sure that is the document? Let me see!" and she took the paper and examined it carefully.

"It is, Edward read it for me! It is done, we own the plot of land!"

Amelia finished reading and looked up, a smile spreading over her face. Richard's enthusiasm was so funny, he looked just like their grandson Dennis when he found a shilling in the dirt. "Yes, you are right, it is ours!"

"My dear, I must hasten to Maryborough, I have some business there that I cannot delay! Is there anything you wish me to get in town for you?" He set about harnessing the horse to the cart.

Amelia gathered her wits quickly. "Richard, I will come with you, and I can visit with Molly while you complete your business. I would love to tell Molly about our land purchase!" and she hurried to get her bonnet and basket.

Molly was thrilled with the news, as it now meant that her parents would be able to build themselves a proper house, which was less draughty that the hut and would have a purpose-built kitchen. Richard was away for several hours, and when he returned from his business he had a cup of tea with Molly and played with his grandchildren before they left.

They sat on the cart and waved to their daughter, who stood on the verandah holding the baby, waiting to see them off. She and James had a lovely house which was made of large sandstone blocks, with a verandah stretching the length of the house. It kept the house cool in summer, and was a pleasant place to have tea on warm afternoons. Amelia loved the house and particularly the verandah.

"Richard, what were you doing in Maryborough, this afternoon?" asked Amelia, "I never asked."

"Never you mind, dear!" answered her husband mysteriously, and sat with a small smile on his face most of the way home, as if he were enjoying a private joke.

Amelia discovered what the business was several weeks later, as Richard asked her to go with him to the plot of land, to start planning out the house he was to build. As they walked up the lane, her husband was strangely silent. They approached the plot and he reached down and took her hand. He led her on to the land, and to her surprise, she found large stacks of bricks and timber already there. She looked at Richard. "It, er looks like a building site," she said.

"My dearest love," said Richard, and he knelt down on one knee. With his hand he took a small packet from his pocket, and handed it to her. "Open it," he said.

The packet contained a small silver ring, with a precious stone in the centre. Amelia held it up in wonder. "My dear Richard, what is this?"

"This is the ring you should have had when we were married, love. I know you couldn't have it then, but I want you to have it now. You have been the one person I have always relied on, the one constant in my life, no matter how bad..." he paused, holding back his emotions, "...things got. I haven't

322

always been the best husband, especially in the early days, and then I led you on this merry chase around Victoria, which I know you didn't always enjoy!" Amelia smiled wryly. That was an understatement.

"I want you to wear this, as a token of my everlasting love for you, my dear wife." He took the ring and slid it onto her finger, and kissed her reverently. Amelia had no time to respond, as still holding her hand, Richard pulled her over to the pile of bricks. "This is my second surprise. I have already engaged two men who are coming from Maryborough to help, and the building of your very own brick home will commence tomorrow, my lady!" and he bowed, grinning with delight.

Amelia remained speechless. The ring was completely unexpected, but the planning that Richard had put into the preparation for building really touched her heart. Richard knew that it was the one thing that she wanted above all else, her very own, brick home. She put out her hand and touched one of the blocks, tracing the hard, rough surface with her finger.

Amelia put up her arms, and they embraced tenderly, an embrace signifying years of endurance and sacrifice, that had brought them to this moment in time.

The house was nearing completion, but Richard would not let Amelia see it until it was finished. Molly had sent a message to say the children were sick with a fever and skin rash, and asked her mother to please come and help. So Amelia decided to go to Maryborough and stay with Molly for several weeks, or as long as it took to help her daughter nurse the children back to health. Richard was happy for her to go, as he was planning to work hard on the house and have it ready for her when she returned. Richard was excited as he had an extra little surprise still in store, which he could hardly wait to show his wife.

Amelia took the horse and cart to town and spent three weeks with Molly. All the children had the illness and they required constant attention, with cool bathing, bringing drinks and food, and cleaning. Molly too, became unwell, and it was with relief that Amelia could finally see them all improving rapidly. She loved her grandchildren, but found the constant demands rather tiring, and was looking forward to some quiet time with Richard when she returned home. She sent him a note to tell him which day she was planning to return.

On a cold, clear, frosty morning on the fifteenth of June, Amelia climbed up onto the cart and gave the horse a tap with the reins. She waved goodbye to her daughter and grandchildren before setting off down the road to Madman's Gully. It was a pleasant three mile trip, and she would be home in time for a cup of tea with her husband, and to see how the house was progressing.

Amelia trotted the horse briskly, and as she passed through Flagstaff, she felt a strange pain in her arm. She slowed the horse to a walk, and rubbed at it, distracted. A sudden faintness came upon her, and she swooned in her seat. The last thing Amelia Barton knew was the sharp pain coursing through her chest, and she cried out, "Richard! Richard!"

Richard sat comfortably on the chair and looked around in satisfaction. He smiled as he anticipated his wife's reaction when she arrived. He had a neighbour's boy on the lookout for the cart going by, so he could bring her directly to the new house which was now all finished. He was very proud of it. It was made of orange clay bricks, which were made by mixing a small percentage of lime to make them as hard as stone during the firing process. It had four rooms; a kitchen, a living room, and two bedrooms.

There was also a separate little wash house at the back next to a fenced vegetable patch, and a pen with five chickens. But best of all, the verandah where Richard now sat extended along the length of the house, facing north to catch the morning sun. It was wide with a floor of boards, and the roof stretched out over it to keep the rain off.

Suddenly, the big man stood, as he saw the boy running very fast down the lane toward him. That is strange, thought Richard, where is Amelia and the cart?

Richard Barton gave his old hut to his friend Paddy, and the three men sold the gold mining equipment for a good price. Edward, along with his wife and child, moved into Maryborough near James and Molly, and he tried to convince his old friend to go too. But Richard could not bring himself to leave and he lived alone in the new brick house for two years.

Every day, after visiting with Paddy, Richard's thoughts drifted to his lovely wife, who had wanted that house so very much but never lived long enough to see it, and he would wander the length and breadth of the goldfield, thinking of her.

It was there on the diggings that Paddy found him, two years later almost to the day after Amelia's death. Richard's broken heart could not survive another winter, and he too, became part of the history that was Madman's Gully.

The barren terrain is dimpled and dotted with holes and mounds, stretching beyond sight. There is no suggestion that the gravelly earth of the gold diggings can support any life other than the thin dry trees, wheezing a tremulous existence from the dust; relics of their ancestors who were so mercilessly cast asunder at the mere mention of gold.

The desolate wasteland of Madman's Gully lays spent and abandoned, yet quivering with memories of the miners who once dwelt there. The madness of the gold fever that gripped the inhabitants ultimately devoured the last vestiges of the soul and left its final victim to die of starvation, leaving behind only the whispering void.

Postscript.

The two heads, one male, one female, carved from solid stone, remain above the door of Saint Luke's Church in Bothwell, Tasmania. The stone figures represent to me the pioneer settlers who survived hard lives with enduring persistence, and then passed on these characteristics to generations of Australians after them.

They look down proudly from on high, as if they were Amelia and Richard Barton who married there so long ago, founders of a huge family of descendants. Lucy's family of fourteen children, Molly's family of eight and Evan's eight children spread over and populated much of Victoria and Tasmania, and now, one hundred and fifty years have passed since the end of their humble lives.

It is fitting for Amelia to be remembered by something that was such a feature of her tumultuous life; a carving of a woman's face, adorning a wall made from solid blocks of stone, with her love, Richard, by her side.

June 15th 2015,
The 148th anniversary of Amelia's death.

References.

1. Convict Lives: Women at Cascades Female Factory (Female Factory Research Group) Research Tasmania 2009.
2. Convict Women: (Kay Daniels) Allen and Unwin 1998.
3. Abandoned Women: Scottish Convicts Exiled Beyond the Seas (Lucy Frost) Allen and Unwin 2012.
4. A Drift of Derwent Ducks (Trudy Mae Cowley) Research Tasmania 2005.
5. The Gentleman's Daughter: Women's Lives In Georgian England (Amanda Vickery) Yale University Press 1998.
6. The Italian Boy: Murder and Grave Robbery in 1830's London (Sarah Wise) Jonathan Cape 2004.
7. Warren James and the Dean Forest Riots: the disturbances of 1831 (Ralph Anstis) Breviary Stuff Publications 2011.
8. Damned Whores and God's Police: Women's Lives in Australia (Anne Summers) Penguin Books 1975.
9. Depraved and Disorderly: Female Convicts, Sexuality and Gender in Colonial Australia (Joy Damousi) Cambridge University Press 1997.
10. The Floating Brothel: The Extraordinary Story of the Lady Julian and its Cargo of Female Convicts Bound for Botany Bay (Sian Rees) Hodder Headline 2001.
11. A Brief History of Worcester, England (Tim Lambert) website
12. www.capitalpunishmentuk.org/1800.html
13. Chronology: or an Introduction and index to universal history, biography and useful knowledge ... To which are added.
14. The Diary of a Shropshire Farmer: A Young Yeoman's Life and Travels 1835-37- By Peter Davis.
15. Wikipedia: 'History of Rail Transport in Great Britain 1830-1922'
16. A Narrative of The Bristol Riots: A full report of the trial of the Bristol Rioters (WH Somerton) 1831

17. Reluctant Travellers (CF Wicken) Tewkesbury Historical Society
18. A History of Worcester (J W Willis-Bund) 1901
19. Free Settler or Felon Database (http://www.jenwilletts.com/index.htm)
20. http://www.ballaratgenealogy.org.au/resources/stock-brands-1855-1860s
21. http://trove.nla.gov.au
22. Convict Labour and Colonial Society in the Campbell Town Police District: 1820-1839. Margaret C. Dillon
23. http://www.inprisys.net/hosted/holobooks/TasmaniaItinerary21.pdf
24. Bendigo: A History, by Frank Cusack
25. The Chambers Letters: A Family's Letters From The Victorian Goldfields, by Janet Marion Epps
26. Bothwell Revisited (Bothwell Historic Society)
27. http://www.law.mq.edu.au/research/colonial_case_law/tas/cases/case_index/1830/notices_concerning_aborigines/notice_6_1830/
28. http://trove.nla.gov.au/ndp/del/article/8647567
29. The Gold Rushes of the Fifties (W.E Adcock)
30. Dunolly: the story of an old gold diggings town (James Flett)
31. The History of Gold Discovery in Victoria. (James Flett)
32. http://www.oldworldbricks.com/history_local_brick_making.php